SAMS
VS
LESTER

SAMS VS LESTER

ARTHUR THOMAS

PALMETTO
PUBLISHING
Charleston, SC
www.PalmettoPublishing.com

Copyright © 2024 by Arthur Thomas

Paperback ISBN: 979-8-8229-4827-3

1
NEW SEASON

The dinner was thoroughly enjoyable. Jim was pleased with the way his daughters accepted Liz and included her as if she was already a member of the family. His grandchildren took a bit longer, but they finally came around. Jim was satisfied with the evening and felt that he and Liz would be comfortable as their relationship developed.

It was getting late, so Jim said, "I think it's time to wrap things up. Liz and I have to drive back home, and I need to get up bright and early tomorrow morning to work on recruiting." The farewell and hugs took longer than Jim expected.

When he and Liz were finally in his car and on the road, Liz said, "Your family is genuinely sweet. They seemed to really care for you and were very kind to me. I've seldom felt so welcome."

They both relaxed for most of the drive home. Not far from her house, Liz moved a bit toward Jim, put her hand on his leg and said, "Are you sure you need to go to work early tomorrow?"

"Not really. I was happy with the whole dinner, having you get to know the family and them getting to know you. But the longer we were there, the more I wanted to be with you, alone. I would say that getting to work early tomorrow will depend on what we can think of doing for the rest of tonight."

"So maybe you need to be in your office around noon?" she teased. "I'll try my best to come up with a few things that will keep you busy tonight."

The first thing Liz did after they pulled up to the front of her house was to let her dog, Queeny, out. Jim was getting a couple of things out of the back seat when Queeny forced her way between him and the car. "Hey there pup. Have you missed us? Have you been good?" Jim said while he reached down and roughed-up her coat. Queeny turned and headed into the house looking for Liz.

Jim found both of them in the kitchen where Liz was feeding her dog. He waited for her to finish and took her softly into his arms asking, "Do we need to spend some time with her before we go up to the bedroom?"

"That would probably be a good thing to do, if we want any privacy tonight," she responded.

All three of them settled on the couch in the living room and found the last of a fishing show on TV. Neither of them was at all interested in the show. Liz pulled Queeny next to her right side and began to pet her, while Jim snuggled next to her left side and put his arm around her shoulders. He leaned in and whispered in her ear how much he loved her and how much he wanted her with him.

After a short while of rather awkward hugging and feeling around, Liz pushed both Jim and Queeny away, stood up and announced that it was time to retire to the bedroom. It was late and being frisky was more of a chore than exciting. They both resigned themselves to crawling under the covers, getting as close to each other as possible and gradually falling asleep.

Jim was first to wake up in the morning. After a visit to the bathroom, he returned to the bedside and enjoyed the sight of Liz sleeping peacefully. He decided to make her breakfast before getting back in bed with her. He knows he's not a great cook but thought a couple of eggs over easy, some wheat toast and a glass of orange juice would be just fine.

He fed Queeny and let her outside before taking breakfast up Liz. She was just waking up as he entered the room. The smell of what Jim had prepared was enough to bring her wide awake. "Oh, that smells good. Boy, I slept well last night. How about you?"

"I slept like a log last night. We must not have realized how tired we were. I let Queeny out a few minutes ago and I need to get her back in the house," he said. Once that task was done, he sat on the edge of the bed and watched Liz eat her breakfast.

When she finished, she put the dish and glass on the bedside table and visited the bathroom. She returned in a few minutes, without her nightgown and invited Jim to join her.

Most of the next hour was filled with love, lust, and pleasure. They both then slept for another hour.

Jim approached the athletic building and parked in his usual spot. There were a lot of other cars already parked and it took Jim a short time to figure out why. Football, soccer, and track and field all had summer workouts. The extra cars must have included athletes in addition to coaches. On the way to his office, he stopped to visit with a number of secretaries, but none of the coaches' offices were occupied, which was fine with him.

It was approaching one o'clock in the afternoon as Jim sat down in his office. His first priority was to complete his volleyball team's schedule for the coming season. As always, he wanted to play strong teams during the preseason in order to get his players used to competing at a high level. However, he encountered a number of strong volleyball programs that were unwilling to play Cascade University in single matches or at tournaments. Jim figured that the reluctance of some of the stronger teams was because of his team's success last season making the NCAA playoffs. However, he was able to schedule Florida, Tulane, and Purdue earlier and he'd entered two preseason tournaments, leaving five spots to fill.

His first phone call was to the volleyball coach at Minnesota State, Carol Grimes, who he'd known for fifteen years. "Carol, this is Jim Sams. Long time no see. How are you doing?" he asked.

"Carol is no longer working at Minnesota State. This is Bradford Clarke; I've just been named head coach, replacing Grimes." He responded.

"Oh, I beg your pardon. I was not aware of a coaching change. Would you know how I might be able to get in touch with Carol?" Jim asked.

"I have no idea. This is my first day in the office and it will be some time before I get my feet under me. Would you like me to transfer you to the Athletic Director?" he offered.

"That would be great, but before you do that, since you're the new head coach, I'd like to schedule a preseason match with Minnesota State, either there or at our school, Cascade University in Oregon. Maybe after you've looked at this coming season's schedule, you can get back to me. What do you say?"

"I'll give it some thought. How about transferring your call to the AD?" he said in a rather blasé manner.

"Yes, thanks. Good luck this coming season." Jim said trying to be as pleasant as possible.

"Hello, this is Director Sebastian's office, may I help you?" the voice on the line asked.

"Yes, thank you. This is Jim Sams. I'm the head volleyball coach at

Cascade University in Oregon and I just learned that there's been a change in the Volleyball Head Coach at Minnesota State. I just spoke with Coach Clarke about how I could contact Coach Grimes and he suggested I call the Athletic Director," Jim said.

"Director Sebastian is out of the office for the next two weeks. Is there something I can help you with?

"Yea. I'd like to contact Coach Grimes, but I don't have a phone number for her. Whenever I've needed to speak with her, I would just call her at your school. Would you be able to give me her personal phone number?" Jim asked.

"I'm afraid it's against the University's and Athletic Department policy to give out personal phone numbers," she said.

"So, no exception to the rule for a coach trying to contact another coach?"

"That's correct. Good-by sir!" she said rather sharply.

Jim was surprised at the lack of help from either the new coach at Minnesota State or the Athletic Department's receptionist. He wrote a personal note about the whole conversation and filed it away for future reference. Oh well, he thought to himself, just forget about it and hope Coach Grimes lands on her feet at another University.

The next call was to Texas Christian University and their new head coach, Jaydon Wilson. Jim developed a friendship with him over the years while at a number of NCAA D1 National Championships. The offer of a head-to-head match would allow them to catch up with one another and for both of their teams to be tested.

"Hello, this is coach Wilson."

"Hey Jaydon, it's Jim Sams. How've you been?"

"Jim! I've been fine. Man, it's good to hear your voice. I saw what your team did this past season. Congratulations."

"Yea. We kind of came together at the right time. I'm disappointed that we couldn't close out our last game. Congratulations on getting the TCU job. Have you put your staff together yet?"

"Yes. I've got all my assistants on board and all of the program's support staff. Listen to this, my first assistant is a former member of the AVP Outdoor League. He was a pretty good player indoors at Pepperdine, and outdoors after that, and he coached four female players on the Women's AVP tour. My hope is that we can field a Woman's Team for the Tour. This University is 'first class'. I'm just hoping I can live up to their expectation."

"Well, it looks like you've inherited a really strong group of players. If you get your players out on the Tour, it will help your team exponentially. I doubt that you or your players will disappoint the AD. One of the reasons I've called you is to see if you would consider scheduling a match this coming season. We can do a home and away arrangement if you like."

"Oh man. That might be more than we can handle this season," Jadon said.

"If it makes you feel any better, you should know that I'm losing our setter to graduation. She started every match for the past four seasons. Add to that, I've got one of my players on probation, for a major violation last season and all of this summer. At this point she's a question mark for ever playing in this program again."

"Well. Now I might be interested. I've got three open dates to fill. Which of us would host the first season?" Jaydon asked.

"I'll let you decide. Just pick what works for you and it will be fine with me," Jim said.

"OK. What open dates do you have in your schedule so far?"

"I need matches on August twenty-seventh, September thirteenth, September twenty-nineth, October eleventh, and October twenty-eighth," Jim said.

"The only one of those dates that works for us is September thirteenth. I think I'll chose to come to your place. That might be a good thing if we should get crushed by Cascade. I certainly don't want to lose in front of our home crowd in the preseason," Jaydon said.

"Hey, I know what you mean. I don't want to lose, ever. But that far into the preseason, with a strong group of women that have played together for a season or two, I'd bet your team will be really strong," Jim said. "Ok, I have you down for a match on September thirteenth, starting at 7:30 pm. I'll have our match coordinator send you a list of hotels and restaurants in the area. She will also meet you on arrival at the gym and escort you to your locker room. If you'd like, you can also conduct a practice the night before the match. Following the match, we would appreciate it if you would attend a post-match interview with the local TV station and newspaper."

"Wow! That all sounds great. I'm impressed. I'm going to remember all of this so that our program is sure to conduct first-class home competitions. Thanks a lot for the invitation and opportunity to visit the northwest. It's been great talking to you Jim. Take care," Jaydon concluded.

That wasn't too difficult. Now just two more matches to go, Jim concluded. He glanced at the clock and decided to call it a day. As he walked out to the parking area, he noticed that most of the cars that were in the lot when he'd arrived earlier were gone. But there was one car still in the lot that he did recognize as the grey sedan that Krats and Wilkens, the Corvallis Detectives, always used. It was parked close to the entry and there was only one person in the car, and he was a large, scary looking fellow.

"Now what?" Jim thought to himself. "How does someone who looks so menacing end up in a car that brings back such bad memories?"

As he left the parking lot, he headed for his house by the most circular rout he could think of. The grey sedan followed him for about ten minutes and then disappeared. Jim continued to drive around, away from his house and only headed for home after thirty minutes. He pulled up to the curb, three houses away from his house, turned off all the lights and waited another twenty minutes before walking to his back door. Inside, he went into the living room and watched the street thru the front curtains. Satisfied that the grey sedan was nowhere to be seen, he turned on the lights and made himself dinner.

After dinner, he sat in the living room and watched the TV for about forty minutes, without ever turning the set on. He was thinking back about all the trouble he'd experienced with the Corvallis detectives and the Salt Lake City thugs. How could it be that the grey sedan should appear now, after getting rid of Lester? He knew he was super cautious and doubted if anyone had seen him return from Salt Lake City with Lester or send him thru the blackberry vines. Now Jim realized he had to be more cautious than ever, if in fact, the grey sedan was driven by one of Lester's henchmen.

2
WORK

As Jim was making his breakfast early the next morning, his focus was not on food. It was still on the grey sedan and the Corvallis detectives. After cremating two eggs and putting them in the trash, he snapped out of replaying everything he remembered about how cunning Wilkens and Krats were. He managed to get two eggs and a piece of toast cooked and sat down to eat.

He knew that he could go to his office and complete the volleyball schedule and that would take his mind off of bad memories. As he drove into the parking lot adjacent to the athletic building, he looked carefully at the cars already there. There were just a few cars in the lot this early and Jim was relieved to not see the grey sedan.

There were only a few secretaries at their desk this early and he smiled to each as he walked to his office. Thinking about a number of colleges and university as he drove to work, he'd decided to start with the University of Wyoming and New Mexico State University. Jim had never met either of the coaches at these two schools, so he decided to make cold calls to each one.

His first call was to the University of Wyoming. "Hello, this is Coach Sams from Cascade University. Would you be able to connect me with the head Volleyball coach, Roberta Ashley?" he asked.

"Oh. Hello. I'm Molly McKale, Ms. Ashley's Director of Operations. May I ask the reason for your call?"

"Certainly, I'm interested in scheduling a match with Wyoming for this coming season. Is that something that you do, or should I be connected with Coach Ashley?" she asked.

"That's something that only Coach Ashley handles. Please hold and I will ask if she can take your call. Could you please give me the school you're at and your name again?"

"Sure. I'm Coach Sams and I'm the Head Volleyball coach at Cascade University in Oregon."

Following a short wait, Jim heard the line come alive. "Hello Coach Sams. This is Ashley. My Director of Operations informed me that you have an interest in scheduling a match for this coming season."

"That's right. I don't know much about the Wyoming Volleyball program, but I'm interested in learning. What would you say to scheduling a home and away match for this year and next?"

"I do have a couple of open dates on our schedule. Actually, I don't know much about your volleyball program either. Maybe we should both just agree to schedule home and away matches and hope for the best?"

"That sound good to me. I already like your style! This year I can come to you if you like, or you can come to us. You decide," Jim offered.

"Well, first off, we're hosting a four-team tournament on August twenty-seventh, if you're available and interested." Ashley said. "I have two teams committed right now and having you in the tournament will round us out at four teams."

"Believe it or not, August twenty-seventh is one of my open dates. That works for me. Who are the other two teams?" Jim asked.

"The University of Colorado–Denver, and Gonzaga University,

both NCAA Division one programs. Are you ok with these two opponents?" she asked.

"Yes. They're both up and coming programs as far as I know. Sounds like fun. I'll put the tournament on my schedule and include each tournament team. When I get my last match scheduled, I'll send you a final Cascade Volleyball Schedule. Hey, it's been nice talking with you.

I look forward to meeting you at your tournament." Jim said.

"Thanks for the call today, Jim. I look forward to meeting you as well." Ashley said.

Jim was pleased to get into the tournament at the University of Wyoming and decided to work on the last opening on his schedule after lunch. He spent a bit over an hour going thru his two most important file cabinets. There were a lot of things in those files that reminded him of some great times last season, but they needed to be discarded to make room for the coming season.

When he was done, he checked the clock which read a quarter to one. He really had only one final project for the afternoon, so a late lunch was no problem. He chose to eat at the Mexican place run by the big, red-haired Irishman.

He pulled into one of the few parking places at the restaurant, parked and walked inside. A grey sedan parked out on the street caught his eye after he'd ordered. Once he got his food, he found a seat a bit away from the street window where he could check out the grey car without being seen by anyone outside.

Sure enough, it was the two Corvallis detectives and the large, scary guy inside the car. They appeared to be talking with one another and gesturing every once in a while. Jim tried to eat and enjoy his two tacos, but he was unable to keep his mind on the food.

The scary guy got out of the car and headed for the back of the building. Kratts and Wilkens walked into the restaurant and ordered at the counter. Jim knew they'd seen him park and walk inside, even though they didn't appear to be in any hurry to approach him. Jim decided to pack up the remainder of his second taco and get back to the office as quick as he could.

He didn't see the scary guy outside, so he backed out of the parking spot, drove out of the lot and headed back to his office. About three blocks from the Athletic building, he noticed that his steering wheel was getting difficult to turn. When he got to his parking spot at his office building, he looked at his tires and saw that the two front tires were just about flat. Jim realized that the big scary guy must have gone around the building and punctured the tires while he was occupied watching Krats and Wilkins.

Jim went up to his office and got a camera to take photos of the damaged front tires and decided to wait a bit to take pictures. That way he could also take photos of the Corvallis Detectives and the scary guy if they were outside. He called the front office to see if Henry Talbot, the Cascade Director of Athletic, or Robert Paige, the Assistant Director of Athletics were available.

The receptionist said, "They are both still on vacation."

"When are Talbot and Paige due back in their offices?" Jim asked.

"It will be five more weeks," she said.

Jim asked, "Are any other administrators available?"

"Not for the next two weeks."

"And who would that be?" he asked. as his patience was beginning to diminish.

"Evert Sloan and Janis Stafford," was the curt response.

"Ok. Thanks for your help," Jim said.

Frustrated at not having anyone immediately available to discuss his concerns about the Corvallis detectives and the new addition of the big, scary guy, suddenly showing up near

campus, Jim decided to try and settle down by working on finishing his playing schedule.

Jim thought that the New Mexico State University volleyball program, a fairly strong member of the Western Athletic Conference, would be a challenging opponent and a good test for Cascade. He'd met their Head Coach at the American Volleyball Coaches Association Convention a few years back and was impressed with his team's accomplishments.

"Hello. I'm Jim Sams, the Head Volleyball Coach at Cascade University in Oregon and I'd like to speak with Benny Wayne, your school's head volleyball coach."

'No problem. Hold on and I will transfer you to his phone," a rather scratchy voice said.

"Hello. This is Coach Wayne. What can I do for you?"

"Hey, Benny. This is Jim Sams. Do you remember meeting me a couple of years ago at the AVCA Convention?" Jim asked.

"Not really. Refresh my memory."

"I'm the head Coach at Cascade University out in Oregon. We sat next to each other at the semi-finals of the National Championships in Omaha three seasons ago. Does that ring a bell?"

"Vaguely."

Jim decided to get right to the point. "I'm calling to see if you would be interested in scheduling a match this coming season."

"We're not able to do that this year. Our schedule is set. Maybe another time," Coach Wayne said.

"Wow, you're really on top of scheduling. I'm sorry to have bothered you," said Jim. "Nice talking with you." Jim jotted down another note about never trying to schedule this school again!

Jim decided to call Liz. "Hey Liz"

"High Jim! How are you?" Liz asked.

"I'm ok. Thanks. And you?" he responded.

"I'm a little tired. I took Queeny for a long walk this afternoon. She's asleep on the back deck right now."

"Say, would you be able to come pick me up at Cascade and take me to my house?"

"Do you mean right now? Is something wrong?" She asked

"You could say that. I've got two flat tires on my car."

"Why yes. I'll be there as quick as I can. Where do I meet you?" she questioned.

"No need to rush. My car is in the parking lot, outside the Athletic Department. I'll be in the car waiting. Thanks. I love you." Jim said.

"Same here. See you soon," said Liz.

Jim grabbed his digital camera and went to as many windows on the second floor as he could access, that provided good views of the parking lot. He took photos from every angle of the lot that he could think of and of areas on each end of the lot. He went back to his office and transferred copies of the photos onto a thumb drive. While inspecting each photo, Jim saw the grey sedan parked in the far corner of the lot away from the only entry. He was able to clearly make out the individual inside the vehicle, Mr. Scary!

Jim returned to his office and called Liz. "Liz? This is me again. How far from the University are you right now?" he asked in a serious voice.

"Fifteen minutes. Why?" she asked.

"There's a car parked in the lot where I always park that looks like trouble. I want you to meet me at the Volleyball Gym where we play our home games. I'll explain everything on the way home. OK?" he asked.

"No problem. See you soon." Liz said.

Jim waited ten minutes and departed out a basement door on the other side of the Athletic Department office building and walked quickly to the Gym. Liz arrived a few minutes after Jim and they both drove away towards Jim's house without being seen by the guy in the grey sedan.

"Liz, thanks for getting here so soon. Is it alright if we go to your house now instead of mine?" he asked.

"Certainly. I've never seen you like this before. Is all this just because of two flat tires?" she questioned.

"In a way, yes," he said. "There's a man back there, in our parking lot in a grey sedan. I've seen him before with two Corvallis d\detectives that have hounded me for more than a year about a female body I discovered on the bank of the Willamette near Harrisburg. I saw what first looked like a pile of clothing up on the far bank of the river as I was fishing from my drift boat one day. When, I went over to that side of the river and up to the road, I looked down into the blackberry vines. That's when I saw that it was a woman."

"My Athletic Director, University lawyers and my staff all supported me and worked to clear me of any wrongdoing. I thought I was done with them by the beginning of this summer. Yesterday, after work when I left the parking lot, I saw the sedan again, but this time there was just one individual in the car – a big, scary person. He was parked near the exit driveway and began to follow me as I drove home. I was able to elude him with no problem which led me to think he was new to this area."

"Oh Jim. I had no idea. Why didn't you tell me about this after we'd met?" asked Liz.

"Liz, I think I fell in love with you the very first time we met up on the hiking trail in the Coast Range," Jim said. "There was no way I was going to take a chance on you thinking I was a murderer. We've been together long enough now that I think you know I would never harm another soul."

"I'm so sorry. I had no idea you were under such pressure," she said.

"Please don't hate me for keeping this from you. You mean the world to me. I felt terrible not telling you. The two detectives are really nasty bastards, with no scruples. I would have been worrying all the time about you. Now there is this large, scary guy that I've never seen before, but if he's associated with the two detectives, that must mean trouble."

3
STAFF CHANGES

After dinner, Jim and Liz talked more about the implications of being harassed by the detectives going forward. He did all he could to assure her that the school's attorneys would deal with any legal matters and that they just needed to move on with their lives.

The next morning, before daylight, Jim had Liz drive him to his house so he could load his two snow tires into her car. They proceeded on to Cascade University and first drove past the parking lot to see if the grey sedan was anywhere to be seen. After confirming that it was clear, they looped around and entered the parking lot. Jim jacked up his car, removed the two flat tires and installed the two snow tires. They were both out of the parking lot just as the sun was coming up, Liz headed for her house and Jim headed to a Les Schwab Tire Center on to the east side of Interstate Five.

Jim went into the tire center and asked the fellow at the counter how long it would take to install two new front tires. The serviceman asked what type of tire and the price range he wanted.

Jim responded, "Anything as close to bulletproof that you have."

"We do carry a line of bullet proof tires and they run two hundred-fifty dollars each." The serviceman told Jm he could have two new tires on his car in forty-five minutes.

"That sound great. I'm going to go across the street and get some breakfast at Shari's."

He downed a large stack of pancakes, a glass of orange juice and two cups of coffee and then walked back to the tire store.

They were just preparing the paperwork as Jim approached the counter.

"Ah, you're back. Your car is ready to go, but I want to caution you about the ride you're going to notice as you drive. I apologize for not warning you before we installed the tires and I should have discussed this with you," the serviceman said.

"No, don't worry about anything. In fact, since you brought this up, I'll take a set of the same tires on the rear end. I'll wait if you can get those on as fast as the first two. Oh, I've got another request. Do you think you can get the four tires that came off into the back of my rig?" Jim asked.

"Yes sir! We have two more of the exact same tires in the back and I'll be sure to load the original tires into your car. I'll put a rush on everything for you. Thank you, sir."

The Serviceman was true to his word and Jim was on the road in just under an hour after paying for the four new tires.

As Jim was driving back to Cascade University, he noticed that the steering wheel was stiffer to turn and that there was more road noise inside the vehicle. He entered the parking lot just before nine am and there was no grey sedan to be seen.

Walking to his office and smiling as usual at each secretary, the last secretary stopped him and said, "You've got two people waiting for you somewhere down near your office."

"Do you know who they are?" he asked.

"I think they're members of your staff."

"Great, thanks," he said with an internal feeling of relief.

As he approached his office, he saw Mickael Banks, his second assistant coach and Pokie, his stat person, sitting on some nearby chairs.

"Hey, you two, it's a bit early to start working. What's up? Don't tell me you're here to invite me to your wedding?"

"No. Nothing like that – but soon hopefully," said Michael.

"Coach, that's all I hear from this guy. How's everything with you?" asked Pokie.

"Not bad at all," Jim said with a big smile on his face.

"Well," said Michael, "We need to inform you that we've both taken another job, at a pretty good school."

"Oh, rats! Sounds like a loss for our program and a great opportunity for you two. Are you going to tell me what school you'll be at?" he asked.

"Absolutely. But I want you to know we're very excited about this opportunity. I will have the position of Co-Head Coach and Pokie will become the new Director of Operations," Michael said.

"Wow! I think you've both just hit the jackpot. Going from your positions here with our program, to the top of the pile at another 'pretty good school', as you called it, is outstanding. When exactly are you going to let me know the name of this school?"

"Promise to not laugh?" Michael asked.

"Michael, no matter where you're both going for jobs like you've described, is no laughing matter. You both need to know that I'm proud you. I'm sure your new school's volleyball program will make a huge jump forward. Enough stalling, what's the name of the school?"

"Mississippi State University, in Starkville, Mississippi." Michael said.

"Ok, I'm familiar with the school and the town it's in, but I don't know anything about their volleyball program. I do know they have a fine football program. Tell me a bit about your research for this job," asked Jim.

"Well, we each just sent out applications to a lot of universities and colleges. There was very little response, and we were both pretty bummed. Then, Mississippi State's Athletic Department sent us a letter asking us to come to their school for an interview. I called the head coach right away and had a nice conversation with her. We were on a plane three days later and got the royal tour of campus, their athletic facilities, and the City of Starkville. It was pretty nice, really. A Few days after our visit, we were offered the jobs. The only thing that Pokie and I discussed before accepting the job was if we wanted to live in a place with such unpleasant humidity. We figured that, number one, it can't be humid all year long and, number two, tons of people live there, so maybe we'll get used to it. Plus, every facility and building we were in, was air conditioned."

Jim asked, "Are you two satisfied with the salary's you'll be starting out at?"

Poke answered, "Both our salaries are way, way more than we'd expected. We figured that the

Coach must have had a hand in offering a lot of money so they'd be sure we would take the job.

If that's the case, she was correct."

"And what about other things like medical Insurance and life insurance, school provided cars, vacation time, program budget for supplies, team travel, recruiting expenses, camps, professional development opportunities, things like that for each of you?" asked Jim.

Michael answered, "Coach I can't think of anything we didn't get. We got everything you just asked about, plus bonuses for getting into the NCAA national championship, and more money for each time we win a match in the championship, until were knocked out. We're getting our offices refurbished and new meeting rooms with everything needed to host meals, if needed. We get money for speaking before service clubs like the Kiwanis Club, the Lions Club, and the Rotary Club when we visit. Then retirement homes whenever we visit and talk about our sport. The list goes on. The University wants coaches to get people in the city interested in the athletic programs. They also want us to be available to talk to the big money doners."

"Geez, now I'm jealous of you two. You each must be in seventh heaven. I'd like to have a job like that someday," he teased.

"I don't know about that. I've always thought your job was one of the best in the country," Michael said.

"Yea. I think so too. But now two of the best people I've ever worked with will have great jobs too," Jim said as he approached Michael and shook his hand. He then hugged Poke and asked, "When will you two be leaving for Starkville?"

"Silvia, the current head coach, asked us to be there by the eighteenth of July. I'm sure we can pack our stuff and be there by then. She's also planned for us to live in a campus house until we find a house to buy or rent. Pretty nice, eh?" Poke said.

"Yes, that's great. She sounds like a really nice person. You two don't have much time then to get packed and sever all your ties in Oregon. It has been a pleasure to have had each of you in our program. I know you will be missed. I wish both of you all the luck in the world," Jim said as he walked them about halfway to the building's exit.

Returning to his office, Jim looked at his clock and was surprised to see it was a quarter to eleven. He decided to take an early lunch and drive down to Liz's house, hoping she would be willing to discuss the situation with the Detectives and their new friend.

Liz was out working in her front yard flower garden when Jim drove up to her house. "Liz don't work too hard. It's going to get really hot this afternoon," Jim said.

"It's not too bad now, I'm about done here. Are you here for an early lunch?" she questioned.

"That and a couple of other things."

"Before or after lunch?" she asked, in a playful manor.

He walked over and took Liz in his arms, and said, "I'm interested in how you would sooth the savage beast, if you get my drift?"

"Oh yes! I'm getting good at 'getting your drift'. I need to clean up before the fun begins if you get my drift!"

An hour later, they both took a shower together and then went down in the kitchen. Queeny was staring in through the window on the back porch and looked anxious to get inside. Jim opened the slider and Queeny went right to him. "She seems happy to see me," he said to Liz.

"I think so too. She's begun to treat you about the way she was when my husband was alive.

I've never heard you talk about pheasant hunting, but I think she would be a good companion for you when you're out fishing," she said while making lunch.

"You know, that sounds like a good idea. I'll give it a try before too long," he said. "What are you making for lunch?"

"Tomato soup and toasted cheese sandwiches. I hope you're a fan of Tillamook cheddar cheese. That's the only brand I eat. We discovered it when we first moved to the Willamette Valley," Liz said.

"Hey, I'm with you. That sounds great."

When lunch was over and the kitchen was cleaned up, Jim said, "Liz, would you mind talking with me some more about the situation with the Detectives and the other guy. I'm really uncomfortable trying to go about my work, and our relationship, with them back in the picture. I don't ever want anything bad to happen to you, or my family, and our friends."

"What friends?" she asked, smiling.

"My daughters and their kids for example. Over the years, as a coach at Cascade and with all the traveling I've done, I'm friendly with a lot of people. More than ninety-five percent of the women that I've coached over the years are still friends."

"Jim. I was just teasing. If anything, I was referring to myself. You are my best friend and now that I think of it, my only friend," Liz said, with a sincere smile.

"It had to be because of the circumstances your husband placed on you. Not knowing if or when he would be at home or gone somewhere definitely left you in limbo. Right now, I'm really worried that the issue of the Detectives and the other guy might evolve into something unpleasant. I don't ever want anything bad to happen to you," he concluded in a soft voice.

"Well, what do you think we should do to stay safe? And by all of us, I mean you, me, and your family," she asked.

"Ok. I've done a little thinking about this. In fact, it's about the only thing I've been thinking about these last few days. I doubt that going to the Corvallis Police Department and expressing my concerns will do any good. In fact, it may make the situation worse. I also distrust the Eugene and Portland police departments. In fact, I don't trust the county's Sheriff's departments or the State Police. In the little research I've been able to do on this subject, the consensus is that the police, sheriffs, and state police captains all protect their officers, regardless of any negative repercussions."

"You really have been thinking. What's the next step. Who do you think can help us?" Liz asked.

"Only the Department of Justice, at the Federal level. That is something that our lawyers at the University will handle, if eventually needed. Probably the first thing would be to get a restraining order on Wilkens, Krats and the new guy – old what's his name? The lawyers at the University would file a complaint about harassment from the Detectives and then after an investigation there would be a decision on the complaint. Stuff that is way out of my league," Jim said.

"How long will something like that take," Liz asked.

"Probably somewhere between one and two months I guess," said Jim. "I don't really have any idea. I'll find out as soon as my Athletic Director returns from vacation in a few weeks."

4
CAMPING

The next morning, Jim followed his normal routine as he entered the athletic building, except for stopping at the desk of the secretary to Henry Talbot, the Athletic Director. "Good morning, Julie. I need to contact Henry as soon as possible regarding an unforeseen issue with my coaching staff. I would appreciate it if I didn't need to wait until he returns to work. I want to get things resolved as soon as possible. If he could call me, I'm sure we could figure things out over the phone."

"Ok, coach. I'll get right on it. Are you going to be in your office all day today?" she asked.

"I'm not sure. Maybe you could just give him my personal cell number. That way, in or out of the office, we could get things done," Jim said.

He settled into his office and got right to work attempting to locate a new second assistant coach to replace Michael. There was a Junior Girls Club coach that he'd been impressed with, while he was out searching for players that could compete at the Division One level for Cascade. The few times I've watched the coach's team compete in tournaments, I was impressed with the club coach's demeanor and the quality of his players. He looked up the phone number for the

Kansas Lightning Volleyball Club and made the call, knowing that it was two hours later in Kansas.

"Hello. I'm coach Sams with Cascade University volleyball. Is Coach King in today and if so, can you connect me to him?" Jim questioned.

"He is in and if you'll hold on, I'll try and run him down for you."

"Sounds good. I'll hold."

A few minutes later the phone crackled back on. "Hello, this is coach King. What can I do for you?" he asked.

"Coach King, this is Coach Sams, from Cascade University in Oregon. First, can I call you by your first name?"

"Yes, that's fine. My first name is Mark."

"Great. You can call me Jim. I've got an opening in my staff for an assistant coach and I've had my eye on you whenever I've watched you coach your club team. You've impressed me with your style, and I'd like to know if you might have an interest in coaching in our program. We're an NCAA, Division One school that has been quite successful over the years. We just suddenly lost one of our assistants and I'm beginning a search for his replacement. You're the first coach on my list. Any thoughts?"

"Oh my. This is certainly a surprise. I'm overwhelmed that you're calling me," he said.

"Don't worry, I'm not going to try and push you into something you might not be interested in. It's just that I think you've got the things I value in a coach, and I want to talk with you before someone else discovers you," Jim said. "If you'd like, you can ask me some of the questions that are going thru your head right now and, after this conversation, I'll call again in a few days to answer any other questions you may have. What do you say?"

"Ok. I've got a bit of time to talk now. So, the first thing that I'd like to know is, for what reason did you lose the assistant that I would be replacing," asked King.

"He informed me yesterday that he'd just accepted the Co-Head Coaching position at Mississippi State University. I also learned that our stat person, his girlfriend, accepted the position of Director of Operations at the same school. They are each great people and I'm happy for them," Jim said.

"You're not upset at them for leaving for another school on such short notice before the new season?"

"Not at all. Like I said, I'm really happy for them. They were both loyal to the Cascade program for a number of years and they were very good at their jobs here."

"Ok. If I were to accept the position on your staff, how quickly would I need to report?"

"Once you indicate to me that you're interested in the assistant coaching position, we will arrange for you to visit Cascade University. You will also get a tour of our town of Dallas, not Dallas, Texas, and hopefully get a sense of the lifestyle and beauty of the Pacific Northwest."

"I'm interested in what you were talking about when you mentioned the stat person, as my fiancé will weigh heavily in my decision. She was a collegiate volleyball player at the University of Kansas, and she knows the game forward and backward. Would there be any chance she could be considered for the stat position, or is it filled already?" asked King.

"Frankly, I haven't even thought about that position yet. But certainly, we'll bring her in with you on your visit and I'll have an opportunity to discuss the position with her. Next?"

"Can you give me an idea of the salary I'd receive if I accept the job? Also, if Chris is ok with you for the stat position, what would her salary be?"

"Well, I can tell you what the positions paid last year. My assistant made sixty-one thousand five hundred dollars. The stat person made thirty-seven thousand dollars last year. I think there will be a bump in salaries this season, but I need to discuss both you and Chris with my Director of Athletics before you are presented with contracts for the coming year," Jim said.

"OK, what's Oregon like," King asked.

Jim was getting the impression that King was becoming more interested. "Oregon is the best kept secret on earth. It's green and lovely, with wide open spaces east of the Cascades, there are mountains on the west and east side of Willamette Valley, where we're located. It's just an hour's drive from the valley to the Pacific Coast, the state has strong academic schools, it's a great place to raise a family, and there's a universal 'can-do' attitude among the state's population. I must sound like a car salesman to you," Jim said.

"No, not really. But the one thing I've heard about Oregon, is that it rains all the time. Any truth to that?" asked King.

"Actually, it's a different type of rain than you have in the mid-west. By that, I mean most of the time when it does rain, it's more like a drizzle. Seldom do we have heavy downpours. And I've never heard of a tornado in Oregon. Also, I've lived here for most of my life, and I can count on one hand the number of times we've had any heavy snow in the Willamette valley. If we do get snow in the valley, in the winter, it usually melts off the same day. I'm an avid fly fisherman and I've spent a lot of time outside. It does get a bit cold in winter here, but nothing like the mid-west."

"Coach, I'm kind of overwhelmed. I've got a lot of thoughts in my head right now and I don't want to forget anything you've told me during our discussion. I really need to sit down with Chris and tell her what you've offered. She's very sharp and a thoughtful person and I know she'll have a lot of questions regarding our future. How about if we talk again in a few days?"

"Mark, that's exactly what I wanted to hear from you. Thank you. What time of day is best to call you?" Jim asked.

"I'm up early every day and I'd prefer to receive your call-back as early in the day as possible. Say, eight o'clock in the morning, my time? That way, I can work the rest of the day with a clear mind. Otherwise, I'd be asking myself questions all day," Mark said.

"That works for me. I'll call you in three days at eight o'clock in the morning, your time in Kansas. I've enjoyed talking with you today, goodbye," Jim said and then turned his phone off.

Pleased with his conversation with King, Jim wanted to clear his mind of all the things he had on his plate and take advantage of the great weather. "Liz, I'm calling to propose that you and I gather up some camping gear and spend a few days up in the mountains. Are you interested?"

"Yes. I think it would be good to get away for a while and just relax," she replied.

"Ah, good. I hoped you'd be in favor of going. I'll swing by my house and get what we need and then I'll come pick you up."

When he left the Athletic Center parking lot, he took a long look around for the grey sedan. Nothing. His head was on a swivel all the way to his house and still there was no sign of the car, which was a great relief.

His stress level was almost nonexistent as he gathered everything needed for a comfortable stay in the mountains. He decided to leave his fishing gear in the garage, so he could focus solely on Liz. He'd decided that he would drive up the McKenzie River, turn up the road to Cougar Reservoir, and drive up beyond the far end of the reservoir on the South Fork of the McKenzie River. Once they found a campground, with an open spot, close to French Pete Creek, they would then be situated near one of the greatest hiking trails in the country. The trail led up into an area that was all virgin timber and had never been logged. It's just as it was before the white man decided to cut the trees down for lumber. The more Jim thought about the camping trip, the more excited he became.

Liz loaded her personal things into Jim's car and said, "This is exciting. I can't remember the last time I've been camping in the mountains. Do you have some place in mind?"

"You bet! We're going to drive up the McKenzie highway, then go up behind Cougar Reservoir where we'll stay in a campground right next to a beautiful little stream. Tomorrow morning I'd like to take you on a hike that's like no other. You will see huge fir trees and a forest that has never been disturbed by man."

"Sounds good. What will we do after that?" Liz asked.

"We'll spend most of the day tomorrow going up, looking around, and getting back a couple of hours before dark. I don't like fixing dinner at night, under a lantern," Jim said.

"Is there that much to see on one little hike?"

"Just wait until tomorrow and ask that question again," Jim said with a big smile. "The following day, we'll go see a couple of natural hot springs, alpine lakes hidden way up in the mountains, lava flows, and a place known as the 'Blue Pool'. Basically, the beauty of some of nature's gifts," Jim explained. "We'll also cook over an open fire, drink pure water and try to stay warm at night."

"That's no problem! I'll take care of keeping us warm," Liz said with a big smile on her face.

They made the drive up the McKenzie River and past Cougar Reservoir to the camping area Jim talked about. He arranged the camp area, which was super simple. A fire pit and a place for their tent fairly close to a small stream under a couple of tall fir trees. Jim unloaded his cooler and laid out the things he brought for the evening meal on top of a table provided by the forest service. After dinner they sat by the fire and talked mostly about their future.

The next morning, Jim snuck a peek outside the tent door and saw that it was overcast, but he knew there was little chance of rain. Liz was still sleeping, so he got dressed, and went outside to get a fire going. He fumbled around in one of the bags they'd brought and found a pot so they could have some tea with breakfast, before beginning their hike up into the French Pete

Wilderness. "Liz, time to wake up," he said softly, trying not to startle her."

"Oh, is it really time to wake up? It's too early," she said as she rolled over.

"No, no, it's just the right time. We can eat a big breakfast and get on the trail before it gets too busy. I'll get breakfast started. The tea's almost ready," he said, trying to encourage her without being pushy. "Do you want me to fix you a cup of tea right away?"

"Ok," she kind of moaned. "That's probably what I need this morning, after last night."

"Yea, I know what you mean. I was never cold at any time last night, thanks to you."

A short time after they finished breakfast and extinguished their campfire, Jim and Liz made the short walk from their campground to the starting point of the French Pete Creek trail. Jim did not want to wear Liz out at the beginning of their climb, so he set a slower pace than he was used to. There was also the issue of blisters whenever shoes and socks didn't fit correctly, or a person's feet were not accustomed to long walks on an incline. Coming down a trail can also be hard on a person's thighs and toes. He coached Liz a bit on the correct use of the two hiking staffs they each carried as they began their walk up to virgin timber.

They hiked for about two hours and began to see the edge of the virgin timber. "Oh my," Liz said in a soft voice. "Are these the trees you were talking about?"

"Yes. This is just the west edge of a huge area of true wilderness that is roughly ten square miles. It gets better the further in we go. On the far side, we'll come out above timberline, and you'll see some peaks at the top of the Cascade mountains called the Three Sisters."

At mid-day, they stopped at an opening in the woods to eat and refill their water bottles from an alpine stream.

"This is really spectacular. You were correct when you were praising this place. When will we get to see the peaks?' Liz asked.

"Timberline is not too much further. Where the trees stop, there is only rock. The altitude Is just too high for most trees to grow. However, we may see an occasional Juniper or pine trying to survive where there's hardly any nutrient in the soil and hardly any water after snow melt."

After a lunch of beef jerky, bananas, and marionberry's, they finished the hike up to timberline, and spent some time walking around on the rocks, which went off in the distance along the tree line. Jim was getting concerned about Liz's stamina and suggested that they begin their descent. "We should start back down the trail now if we are going to be in camp with enough time to fix dinner before dark," he said. "We'll take a different fork of the trail going down so we can see some of the other parts of the forest. How are you doing?" Jim asked.

"Ok, I guess. I'll have a better answer tomorrow morning," Liz said.

"Tomorrow won't be as taxing as today's hike. We're not going to do too much of the uphill stuff. It's mostly visiting some of the other beautiful places in this area of the Cascade Range."

The next morning, they both slept in longer than Jim wanted. "Hey Liz," Jim whispered in her ear. "It's after ten. Time to get moving. There are a lot of things left to see today."

"Alright," she said in a quiet voice. "I can't believe how sound I slept last night or how sore I am this morning."

"Once we get up and start moving around, we'll both feel a lot better. I hope you're hungry enough for me to make a full breakfast this morning?" Jim said.

After a slow morning, they both got in Jim's car and headed out. He decided to stop first at one of the secluded hot springs he'd discovered years before while fishing the south fork of the McKenzie. A short drive took them to a small turn-out in the dirt road. They walked about fifty yards into the timber which brought them to a series of three small pools where the water fell from one pool down to the next. "What do you think?" Jim asked.

"It's beautiful. Can we get in?" Liz asked. "Or are we going to have visitors?"

"I can pretty much guarantee you won't see another sole until late this afternoon. All the times I've been here, I've never seen anyone until about four pm."

He began to take his shoes and clothes off and Liz asked, "Are we going in naked?"

"Yea. I don't want to drive around in wet underwear. What do you say?"

"Well, I'll give it a try, but only because I think a warm soak will relieve my sore body."

"I'm sure it will," Jim said, as he entered the pool. Once Liz was in with him, Jim could not keep his eyes off her wet body. "How does it feel?"

5
TROUBLE

The balance of the afternoon was spent driving around the area east of Cougar Reservoir, looking at lava fields and the Blue Pool. Before Jim could take off for the next area he wanted to visit, Liz asked, "Jim, would you be disappointed if we headed home this afternoon?"

"Not at all. I've had a great time showing you the things I like about this part of the Cascades, It's your call. We can break camp, go back, and be home in a couple of hours if you'd like. How does that sound?"

"That would be great. The next time we go camping, I'm going to be in better shape. I promise!" she said.

Three hours later they were home, showered and heading out for dinner. Jim decided on a winery named 'Left Coast Estate', north of Liz's house, that served dinner outside on a patio in amongst some century old oak trees. They arrived about an hour before sunset and after being seated, Liz, exclaimed, "This place is gorgeous. How do you find all these special places?"

"Remember Liz, I've lived here most of my life. And, I usually have two months off each summer. I've tried to see as much of Oregon as I can. It's been years since I've seen a lot of the places we've seen these last two days. I really enjoyed showing them to you."

"That's so sweet. I'll go anywhere with you, anytime!" she said, as she took his hand in hers.

The view improved the later it got. After a delicious meal and the sun setting, they went home and snuggled in bed for a good night's sleep.

The next morning, Jim was back at work and made the call to Coach King at exactly six in the morning, Oregon time and eight o'clock, Kansas time.

"Hello, this is Coach King, may I help you?"

"You sure can. This is Jim Sams. Have you and Chris come to any decision about coming out to Oregon for a look-see?" asked Jim.

"Yes. We've decided to take you up on the offer to visit Cascade University and Oregon. She and I spent a lot of time discussing everything you and I talked about the other day. We also spoke with both of our parents, who were reluctant to have us leave Kansas and go out west. But Chris and I can see what a great opportunity this is. So, what's the next step?" Mark asked.

"I need to speak with my Athletic Director today and convince him that you, and more than likely Chris, are exactly what our program needs right now. I'm sure he will approve your trip to fly out and look around. I will also discuss your salaries with him and have contracts ready if you both decide to accept the offer," Jim said. "I will also secure accommodations for a two day stay, which will include a vehicle for you to drive. My thinking is that you may want to get out on your own and look around. Next, if you accept the position, I'll have the University arrange for one month of housing, at no expense to you."

"Oh man! I'm going to call Chris right after we hang up and tell her we're on for the trip to Oregon. How long before we leave Kansas to fly out there?" Mark asked.

"Once I've got everything approved and before I can make any of the arrangements I've just mentioned, I'll need to get your flights booked – out and back. I'll then call you again, first thing in the morning - your time. Let's see here, today's Friday, so I'll work on getting your flight out this coming Monday and your return flight Thursday. That way you will have two full days here. How does all that sound to you?" Jim asked.

"That's perfect. It sure sounds like a lot of work on your end. I really appreciate everything you're doing for us." Mark said.

"It goes with the territory. This University is what I consider a 'first-class operation' in everything they do for their students, professors, staff, coaches, and employees. My hope is that you and Chris feel the same way after your visit." Jim said.

"Thanks again Jim. I look forward to hearing from you soon." Mark said.

Jim's next thought was that it's breakfast time. He walked over to the campus Student Center and into the dining hall, where he ate a light breakfast. Back in his office twenty minutes later, he was on the phone to the United Airlines reservations department.

"Hello, I'd like to make reservations for two round trip, economy tickets, from Kansas City to Portland Oregon, and return. The passenger's names are Mark King and Chris Raddix. They need to fly out this coming Monday and return on Thursday."

"Your name sir?" the agent asked.

"My name is Jim Sams and I work for Cascade University, in Oregon. We have an open account with United."

"Ok, sir. What time of day do you want to book? Morning, mid-day, or evening?" the agent asked.

"I'd want morning flights, in each direction. Oh, the passengers names are Mark King and Chris Raddix. That's Mark with an 'M' and the lady's first name begins with a 'C', and I'll spell her last name for you. It's R, A, D, D, I, X."

"Alright. I've got the reservations, booked, and paid for on the Cascade University's account. Has your personal email account changed in the last three years?"

"No. It has always been the same, I've never changed it," Jim said.

"Good, I will send the flight information to your email, and you can give the record locater number to the passengers, so they can print their boarding passes at a kiosk in the United wing of the Kansas City airport. Will there be anything else, sir?" she asked.

"No thank you. You've been great," he said.

Jim busied himself the rest of the morning collecting information for hotels, car rentals, and meeting arrangements for Mark and Chris's visit. It was something that Jim disliked because Kristy, his first assistant coach, had no trouble talking to whoever answered the phone. For items like this, Jim had little to no patience.

Just when Jim was getting ready to go to lunch, his phone chimed. "Hello, this is Coach Sams."

"Hey coach, this is Talbot. I've been told you needed to speak with me. I hope it's nothing serious. You do know I'm on vacation, right?" he teased.

"Yes. I was aware of that, but I've been working on getting a replacement for my second assistant and stat girl."

"Ah. Are there more problems with Banks?"

"No, not at all. In fact, he and Pokie, our stat girl, have both taken great jobs at Mississippi State University. I've started looking for a replacement, so we'll be ready for the new season. Practice begins in a little over a month and I need time to bring the new assistant coach up to speed."

"Yes. That's good thinking Jim. So, what do you need from me?" Talbot asked.

"Thanks. It just so happens that I've had my eye on a young man, who's a Junior Girls Club coach in Kansas City. I've seen him coach his team many times while I've been out recruiting. He has a good attitude and his approach to the game is always positive. He's my first choice to replace Michael."

Jim spent the next twenty minutes outlining everything that was needed to bring in Mark and Chris for interviews. When Jim concluded the list of things, he felt he would be able to hire Coach King, he asked Talbot, "Is what I'm asking for ok with you?"

The Athletic Director responded, "Yes, I'll approve everything you're asking for. I want you to continue to improve your team and someday, bring us a National Championship."

Jim could hardly wait to get back to Coach King with the good news. But his stomach was telling him it was time to eat. He decided to eat at Oscar's delicatessen, out on the far west side of town. The place was crowded with hungry customers and Jim had to wait a bit for an empty seat at the counter.

"Well, lookie here, Hello Coach Sams. How you been doing?" asked the waitress, Ellora.

"Hey, Ellora. I'm doing well, and you?"

"Not bad at all. You had a pretty good season last fall, right?" she asked.

"Yep, it was a piece of cake! All I had to do was work my tail off, day after day. Speaking of cake, are Ruben sandwiches still on the menu?"

"Hey baby, you know they are!"

"Great. That's what I'll have. Plus, a couple of scoops of Tillamook Marionberry Pie ice cream. OK?"

"You got it sugar," she said.

Jim did all he could to finish the Ruben sandwich and ice cream. He felt stuffed. The place had thinned out by the time he was ready to go. He paid, said goodbye to Ellora, and walked outside into the warm midday sun. He left the parking lot thinking he would take his time driving back to work.

Before long, he could feel the presence of a car too close behind him. Jim glanced into his rearview mirror and saw what looked like the grey sedan. As he drove, he checked the side mirrors and his rearview mirror repeatedly, trying to see who was in the sedan. He finally got a clear view of two people in the front seat of the car. There was no sign of Wilkens and Krats, but now there were two big, scary looking guys following him. He took the shortest route possible back to the Athletic Building. He parked, went straight up to his office, and looked up the phone number of the FBI.

"Hello, my name is Jim Sams and I'd like to speak with an Agent."

"Why do you think you need to speak with an Agent?" questioned the lady that answered.

"I think I've got a problem with some stockers. It's a couple of guys who've been following me all over the place. They wait outside wherever I go, like work or home or out to eat," Jim explained.

"Sir, the problem you just explained is not something that the FBI deals with. You need to contact the police department in your city and speak with them," the lady instructed.

"Ok, thanks," Jim said.

Rather than explain the history of his problems with the Corvallis Detectives, Lester and what he did to get Lilly back, he decided to forget the FBI and contact a University Lawyer for advice. Jim called Talbot's secretary and got the phone number of Ira Ehrman, a university attorney. After jotting down his number, Jim had second thoughts about seeking help from anyone, anywhere! He decided to call the Corvallis Police Department and ask to talk to Wilkens.

Jim dialed the phone number he'd hidden in his office desk and asked, "I'd like to speak with Detective Wilkens, please."

"Sir, that's no longer possible, Wilkens was terminated two weeks ago," the desk Sargent said.

"I'm so sorry to hear that. Then may I speak with Detective Krats instead?"

"Nope. Same reason."

"How long ago was Krats fired?" Jim questioned.

"Same day as Wilkens, two weeks ago."

"So, you're saying they've both been let go, on the same day?" Jim asked.

"That's correct. Hey, are you a journalist of something?" the Sargent asked.

"No. Not at all. They left a message for me to contact them, but I've been gone for a month. Thanks for your time."

Jim wondered why they both would get laid off and still be after him. He leaned back in his chair and finally put two and two together. He figured that the two detectives must have been working for Lester. That would explain why those two and the big scary guys are now in Oregon. Jim now understood why they were always trying to pin the girl's murder on hm. Wilkins and Krats, or even Lester, must have killed the girl and dumped her body.

If Jim's thinking was correct, he concluded that he and his family were in real danger. He asked himself how he could protect his daughters, his grandchildren and Liz? How would he be able to keep his players and staff safe?

The next morning, Jim contacted Coach King and told him his AD approved everything they'd discussed for their visit to Oregon. "I'm sending the flight information to your email. The morning of your flight, just find a kiosk in front of the United Airlines ticket counter, at your airport, and enter the record locater number. That's where you'll get the boarding passes for you and Chris, and you'll check your luggage. When you arrive in Portland, you'll be met outside the baggage claim area, by either my first assistant, Kristy Winslow, or me."

Coach King said, "Jim, we are so excited about this. We're really looking forward to meeting you and seeing everything you've told us about Cascade University and Oregon. We can't thank you enough."

"No problem at all. I'm looking forward to showing both of you around. See you soon."

6
IRONS IN THE FIRE

Jim knew he needed to talk with Liz and his daughters about problems he envisioned with Wilkens and Krats not being detectives anymore. Without disclosing what he'd done to Lester, he needed to be very discreet about what he said.

It was still early when Jim arrived at his office without any sign of the grey sedan in or around the parking lot. He sat at his desk for a while as he tried to decide where to begin. His thoughts were broken when his phone rang.

"Hello, this is Coach Sams."

Hey dad, this is Erin. Have you got a minute to talk?" she asked.

"For you sweetheart, anytime. What's up?"

"Well, we've run into a snag with our vacation this year. Roy's boss has offered him the use of his summer home up in Canada, but he doesn't allow dogs. And get this, he's giving Roy a month-long vacation as sort of a bonus. Can you believe that?" she said.

"Wow. You guys have all the luck. So, you want me to take care of your dog?" he asked.

"Sort of. Curley's a 'home body' and he puts up a real fuss if we leave and put him in a boarding kennel. He's an even bigger pain if we leave him with friends. I was thinking you might be able to stay here, at our house, and watch after him."

"Normally that would be no problem. But I've got just over a month to hire and train a new assistant coach. Michael and Poke have both resigned to take good jobs at Mississippi State University. Prospective candidates for their positions are flying into Oregon in a few days and Kristy has not checked in yet, so that leaves it up to me to wine and dine him. If he accepts the job, I've got to train him about how my program operates. He has no prior collegiate experience, so I'm sure it will take longer than normal to get him up to speed. I'm sorry to decline, but I think I might have a good solution. I'll call you back." Jim said.

He dialed Liz, and after explaining what Erin was asking, Liz told Jim, "I'd be happy to watch Curley, provided I can bring Queeny."

Jim called Erin right back to let her know that Liz could take care of her dog, if she could bring Queeny.

"I don't have any issues with Liz's dog," she said. "Thanks dad."

That solved more than one problem. Especially for Jim not needing to worry about Liz, and Erin's family being able to have a great vacation.

Jim returned to thinking about how he could deal with the men who were following him everywhere he went. He knew he had to be extra careful when Mark and Chris were in Oregon for their visit. If for some reason they declined the job offer, the time after they'd leave for Kansas City, until the start of preseason practice was a whole different issue.

Pieces of a plan were slowly forming, and the more he thought about it, the more he liked it.

He decided to take a ride out to the Steens Mountains, in southeastern Oregon, as soon as the visit with Coach King was done. The size and expanse of the Steens might make it hard to locate the mines he'd heard about years ago. However, he knew that finding them before he would be followed by the grey sedan was the best thing to do.

On the day of arrival for Coach King and his fiancé, Jim was parked at the Portland Airport next to the curb outside the baggage claim area. He knew that the sidewalk was always patrolled to keep the area from becoming a parking lot. Before too long, a policewoman tapped on Jim's passenger window. He lowered the window and she said, "Come on buddy, move it along. There's no parking here, just like the signs say."

"Hello officer, I'm the head coach at Cascade University and I'm here to pick up two new members of my staff who are here for the first time. I'm worried that they may get lost if they come out and don't see me."

"Oh! Coach Sams! Now I recognize you. I'm a big volleyball fan. I played at Portland State. Don't worry, you can go ahead and wait here for a bit. How's your team going to be this season?"

"I think we will be better than last season, but it's going to take a lot of work. I've got six first-years coming in and we graduated an all-conference setter. Thanks for the consideration about parking here. Bye the way, we're going to play a tournament at Portland State this season and I can have a couple of tickets waiting for you if you'd like. Just give me a call at Cascade and let me know if you're coming and I'll set everything up for you."

"Oh my. That would be great. I'll be sure to call you. Thanks coach," she said.

Three minutes later, Jim noticed Coach King and Chris walking down the sidewalk towards Jim's car. "Coach Sams. We finally made it," Mark said.

Jim got out of his car and reached out to shake Mark's hand. "It's good to see you," Jim said "How are you doing Chris? How were your flights?"

"Smooth as silk. No problems at all," said Mark.

"You two must be hungry. What do you say to a late lunch?" Jim asked.

"That would be great. What do you have in mind?" Chris asked.

"I know a nice little place in downtown Portland that I think you'll like. It's called the Elephant Delicatessen, and it will knock your socks off with its variety. Interested?"

" Let's go," Mark said.

When they all were done with lunch, Jim headed over to the Nike World Headquarters. Then it was down I-5 to Salem, west on Hwy 22 to Rickreall and on into Dallas on East Rickreall Rd. Fortunately, there was no sign of the grey sedan on the way to the Portland Airport, or on the way back to Dallas.

"I'll give you a quick tour of our town and Cascade University, and then we'll go get you a car to use. Here's the address of the Wyndham Hotel. It's out on the southwest end of town," Jim said.

The next morning Mark and Chris arrived at Jim's office at 9:00 am. The next two days were filled with meetings and visits with a number of professors, coaches, and towns people. Jim did his best to sell the University, town, and state. He included things both good and bad, trying to be as honest as possible to two young people that would need to make a life changing decision if they accepted the positions.

On day three Jim, Mark and Chris met in Jim's office for about an hour before they would all drive up to the Portland Airport. "Well, you two have seen just about everything we have to offer. Oh, by the way, were you able to get out on your own to check out the Cascade Mountains and he coast?" Jim asked.

"Yes. We went one day to the coast and the next afternoon we went up into the mountains," Chris said. "They were both breathtaking!"

"And are each of you satisfied with the salary you will be getting?" Jim asked.

That question brought a smile to their faces. "We were sold on taking the jobs before we knew what the salary would be, but that put the icing on the cake," Mark said. "In fact, we're both thinking about getting married here instead of Kansas."

Chris added, "It will be a hard sell back home, but we'd like our families and friends to be able to see what a wonderful place we're moving to."

"Ok then. You're both telling me that you are going to join my staff. Right?" Jim said.

"Yes. We thank you very much for such a great offer and for all your time and energy showing us around. We really enjoyed meeting the professors, other coaches and the Athletic Director and his staff." Mark said. "I do have a couple of questions for you."

"Ok, shoot," was Jim's reply.

"When will we need to be here to start working, and when does preseason begin?"

"How does ten days from today sound to begin your jobs? I think that should give you enough time to pack up your things and say all your goodbyes back in Kansas. Also, we begin preseason workouts thirty days from today, so that gives you twenty days to learn my coaching regimen. I like things done a certain way, but I'm always open to suggestions. Initially, I want you to do things here the way the players are used to. But I also like the way you delt with your club players. Who knows, we'll try to use the best practices of the both of us," Jim said with a smile. "I think we're done here. We'd better get on the road. Sometimes the traffic on the way to the Portland Airport is really heavy."

The trip up to Portland was smooth until about two miles south of the airport, then it took over thirty minutes to cover the last two miles. When they arrived at the outgoing terminal area, everyone got out of the car and assembled on the sidewalk. "Have a good trip back to Kansas City. I'm looking forward to working with each of you. Feel free to call anytime if you have more questions," Jim said reaching out his hand to Mark and Chris.

Once back on the road headed south to Dallas, he called Liz to let her know that he would be at her house in about two hours. As he drove, he kept checking for the grey sedan all the way to her house. Just to be extra careful that he was not followed, he passed her driveway and continued on up the road to an elevated area where he could park and keep an eye on the road in front of Liz's property. After half an hour of watching, he was satisfied that he was not followed. When he headed back down the road, he entered the road to her house where Liz and Queeny were waiting for him. "Are you Ok?" were the first words out of Jim's mouth as he hugged her.

"Yes, why do you ask?"

"I think we've got bigger problems than I'd imagined at first," he said as he steered Liz and Queeny into the house. "I've seen the grey sedan almost everywhere I've been in the last few days. It's either parked somewhere close to where I park, or it follows me as I drive."

"I don't like the sound of that. Are you worried about what they're after or what they might do?" Liz asked.

"Yes, exactly. But even more, I'm worried about you, my daughters, and their families as well.

I'd like you to take off for Erin's house tomorrow morning and stay there until they return from their vacation in Canada. I'll talk to Erin later tonight to arrange everything. That way I know you'll be safe from these scumbags until we can be rid of them," Jim said.

"Well, ok. Will I be able to see you sometime during the month I'm at Erin's house?" Liz asked.

"Yes. I'll get down to see you as much as I can. I've got preseason practice starting in a couple of weeks, which will limit my visits to Sundays. However, I've been known to give the girls a day or two off to help them recuperate. On those days I'll do my recuperation with you."

"I think that if I need to leave tomorrow, that this evening would be a good time for us to start your 'recuperation'. What do you think?" Liz asked.

Jim smiled and took Liz by the hand and led her into the bedroom, where he began to slowly undress her. She was so eager to get out of her cloths that she tripped over her feet trying to drop her Bermuda shorts. Jim joined her on the floor, where they spent the better part of two hours 'recuperating'. They woke up early the next morning in bed, neither recalling how they got there. Jim complained about how tender his knees were and they both began to laugh.

7
THE STEENS

Jim got up and prepared breakfast for both of them. While they ate Jim said, "Liz, I've got to get back up to Dallas and take care of a lot of details regarding the two new staff members that are replacing Michael and Poke. Please call me when you and Queeny get on the road down to Erin's and again when you get there. Ok?"

"Yes. Not a problem. One thing before you leave, how did you like your 'recuperation' last night?" she asked with a twinkle in her eyes.

"It was outstanding. I think I'll need a lot of 'recuperation' during the volleyball season." Jim dressed, kissed Liz goodbye, and headed back to his house, which took just over an hour.

Again, his head was on a swivel all the way up to Dallas. Fortunately, there was no sign of the grey sedan. It was almost ten thirty when he pulled into the garage. He figured he would be gone for about two days, so he loaded his car with a complete change of clothes, two pair of hiking boots, weatherproof clothing, a helmet, rope, carabiners, accessory cords, and a harness. He also put a good supply of granola bars, pre-cooked mini burritos, string cheese, chocolate bars, some dried fruit, and plenty of water. He thought about bringing a firearm but settled on a machete.

When he entered the parking lot at the athletic building, it was just as he was hoping for – a grey sedan parked in the far corner of the lot. Jim hurried up to his office and found nothing important on his computer. As he was leaving his office to begin his drive to the Steens, he grabbed his binoculars.

The drive to the Steens Mountains would take all of five hours, first up over the Cascade Mountains, and the rest on dry, empty land. He left the parking lot and could see in his rearview mirror that the grey sedan, with Wilkens, Krats, and the two scarry guys, was going to follow him. Jim was concerned about the portion of the trip out in the open area southeast of Burns. It was a two-lane highway with hardly any sign of habitation. He thought the thugs would make some sort of an attempt to get rid of him out there. As he drove, he tried to relax knowing that he would have the advantage once he reached the Steens Mountains and the mine shafts.

There was not much traffic this time of day as Jim headed east on Highway Twenty-two out of Salem. At the far end of the town of Stayton, he saw a large barricade in the middle of the road which said, 'Road Closed due to Fire'. He worked his way back to Interstate Five and south to Albany where he headed east again, this time on Highway Twenty. He only got as far as the east side of the town of Sweet Home and was stopped by another sign exactly like the one back at Stayton. At this point, he became a little worried, having spent the last hour driving around. He was determined to get over the mountains and all the way to the Steens before dark.

The last road that would allow that to happen was Highway One Twenty-six, east out of Eugene. As he turned off of Interstate Five onto Highway One Twenty-six, he checked his rearview mirror to see if the grey sedan was still with him. There it was, keeping well behind his car, but close enough to not become separated. Jim had made the drive up the McKenzie Highway many times to go fishing and knew he could make up some lost time by driving a bit over the speed limit. This was his favorite road up and over the Cascade Mountains because, part way up, he would pass the source of the McKenzie River. After going through the sister city of Springfield, he began to increase his speed. Before long he could see smoke blowing west up above the trees and wondered if he would soon see another road closure sign. Unlike the other two roads he'd tried, there was still west bound traffic headed for Eugene. Before too long he did encounter a sign that warned about heavy smoke ahead due to slash burning. Jim never liked it that logging companies could gather all the branches and debris left on the ground after cutting trees down and then do a controlled burn, even though he understood that slash burning prepared the ground for replanting young trees.

Further up the highway, the smoke was getting so thick it was hard to see very far in front of his car, but Jim knew this road like the back of his hand. He stepped his speed up a notch or two to see how eager the grey sedan was to keep pace with him. To his amazement, the grey sedan was closing the distance on him and even attempting to pass on a narrow curve in the road.

Like a ghost, a fully loaded log truck appeared in the westbound lane and hit the grey sedan head on. The sound of the crash and the brakes of an out-of-control log truck jolted Jim. It was all he could do to stay in his lane without going off the road into the river.

Jim regained control of his vehicle and pulled over. He did not like what he saw when he walked back to the crash scene. The log truck was laying on its side and the logs were spread all over the road. He looked thru the windshield of the truck and saw that the driver was alive, but bleeding. As for the grey sedan, it was a crumpled mess.

The car was compressed to about half its length. Body parts were strewn on both sides of the road near the sedan. Jim was carefull to make sure he accounted for each of the four who were in the car. No one survived.

Cars were piling up in both directions and people on foot began to appear, curious about the crash. One woman asked Jim, "Are you ok? Were you part of this crash?"

"Almost. This grey car was attempting to pass me when the log truck came out of nowhere and hit it head on. I think I'm lucky to be alive," he said in a rather shaky voice as his nerves were getting the best of him.

The sound of sirens was approaching from both directions. Fire trucks from the east and ambulances from the west, were the first to arrive. They were followed by police from Springfield and a State Trooper. The ambulance EMTs went right to work checking on the log truck driver. They were able to stop his bleeding and extract him from his truck with help from the firemen. The police were busy with crowd control and cordoning off the crash scene. A

State Trooper found Jim and began to ask him what he remembered about the crash.

"It's just like I told a person who asked me if I was hurt. The grey car was trying to pass me when the log truck came out of nowhere and hit it head on. It startled me so much I had a hard time keeping my car out of the river."

"Ok, how are you doing now?" asked the Trooper.

"I'm ok now. I was really shaking a little bit ago. Do you need to see my driver's license or something?" Jim asked.

"Yes. That would be good, even though you were not involved in the accident, you are a first-hand witness. At some later date, you may be asked by an attorney for information or to testify in case of a lawsuit."

After letting the Trooper get all the information he needed, Jim asked, "When can I get going?"

"As soon as the tow trucks can get here to clear a lane," answered the Trooper.

Jim went to his car and turned it around so he could be the first to head west when a lane opened up. He sat there thinking for more than an hour about the crash. He felt sorry for the truck driver but was confident he would be ok. Those that he did not feel sorry for were the detectives and the two big, scary guys. He hated to see anyone die. He hated more to be the one that killed someone, which he would have tried to do if they'd have made it to the Steens Mountains. He thought of how hard it would have been on him if he did kill those four scums. How could he ever have coached his team, or even looked people in their eyes again. If he were caught by the authorities, he would have been sent to prison. He knew that Liz would never have anything to do with him after something like that. He didn't even want to think of what his daughters might say if they knew.

It was close to dark when Jim was able to head west to Eugene. He was sure that the evening news on television would talk about a traffic accident on the McKenzie highway. He went directly to Erin's house to let everyone know that he was not hurt.

Erin was a little surprised when she answered the door. "Dad! What are you doing here? We all thought you were headed somewhere out in eastern Oregon. Is something wrong? Are you ok?"

"Yes sweetheart, I'm fine. Have you heard anything about a traffic accident up on the McKenzie Highway this afternoon?" Jim said as he entered the house.

"No. We just sat down for dinner. No one has turned the tv on this evening."

Liz got up and smiled at Jim. She gave him a hug and asked, "What are you doing down here?"

"It's kind of a long story. Let's go into the living room where we can talk without the kids hearing." Erin and Roy, sat down on the couch and Liz joined Jim on an oversized chair. "I started out about nine thirty this morning heading for the Steen Mountains. I first tried to get over the Cascades on Highway Twenty-two, but it was closed beyond Stayton because of a forest fire. So, I headed south to Highway Twenty and ran into the same situation at Sweet Home. Even though time was slipping away, I decided to take the McKenzie Highway, which had no road sign saying the road was closed, but there was a sign saying there was slash burning up ahead. Smoke from the slash burning was flowing west along the road, but still up over the fir trees. Somewhere close to the Rennie boat launch the smoke got really thick at road level. Out of nowhere the car behind me decided to pass on my left side and a fully loaded log truck appears in the west-bound lane and hits that car head-on. I heard a loud crash sound, and I was able to get stopped. I walked back to the crash area and saw the log truck on its sides with logs scattered everywhere. I checked the truck cab and saw that the driver was still alive, but bleeding. Next, I looked at the grey car and there was not much left. Everyone in the car was dead. It was a gruesome sight. There were a lot of body parts out on the road."

"Oh. That's terrible. I'm so thankful you avoided the crash. It's bad enough you had to see such a thing," Liz said.

Erin asked, "What time did this happen?"

"I think the crash was around two-thirty. Maybe a bit latter. Once traffic got stopped and people began to gather, along with the fire crews, ambulance, and police, it was a mess. The actual crash site was bad enough, but to have so many people there milling around was terrible. The firemen and EMTs were trying to extract the truck driver and the police were trying to control the onlookers. They also worked on finding a way for the tow trucks to get the logs moved off the road."

Jim was quiet for a few minutes as he replayed the crash site in his head. "That's about it. I'm curious about what the news shows on tv will have to say about it," he said.

Roy said, "We should all go ahead and eat supper. Jim, have you had much to eat today? Snacks or even lunch?"

"Come to think of it, no. I was so focused on getting over the mountains, and then the crash, I think I lost my appetite," Jim said. "What's for dinner?"

Erin said, "You're here on a good night. I made an Irish Stew with corn bread muffins."

After dinner Roy and Jim went into the living room and turned on the television, while Erin and Liz cleaned up the dining room and kitchen. None of the news channels had anything on about the crash, so Jim decided to head back to Dallas and get a good night's rest. It dawned on him that he would never need to be looking around for the grey sedan again. He said goodbye to Erin, Roy, and his grandchildren in the dining room and took Liz by the hand to the front porch. "I would love to stay with you tonight, but it would be really awkward with my daughter and grandchildren in bedrooms right next to where we would be sleeping."

"I agree. The house will be empty for a month in just a few days. I think we can wait. Who knows, you may be needing more 'recuperation' treatments just after they leave for Canada," Liz said.

They hugged and enjoyed a long, warm kiss. "I'll be back before you know it. I love you," Jim said.

Time seemed to fly by on the drive up to Dallas with hardly any traffic. After unloading his car and putting everything away that he'd packed for the trip to the Steens, he checked the television news channels again for any information about the crash. Finding nothing, he sat down with a small bowl of Tillamook vanilla ice cream and watched a car repair episode on one of his favorite tv shows.

Jim woke up from a great night's sleep at nine-thirty the next morning. It was Monday and there was a lot to do to get ready for his new staff members and the preseason workouts. When he entered the athletic building parking lot, he drove slowly around the perimeter just to make sure that there were no other scary people lurking about. As he walked past all the secretaries and coach's offices, he was pleased to be able to start working on volleyball for a change.

Sitting outside his office was Kristy Winslow, his first assistant. "Kristy! Great to see you. How have you been?" Jim asked, as she stood up and gave him a hug. "Did you play on the AVP circuit again this summer?"

"In early May I was physically ready and really thought this could be the summer when Rosie and I would make it into the top ten. We were about two weeks into our training routine when Rosie blew out her left knee. So, with her out for the season, I began to look for another partner, but by that time all the good players had paired up. I spent the summer reading a lot of books and learning how to surf. Reading was easy, surfing, not so easy."

"I'm sorry to hear that. I'm glad it wasn't your knee and I'm sorry for Rosie."

"Me too. She was a hard worker that was just beginning to produce. I doubt if she will ever want to play on the sand again. Tell me, how was your summer?" Kristy asked.

"It was short and jammed with a lot of surprises. I'm glad that you're here today because there's a lot to talk about. First, Michael and Poke resigned and took the Head Coaching and Director of Operations job at Mississippi State University."

"No way! Seriously? You've got to be kidding!" she said as she began to laugh. "Do you think he's up to a job like that?"

"Only time will tell. I'm happy for both of them. Oh, and their salaries are seriously high for a first-time head coach. Poke is also rolling in dough! I wished them both all the best," Jim said.

"That's just unbelievable. Why couldn't that have been me?" she pondered.

"Well, the first thing one must do to find a job is to start looking. To keep you from looking, I'm going to see if I can convince the AD to increase your salary. How does that sound?"

"Sounds great. How much are you going to ask for?"

"Enough so you'll stay here. Michael and Poke's salaries should indicate how much your position is worth. Like all things here, it will take some doing, but I won't stop until you get more money." Jim said.

"That would be great coach. Anything else I should know?"

"Yes. I've hired a new assistant coach and a new stat person. Their names are Mark King and Chris Radddix. They lived in Kansas City and are getting married before they leave to come here. They both were here for the interview a few days ago and fell in love with Oregon and the University. Neither have any collegiate coaching experience, but Mark was a very successful club coach and Chris played at Kansas State. Needless to say, they understand volleyball," Jim explained.

"Maybe, but why would you hire someone with no collegiate experience? Especially now that we've moved up in the rankings and we have six new players coming in?" she asked.

"Kristy, I've watched this guy coach his players many times when I've been out recruiting. He's done a good job with the talent he had, and he knows how to treat female athletes. I'm sure that he will help our program, especially after you and I teach him how we practice and prepare for competition," Jim said, rather sternly.

"We'll see. What about his wife to-be? Has she ever taken stats before?"

"No. But with her background as a player and your instruction, I'm sure she will do fine."

"Oh my. Anything else I need to know?" she asked.

"The last thing is that I've completed our schedule for this season. We will host TCU and we will go to a tournament in Wyoming. Besides Wyoming, we'll play the University of Colorado-Denver and Gonzaga University. I thought I needed one more match, but a two-day tournament, where you play both days, counts towards the total allowable matches you're allowed. So, our schedule is complete," he said.

"Yea. I guess you've been busy this summer. When do you want me to report?" she asked.

"I'd like you here, ready to go, early this coming Thursday, so you can meet Mark and Chris. Is that doable?"

"You're the head coach. Your wish is my command," she teased.

'Thanks Kristy. I have a feeling this will be a great season for us."

8
CHANGES

Jim spent the next two days laying out a 'to do' list for Kristy, which she knew by heart. Mark's list was considerably longer. It included how to warm up, numerous skill drills, scrimmaging, post-game stretching, and how to cool down. Jim added comments about what to do when players seem to be just going through the motions, like volleyball games, Doctor Dodgeball, Tug of War, and Race Walking. Drills that are added to liven things up.

On Thursday morning, Kristy was in her office at seven in the morning, anxious to meet the new staff members and to see if what Jim said about them was true. Jim opened Kristy's door at seven thirty and said, "Good morning young lady. Are you ready to go? Are Mark or Chris here yet?" Jim asked.

"Not that I know. I haven't seen them this morning."

Mark knocked lightly on Kristy's door and said, "Hello Jim. And you must be Kristy?" Mark said.

"Yes. Nice to meet you Mark, you too Chris. Coach has told me a lot of great things about you two. Welcome to Dallas University and Oregon. I understand you've just married."

"Yes. Actually, we played with the Idea of getting married out here, but our parents and friends insisted that we get married before we moved. It all worked out fine."

"Hey, guys. How did your move go. Are you settled in your new digs yet?" asked Jim.

"Sort of," Chris said. "We still have a lot to unpack. The house we're in is nice, but we don't want to get too attached to it. We'll start looking for a house in a few days."

"OK, we'll have our first staff meeting at one o'clock today in my office. Right now, I'll show you to your offices," Jim said, as they left Kristy's office.

As they walked Mark asked, "Offices? We were hoping we could share one office, like we did back in Kansas."

"I think two offices would be best Mark. You'll have a lot of meetings with players that should really be with just you. You will also be meeting with other people in the Athletic Department. One of your responsibilities will be meeting with shoe and clothing salesmen. Individual offices will let you focus on your own area of responsibility," Jim said.

"Yea. I see what you mean. Sorry to be pushy," Mark said.

"Don't worry about it. You may find a lot of things that are different at the Collegiate level than what you're used to. After you each check out your offices, come see me. I put together a list of responsibilities for each of your areas. You may have questions regarding those areas that I can elaborate on before our staff meeting," Jim said smiling.

Next, Jim called Kristy and asked, "How about lunch?"

"What about Chris and Mark?"

"I'd like to talk to you about them with no University ears around.

I know it was your first impression, but your opinion is important to me. Are you ok with Oscars' Delicatessen?"

"Always! It's been ages since I've eaten there. Do you think it's still good?"

"I know it's still good! I ate there not too long ago. Do you remember Ellora?"

"Yea. Who could forget Ellora? It'll be fun to see her again. What time will we leave?" Kristy asked.

"Ten. I want time to talk and eat without rushing. We need to be back for this afternoon's meeting at one o'clock." Jim said.

"Who's driving? You or me?" she asked.

"I'd like you to drive if you don't mind. I've been driving so much lately I need a break. I just want to sit and look out the window," Jim said.

As they pulled into the parking lot at Oscars', Jim's phone rang. "Hello, this is Coach Sams."

"Coach? This is Trish, you remember, Lilly's friend."

"Just a minute. I need to get out of the car so we can talk," he said while covering the phone "OK Trish? Certainly, I remember you. What's up?" Jim asked.

"I may have a serious problem. You remember the bastards that were always around Lester? I think they've figured out who I am."

"No! Don't tell me. How on earth could they? Trish, this makes me sick to my stomach," he said. "Tell me what's been happening. What have they been doing? Have they assaulted you? Are they stalking you? Have they threatened you?" he asked.

"Not so far, they just sit outside my house all the time. Whenever I go anywhere in my car, they're right behind me. If I go shopping for food, they follow me around in the market. If I go out to get the mall, or out to eat, they follow me," Trish said.

"Have you reported them to the police yet?"

"No, I wanted to talk to you first. I just don't know what to do," she said as she began to sob.

"Oh Trish. I'm so sorry. Wipe your tears. I'm going to tell you my home address. I want you to memorize it. Can you do that?"

"Yes. Go ahead," she said.

After giving her his home address, he asked, "Are you driving now, or are you at home?"

"I'm at home. Why?" she asked.

"Ok. Pack some clothes and put some food in a paper bag so you can eat while driving, then drive straight to my house. If you need to stop for gas while it's still dark outside, only stop in busy gas stations that are well lit. You need to leave your house immediately?" Jim stressed.

"Right. Thank you, Jim. I'll see you sometime tomorrow," Trish said, while still weeping.

Inside Oscars Jim spotted Kristy talking with Ellora. "You two catching up?" Jim asked trying to be as cheerful as possible.

After ordering lunch, Jim asked Kristy, "What do you think of Mark and Chris so far?"

"That's a hard question to answer. I don't know them at all, and I only spent a few minutes talking with them this morning. Seems like they'll be OK, but I'd rather answer your question after this afternoon's meeting," Kristy said.

"Fair enough," he said.

Jim's outlook for being able to coach his team without any distractions just got shot down, as his mind spun with questions. How could he keep Trish from his staff, or Liz? As much as he would be traveling with his team, how could he protect her? He began to think about helping her get relocated to another part of the country. Maine, maybe. Canada, Alaska, or Louisiana all popped into his head.

It was almost one o'clock when Kristy and Jim arrived back at his office. Mark and Chris were waiting outside and seemed eager to start. "Good we're all here. Come inside and make yourselves comfortable," Jim said. "The four of us each have specific jobs to do to make this team successful. It's very important that we communicate with one another and our players. If there are problems with either your specific area or with any player, you are to let me know, immediately! We will talk about the issue at hand, and I will decide if, after we come up with a solution, you or I will communicate with those who are involved. This applies most directly to our players. By that I mean serious problems about grades, behavior, punctuality, substance abuse, lack of motivation. You get the picture. Any questions so far?"

Mark asked, "What type of warm-up do you want me to use before practices and matches?"

"We use a dynamic type of warm-up. Are you familiar with that?"

"I wouldn't know it if I saw it. We just stretched and played pepper with a partner. Then we went into drills and playing," Mark said.

"We use stretching after practice. Everything we do to get ready before practice and games has movement. Beginning tempo is slow and it progresses to quickness. Then pepper, serving, ten-foot-line hitting, drills, and finally game situation work," Jim said. "I'll walk the players through the whole warm up and practice the first time, then it will be all yours?"

"Sound good," Mark said.

The group discussed each person's area of responsibility for the next three hours. Most of the time was focused on Mark's and Chris's responsibilities, which would be expected. Jim was pleased with the questions and answers that developed and felt that each person new what they must do.

Jim said, "Our players will be arriving on campus in three weeks.

They need to meet our new staff members and each other, due to six new first-years. I haven't fully realized the fact that we will have so many really good players. Not only do they need to learn our way of practicing, but they also need to become comfortable as part of our team. Do you have the new girls rooming with the older girls?" Jim asked Kristy.

"Yes. As far as I could. A couple of the older players asked me last season if they could room with their best friend this season. There may be some switching around early. Time will tell," Kristy concluded.

"Good. I'll see you guys at ten tomorrow morning," Jim said.

He was anxious to get home and wait for Trish, knowing that she could arrive at any time. He spent most of the evening straitening up the house and preparing dinner. At midnight, he made sure the porch light was on and decided to go to bed. He was awakened the next morning at six fifteen by the sunlight coming thru a window. After looking around the house and outside for Trish, Jim began to think that something bad happened to her. He tried calling her but got no answer. Knowing he needed to be at his office by eight, he left the front door unlocked and decided not to leave a note on the coffee table asking her to call him.

The first half of Friday was spent working with Kristy and Mark on how different drills were conducted. The afternoon focused on defense with about half the time on blocking and the other half on digging. "Mark, are you getting a feel for the way I want our players to perform?" Jim asked.

"For the most part. I may need to coach it for a while, so it becomes habitual," Mark said.

"Ok, that will do it for today. I hope each of you have a good weekend. See you Monday."

Jim became increasingly worried about Trish. He finally resorted to an old technique he used to find information about a former player. On Saturday he went down to Albany and visited the town library. He used one of their computers to pull up the newspaper for Twin Falls, Idaho. There it was, the Times-News. He worked backwards in daily editions and found a short piece about a woman in a burnt car being killed just north of Twin Falls. The occupant was identified as Trish Kingery, and the police suspected that she was dead before the car caught fire. Jim's stomach turned when he read that. He reflected briefly about how helpful she was when he'd abducted Lester. He said a silent prayer for her.

He was in a daze driving back to his house when he realized he still had half a day left. He changed directions and headed to Erin's house hoping Liz could take his mind off the seemingly endless complications those bastards from Salt Lake City have caused.

9
SUSPICION

"Well, hello Jim," Liz said as she opened the door. "Come in, I'm about to start dinner."

Jim stepped into the house and took her in his arms. Their embrace was long, and it made Jim feel better. "I've missed you!"

"Is something wrong?"

"No. Not at all. It's just been really busy getting my new assistant coach and his wife up to speed. I miss you and I needed to unwind a bit. How about going out for dinner tonight?"

"That would be fine. Let me turn the stove off and change into something nice."

"I'll be right here," Jim said as he sat down.

"Hey Jim, could you help me get the back of my dress hooked?" Liz asked.

He went into her bedroom and began to fiddle with her dress. "I thought we were going out for dinner. Don't worry, there'll be plenty of time for that when we get back," she said.

They spent Sunday morning in bed together. "Are you awake?" Jim asked softly.

"Somewhat," Liz said. "What time is it?"

"It's almost ten. What would you like to do today?" he asked.

"Would you be interested in driving over to Newport and having lunch at the South Beach Fish Market? Have you ever eaten there?"

"Yes, many times. I love that place. It has the best halibut fish and chips on the planet. Great choice by you."

Besides having a nice lunch, they spent time on the beach in front of the Inn at Otters Crest, which was their favorite beach in all of Oregon. They were back at Erin's house by six thirty and just had nachos for dinner.

During the next three weeks each member of the coaching staff worked on their separate areas of responsibility. Jim gave Mark and Chris a couple of days off each week so they could look for a house. Jim spent weekends with Liz, leaving Dallas early on Friday afternoons and returning early on Mondays. Kristy was always doing something in her office but knew she could take some time off if she asked.

Report day arrived and Kristy's job for the next two days would be to make sure all the players had arrived and were checked into their dorm rooms. Jim asked Kristy during a lull in the check-in process, "It's a gorgeous day outside, wouldn't it be fun to spend the first week outside on the sand courts?" Jim said

"It would be fun, but I don't think we can afford messing around outside when we have so many new players and new staff members," she said.

"Yea, you're right. I sure hope the players will be fit to go hard right from the get-go."

"Coach, I don't think it would be a good thing to push too hard the first week. There are just too many new players this season. I think if we go hard right away, most of them will try to keep up or even outdo the older players. Last year you took it easy the first few days and we had zero injuries. Remember?" she said.

"Yes, I remember. But I also remember telling all the kids coming back this season to be in tip top shape. Maybe I should just forget that bit of advice in the future?"

On the first day of practice Jim was in his office at seven am. Kristy, Mark, and Chris arrived at seven-thirty and talked for a bit with each other. The whole staff walked into the gym at seven forty-five, pleased that every player was there, dressed, and ready to go.

"Ladies, I'd like you to meet our two new staff members, this is Mark King, and this is Christy King. I'm happy that each of you are on time. The one thing that we need to tell you, is what the punishment is for being late to practice. There is no reason to talk about that now. You will find out If and when one of you is late. I'm going to run the warm-up this morning. Tomorrow and thereafter, Coach King will be in charge of getting you ready. The same warm-up routine will apply to both practice and pregame preparation."

Warm-up took a little longer than usual due to the six new players. However, everyone was sweating and eager to move on to pepper. Kristy administered that phase, seeing that the new women were each partnered with an experienced player. During pepper, the focus was on having a high point of contact when hitting and aiming at the platform of their partner. Then, the goal of the person receiving the hit is to pass the ball back up so that it can be set, allowing for the other person to then hit the ball.

Mark next worked the team through various skill drills, ten-foot hitting, and blocking which each of the experienced players were familiar with. The new players caught on quickly and showed a lot of promise, especially in hitting from the ten-foot line.

Jim conducted the last area which was game situation work. He started by placing the six players, that he thought would start the first match of the season, on one side of the net and the next six best players on the other side. "OK, ladies. Look around. Get to know who is next to you, who is in front of you, and who is behind you. It's important that you know why each player is on the court. Are they strong side hitters, middles, weak side hitters, servers, passers, or defenders. I'm sure there will be position changes made throughout the season. It may be due to ability, injury, or just to get everyone some playing time. The six best players on this team will always start a match. Consistency and production are what I mean by best. They may not hit the ball as hard as another player, but their hitting percentage is higher. They play better defense or are better passers than other players."

With that, he put the strongest six on defense and the next strongest on offense and had the defensive side serve for about fifteen minutes. After a water break, he switched and put the strongest team on offense and the next strongest on defense. After that arrangement worked for fifteen minutes, he gave them another water break and subbed in the rest of his players on one team or the other and let them play for the next twenty-minutes.

"OK ladies, good job. That's it for this morning. Mark and Kristy will conduct the post-practice cool down. We will see each of you at three this afternoon."

Each succeeding day, the staff thought the team was looking better. Despite the fact that Jim forgot to ease them into their early work outs, there were no overuse injuries. Most of the players experienced varying degrees of soreness early in the first week, but treatment by the trainers solved the aches and pains.

The first match of the season would be on a Friday, two weeks before Cascade starts classes. On the seventh day of practice, Jim asked his assistants, "What would you guys think of some sort of get-together the Wednesday before our first match?"

"For as hard as we've been pushing this group, I think that's a great idea. They need time to bond as friends and classmates, not just teammates" Kristy said.

Mark said, "I think you're right Kristy. Coach, what you're suggesting will go a long way in helping each player know that every other player has their back."

"OK then. We will use the afternoon practice on the last Wednesday before our first match for the party. As soon as you two put everything together, let me know what we'll need from catering and facilities management. They'll need at least a week to get everything we ask for," Jim said.

Jim was pleased with the progress of his players during the preseason practices. The party for the team was a huge success, and he was satisfied with how much the team had come together in three weeks. He was especially happy that Martha was accepted back on the team by the players. She had done everything Jim asked of her when he put her on probation last spring.

Jim called a meeting early on Thursday morning, the day before their first match, with all the coaches, players, stat crew, and announcers. When everyone got settled, Jim began, "The Dallas Classic Volleyball Tournament will begin at nine in the morning tomorrow. Our first contest of the season is at noon. I know that our players are well prepared." He looked at his players and said, "I want each of you dressed, in and out of the training room if needed, and on the court by eleven o'clock to begin warmups. We don't know a great deal about any of our three opponents, but we will adjust as needed." He turned to the others in the room and said, "I've spoken briefly with the stat crew, those at the score table, concessions, and the announcers. Coach

Winslow will meet the referees as they arrive and show them to their locker area. All matches played in this tournament will be televised on ESPN+. Do any of you have questions?"

One person from the score table crew asked, "What do we do for lunch each day?"

"We have the Newman Room set up to provide lunch for the visiting team's coaches and everyone else working this tournament, except those working concessions, the trainers, and the television crew. They each will be too busy between matches selling food, treating athletes, and broadcasting. The tv crew, trainers, and concession workers can start a tab at concessions for their food. Our players and coaches will eat at the school cafeteria, which is opening just for this event. Are there any more questions?" he asked.

"Who are the teams that will be in the tournament, besides us?" asked an announcer.

"Washington State University, University of Idaho, and the University of Nevada-Las Vegas. This will be a strong tournament because of the strong teams. It will be a true test for each school, and it should be very entertaining for the TV audience. Any other questions? Alright then, each of you should know when you need to be here to get set up. If, at any time before or during the tournament you have questions, speak only to me or Kristy. We will address your questions and correct any problems. Also, for our players, we will not practice this morning or afternoon. So, relax and get a lot of sleep tonight? Thank you all for attending this meeting."

Just as Jim entered his office, his desk phone rang. "Hello, this is Coach Sams."

"Mr. Sams, this is Agent Wallace of the FBI. I'm based in the resident agency in Boise, Idaho. I would like to ask you a few questions regarding an auto accident that happened just north of Twin Falls, Idaho. Do you have time to talk?"

"Certainly. I'm curious though. Why are you calling me about an auto accident in Idaho?" he asked.

"Information about the circumstances of the accident, given to us by the Idaho State Police, prompted us to contact you. A woman was found dead in a car, and we believe she was killed before the car was set on fire. We were just able to read the numbers on a charred piece of paper the State Police gave us. We discovered that the numbers were your address. From that, we obtained your phone number," the agent said.

"Wow. Who was the woman?" Jim asked.

"At his point we don't know. Everything in the car was burnt, except the piece of paper I just told you about. With any luck, forensics may be able to identify her. We were hoping you would know her."

"The only women I knew who lived in Twin Falls, were a player that I coached on my volleyball team, her mother, and a friend of theirs. Unfortunately, my player and her mother were killed in their home. I recall that their house was burnt to the ground, because their friend called and told me. Trish was her name."

"Do you know this Trish woman's last name?" the Agent asked.

"No. I'm sorry. I just know her as Trish," Jim said. "In fact, she called me yesterday about mid-day. She was panicked about some thugs who'd been following her everywhere. The only thing I could think of was to give her my address, so she could get away from Twin Falls. My intent was to have her get out of town so she wouldn't be followed. I felt sorry for Trish, being all alone and scared. I've been waiting all morning, thinking she would arrive before noon."

"We'll follow up on that name. Thank you for taking the time to talk with me today. I'll contact you again If the need arises," Agent Wallace concluded.

"Any time," Jim said.

Jim thought that there were too many things happening lately that were of the 'good news–bad news' variety. First, he was trying to help Trish, and now she was out of the pitcher. Next, he wondered if the FBI knew about the thugs in SLC that answered to Lester, and that they would somehow learn why Lester is nowhere to be found. In his own mind, Jim felt he could explain it away.

When he talked with Trish about helping him nab Lester last spring, he did so in person or briefly on a burn phone. When the FBI escorted Lilly and her mom back from Europe, they'd interrogated Lilly about how she'd escaped and made it to the convent. She told them that an old man in Budapest helped her get away and transported her to the convent.

After lunch, Jim's attention turned to his team. He was excited to see how this team would react to starting the season against three tough opponents. He thought that, if the veteran players were steady and played close to their ability, the new setter and the other two new players from Brazil would develop fast. Once every player found their groove, he could begin to think about a return to the National Championships.

Jim had a restless evening due to his mind constantly reverting back to the call from the FBI this morning. Knowing that he would be in jeopardy if they learned about what he'd done to Lester, he concentrated on eliminating anything he could think of that would put him at risk. He decided the first thing, and most important thing, would be to float down to the island where Lester perished. He could then remove and destroy everything he used to eliminate the bastard.

The thoughts of yesterday vanished Friday morning. He arrived at his office before seven, so he could make sure everything was ready for the tournament to begin. Kristy, Mark, and Chris all arrived right at seven, checked in with Jim, and then attended to their areas of responsibility.

At the beginning of the first match, Mark put the players through a good pre-match warmup. Jim seemed to be the only one that showed any sign of being nervous. As the match unfolded, his nerves switched to coaching. Cascade's first game against Washington State was a nail-biter, which they won by a score of 28 to 26. They lost the next two games, which were also close, and rebounded to win the last two by large margins. Needless to say, Jim was delighted that his team performed so well in such a challenging match.

The tournament ran like clockwork and ended with the last match between Cascade and the University of Idaho being a blowout. Jim was able to get playing time for every one of his players without his team letting up. He was surprised that the recipient of the Player of the Tournament was Iliana, Cascade's freshman setter from Brazil. Before releasing his players from the tournament, he congratulated them and told them that there would be no practice on Monday.

10
DETAILS

Early Monday morning Jim got his drift boat ready to float the Willamette River to do a little 'fly fishing'. He put a bag full of tools and cutters on the floor of the boat that he would need to disassemble the water wheel he'd installed. On the way to the blackberry covered island, he fished at four places he considered sweet spots. The number of fish that he hooked and released surprised him a little, due to the unusually shallow depth of the river. As he approached the north end of the island, he could see the water wheel sticking up about a foot above the current. Just as in the past, he paddled around to the west side of the island to beach his boat.

He walked back to the north end of the island, carrying the bag of tools, and waded out to the water wheel, expecting to find the cable wrapped around the small car rim, with the skeleton of Lester hanging there. He looked carefully on all sides of the water wheel above and under the water. There was no sign of a body anywhere.

He walked back to shore and began to rummage around in the dry dirt from the end of the vines to the water. To his surprise, he found the cable that was attached to Lester's chain vest, created to pull him completely through the tangle of vines. Jim next walked along the west side of the vines to find the three areas he'd cut out, in order to get the cable as far as it would reach to the south end of the island. He pushed into the new growth of vines in the cut outs and found cable in the first two. At the last cut out, the cable was harder to locate.

He finally located the cable about eight feet into the vines. He saw immediately that the cable end had been cut. How could that be, he thought to himself? Lester couldn't have accomplished that, considering how Jim had built the cable vest. The only answer had to be that someone must have found him and helped him out of the vines. He began to worry that Lester may have survived after all. Surely someone from the lower end of the Willamette Valley would have made a big deal out of a person surviving such an ordeal. Nothing in any Oregon newspaper, on the radio, or television news programs had mentioned anything about the discovery of a person chained in some vines. He thought that Lester must have been rescued from the vines and that he was still alive somewhere.

Again, more bad news, he thought. Jim realized that the best thing he could do now was to remove the water wheel and gather up all the cable, so there would be no evidence of someone having been trapped in the vines.

Fortunately, no other boats passed by the island as he dismantled the water wheel. Everything attached to the five steel posts was easy to take apart and took only an hour and a half. But removing the posts from the river bottom was a three-hour job. After putting all the parts into his boat, he reeled in the cable, placed it on the ground like a water hose, and secured it with duct tape. After he wiped out any foot tracks, he looked around to see if he'd overlooked anything.

Satisfied that he'd done all he could to leave the area free of any signs that something bad happen on the island, he pointed his boat down river to the takeout point.

For the next three weeks, whenever he had a free day, he would dispose of the contents of the water wheel and the cable. Some days, he would drive up to a couple of lakes, far up in the mountains, and put ingots in the deepest water he could reach. Other days, it was as simple as putting things in the dump. The days he went to the dump, allowed him to get down to Erin's house to be with Liz.

Once he'd disposed of everything from the island, he was able to enjoy his team's performance. They'd won every game thus far and were about to begin conference play. The first team was established, and they were a force to deal with. Their strong play allowed Jim to sub other players into games, which pleased everyone on the team.

Concurrent with coaching home and away games, he and his staff worked on recruiting. Only two players would graduate this year, so the coaches could focus on getting high quality players, instead of simply a lot of players. Height was one of the strongest attributes a prospective player could have and there were not a lot of them around. As teams increase their rankings, the easier it was to recruit this type of athlete.

Cascade's first two conference games would be a three-day affair. Wednesday, at the end of practice, Jim gathered the team together and said, "We will leave on Thursday afternoon at two and fly to New Orleans, where we will then go by bus back up to Baton Rouge. Friday morning, you can sleep in until nine. Then we will work out at eleven and then play Louisiana State University at seven in the evening. Following that match, we will bus back to New Orleans and check into the hotel. We will have all day Saturday off, to explore the area, do homework, or just rest. We'll decide what to do after breakfast on

Saturday. On Sunday, we play Tulane at noon. Breakfast will be at seven am. You are not to go back to your rooms to sleep. If you have friends or family here, you will be able to visit with them in the hotel lobby during the two-and-a-half-hour gap, between eight and ten-thirty. No one, other than your teammates, are allowed in your hotel rooms. I want you to begin getting dressed and seeing the trainers before the beginning of warn-ups at eleven. The match begins at twelve o'clock."

"Are there any questions?" he asked. "Ok, no questions. Good. The best part of this trip is that we get to use the University's new plane. That means we will be back on campus by nine pm Sunday night, just in time for you get a good night's sleep and be in class Monday morning."

The Cascade volleyball team was excited about flying to Louisiana in the University's new plane. The flight time from Salem to New Orleans was five and a half hours, which included the drive over from Dallas to Salem, and the takeoff and landing. Most of the players were unaware that they would lose two hours flying east, due to the time change. A bus ride is usually not too interesting, but the route up to Baton Rouge gave everyone an opportunity to see a bit of the western part of New Orleans and a lot of the southern flatland in Louisiana.

The match with Louisiana State University was much easier than Jim expected. His team played close to perfect, while LSU was an exercise in confusion and mistakes. Jim tried to be gracious to the new Coach after the match, but there was not much he could say. When he addressed his team on the bus back to New Orleans, he complemented them on not letting up at any time during the match. "Ladies, by continuing to play hard against weak teams is the only way to show them respect. Had you let up, it would have looked like you felt sorry for them. The way you played tonight lets them know what they need to work on."

An hour and a half later, the team stepped off of the bus in New Orleans and assembled in their hotel's lobby. Jim said, "You need to see Kristy for your room keys and room assignments. The hotel provides breakfast in the morning from six to nine am. Be in the lobby at ten tomorrow morning and we will decide what you would like to do."

Jim got the best night's sleep since talking with Agent Wallace. Saturday morning, he dressed and went downstairs to the breakfast area at seven am. At the ten o'clock meeting, when everyone was ready, Jim said, "We have two vans at our disposal today. I will drive one and Kristy will drive the other. First, I'll offer a few places that we could visit and then we'll open it up to anyone who has suggestions. The French Quarter is usually what everyone wants to experience at least once. There are a lot of restaurants where we could eat after walking around the Quarter. There is a lot of music coming out of cafes and bars, but you are not allowed to enter a bar at any time during a volleyball trip. A lot of people just hang out on the sidewalk and listen. My choice for a place to eat in the Quarter would be Houlihan's, but you will have a ton of restaurants to choose from. You are not allowed to have a group eat at one place and another group or two eat at other places. Are we all clear with that?" he asked.

"I only want one receipt for lunch."

"Kristy, do you have any place to suggest for your group?" Jim asked.

"I think we will check out some antebellum homes. There are a couple that are fabulous and worth seeing. It's a part of the history of this country that most people never get to experience. After that, we'll head over to Metairie and destroy some Po' Boy sandwiches."

Marta, the player from Brazil asked, "What's a poor boy sandwich?"

Kristy laughed and said, "It's made out of some of the best tasting ingredients you will ever eat. It has roast beef or fried seafood, usually shrimp, fish, oysters, or crab, all covered with lettuce, tomato, pickles and slathered with either hot sauce or mayonnaise. It's served on New Orleans French bread. that has a fluffy center and a crisp crust. I know you'll like it."

Another player from Jim's group asked, "Coach can we get those too?"

Jim said, "We'll see. Remember, we will be checking out the French quarter. It all depends on where you guys pick to eat."

Both groups enjoyed a great day. After resting in their rooms and getting dressed for dinner, everyone gathered in the hotel lobby, where the coaches were waiting. Jim addressed the group, saying, "I hope everyone had a good time on your outing today. I can't tell you how much I'm enjoying coaching you guys. So, we're going to celebrate the undefeated start to this season. For dinner tonight, I've decided to spoil you a bit by making reservations at Antoine's Restaurant in the French Quarter. I know you will be impressed!"

Dinner lasted for a little over two hours. When Jim announced that it was time to head back to the hotel, no one moved. It was as if they wanted to stay and enjoy every last bit of the ambiance the place offered. "Ok, let's all head for the bus and get back to the hotel. The celebration's over, tomorrow will be a very full day," Jim said.

At the hotel, the players were gathered for another short meeting. "Ok, forgive me for repeating myself, but again, here's the schedule for tomorrow. Our match with Tulane is at noon. Breakfast will be at seven am. I don't want anyone going up to sleep after eating. If your family or friends want to visit with you, that takes place in the lobby between eight and ten-thirty. Only teammates are allowed in your hotel rooms. Be dressed and, if needed, see the trainers before the beginning of warn-ups." Jim said. "We are not going to take Tulane for granted. They are a much-improved team this year. Are we all good?"

The collective response was, "Yes!"

Tulane's gym was not the best representation of a Division One program. It was small, with not much room on the side lines or ends lines. It was also very warm, despite four overhead fans mounted on the ceiling over each corner of the court. The thing that concerned Jim the most was the height of the ceiling.

Just before his team took the court for warmups, he gathered the players together and said, "This is not the fanciest gym I've ever been in, but this is what we have today. We will need to focus on ball handling, particularly on defense, so we don't hit the ceiling. However, if the ball does contact the ceiling, it's still playable."

Even though Cascade won the match in three straight games, it took longer than usual, due to the low ceiling. None of the players complained or tried to blame their play on ceiling errors. After showering, the players and everyone else boarded the bus and headed for the airport.

Their plane touched down in Salem at six pm. Jim had the bus to Cascade stop for dinner at Rudy's Steakhouse, which was close to highway 22. The players seemed tired and took their time eating, as did everyone else in the party. Once back on the bus, you could hear a pin drop.

At Cascade, Jim congratulated everyone for a successful trip and notified the team that they had Monday off.

Jim was shocked when he arrived at what used to be his house. There were four firetrucks, six police cars, and an ambulance scattered all around the charred remains of his home. He sat in his car for about twenty minutes, trying to clear his head. A deputy sheriff knocked on the passenger side window and motioned him to move on. Jim lowered the window and said, "Officer, this is my home. Or I should say, this was my home."

"Ok," the officer said, "Back your car up and park in the next block. Then come back so we can talk."

Jim complied and as he approached the officer, he got a better view of the destruction. He had trouble recognizing anything in the rubble, except for the twisted remains of his drift boat. He asked the officer, "When did the fire start?"

"We received word of a fire here at six this evening. I got here at six-twenty and the fire was burning pretty good. The fire department was on the scene at six-nineteen, and they seemed to have had trouble knocking it down. Looks like they were unable to save anything," the officer said. "I'm going to need to get some information from you."

"Yes. I understand," Jim said in a rather discussed tone. "Can I get your name in case I have a question or two latter?"

"Certainly. My name is Deputy Rafferty. You can call me anytime," he said.

After getting the deputy's name and badge number, Jim thought for a bit about where he could spend the night. It was too late to drive down to Erin's house, so he checked in to the Best Western on Orchard Drive, in Dallas. Following a restless night, he drove back to his house to have a look around in the daylight. It was just a dirty, smoldering mess. He picked up the remains of a rake handle and began moving the burnt debris around, trying to see if anything at all survived the fire. A small black, steel safe that he kept important papers in caught his eye. Unfortunately, the brass key to the safe was nowhere to be found. After searching for two more hours in what used to be his house, he called Liz.

"Jim, how's everything? When did you get back?" she asked.

"I got back around nine last night and learned that I don't have a house anymore."

"What?" she exclaimed!

"It was burnt to the ground. There were firetrucks and police cars everywhere, but they were unable to save it. When I say it burned to the ground, I mean to the ground! It was just a bunch of chard wood and electric wires. I spent last night in a motel and went back this morning to see if I could find anything in the daylight. I did find a small safe that has some important papers inside, and it was as black as coal, but I couldn't find the key to open it. I'll need to get another one made so I can see if anything inside survived. Are you still at Erin's house or are you at home?"

"I'm back at my house. Erin's family arrived last evening, so I left to let them have their privacy."

"I wanted to ask if I could come stay with you until I build another house?" Jim questioned.

"I would love that. In fact, you can live with me for the rest of our lives, if you'd like," Liz said

"Thank you. We'll have that discussion sometime after I find out what caused the fire. I need to get away from here for a bit. How about if I come take you out to dinner tonight?"

"That works for me," she said.

Before leaving for Liz's house, Jim called his Athletic Director. "Hello, this is coach Sams, is Henry available?" he asked the secretary.

"Yes, let me see if he is available." After a short pause, she connected Jim to Mr. Talbot.

"Jim, nice going on your trip to Louisiana. Two more big wins for our program," he said.

"Yes, thanks. The more I watch these kids play, the more I'm liking this group of athletes. We'll see how long the undefeated string lasts. The reason I called this morning is to let you know that my house burned down last night. So far, the authorities have no idea of what caused the fire. I'm going to need to talk with my insurance people and see about rebuilding."

"Oh my. That's terrible! We were all wondering where the sirens were coming from last night. Where are you going to live? Would you like me to arrange a place for you on campus?"

"That's a very generous offer, thank you. However, I've already decided to stay with a friend that lives a little south of Dallas. If I'm able to rebuild, I'll get back in town."

"Ok. That sounds good. If there is anything we can do for you, just let me know," said Talbot "Will do. Thanks again Henry."

11
TOGETHERNESS

Jim pulled into Liz's property, close to one o'clock. Liz opened the front door and she and Queeny waited on the porch for him to park. As soon as he opened his car door, Queeny was at his feet.

"Yes, yes, I know," Jim said as he patted and stroked her coat. Liz was now next to Jim and their embrace seemed to last forever. "I really missed you. It will be so great to be near you every day and night. I may stall on building another house," he said, smiling.

They went into the house and sat down next to each other. Queeny joined them by laying down next to Jim. Liz said, "Tell me about your trip. Was it fun? Did the players enjoy themselves? What do you think about this team?"

"Hold on," Jim said, with a smile. "Let me answer your questions one at a time. Yes, the trip was a lot of fun. None of the girls had ever been to the south, much less to New Orleans or Baton Rouge. They had all day Saturday to explore. Half of them went with Kristy in a van and they saw a couple of antebellum homes and a bit of the French Quarter. The other half went with me in my van. We ate a midday snack at the Cafe' du Monde and spent the rest of our time in the

French Quarter looking at shops, listening to music, and enjoying a wide variety of people. For dinner, we all ate at Antoine's Restaurant, an over-the-top, super posh place in the French Quarter. Yesterday, they were dead tired by the time we got back to Salem, even though we used the University's new plane, there and back."

"It sounds like you had a great trip. Plus, you won both games. It's really a shame about your house."

"It would have been a better trip if you were able to be with me. You would have loved being around the girls. I need to find out about the house burning down and having it replaced. Would you mind if I called my insurance company now?" Jim asked.

"Not at all. I'm going to take a shower and get ready for tonight," Liz said.

Jim spent more than an hour talking with his insurance agent, who he'd been with for over twenty years. The policy that he had, always paid claims quickly. Finally, some good news. He learned about a new feature that was added to his policy. It stated, if his house was totally destroyed, they would pay him the value of that house. If and when he built a new house, they would compensate him at current prices. His agent said that the same applies to all of the furniture, clothing, tools, and valuables. He was told that an inspector from their firm would need to inspect the property to determine the extent of damage. Once that was completed, he would qualify for coverage of a new house and would be able to start construction immediately.

After Jim explained to Liz what the agent told him, Liz responded, "In some ways you must live a charmed life."

"Yea. I felt that way shortly after you and I met. Losing my wife was devastating, but finding you was truly a gift from the good Lord."

"Thank you. I feel the same way," she responded and kissed him. "I've been thinking about where we could eat tonight. What would you think about driving down to the King Estates Winey?"

"Whatever you want. I'm up for trying new places. What's the menu like?" asked Jim.

"The first thing you should know is that it's spendy, really spendy! The menu is 'fancy chick'. It's more about flavor than quantity."

"No problem. Let's go."

Their meal was exactly as Liz explained, and the service was outstanding. There was no way Jim could complain about quality, service, elegance, or taste. "This was a great choice by you," Jim said.

"Thank you. I'm really glad you enjoyed it. Can you believe the size of this place. There are just acres and acres of grapes."

"Yea. You'd think I would have discovered this place a long time ago. I'm sure happy you suggested coming here."

Jim was up early Tuesday morning and left a note for Liz, saying he needed to be at the University by seven. Cascade's next opponent was San Diego State University, and he knew they were the type of team that would be difficult to beat. Kristy, Mark, and Chris were all sitting outside his office when he arrived. "Well, it's nice to see everyone here so bright and early. Have you recovered from our trip to Louisiana?"

Kristy said, "We're good. The question is, how are you"?

"I'm doing Ok, but my house took a beating while we were gone," he said, trying to lighten the air. "It's just one of those things. You never know when something like this will happen. I've talked to my insurance agent, and it looks like the cost of building a new house will be completely covered."

"How long do you think it will take to construct your new place?" asked Mark.

"Probably three or four months, if the weather cooperates. I'd like to build a single-story house on a 'zero-entry' slab. I'm sure I can start construction once the lot gets cleaned up and compacted," he said.

"What's a zero-entry slab?" asked Mark.

"That's where your doors to the inside are all at ground level. In other words, the front porch and the back porch, or patio would allow a person in a wheelchair to go inside without needing to deal with steps."

"Are you thinking you'll need a wheelchair before long," Kristy asked, smiling.

"I hope not. I'm just thinking about resale value. I think it would open up the market to more people."

"Coach, Chris and I will be needing to find a home before long and we've been thinking about building. Maybe you and I could talk sometime about all that's involved with building a house?" Mark asked.

"Sure, no problem, but enough of this. Let's get started with the evaluation of the matches against Louisiana State and Tulane," Jim said.

The group spent the next two and a half hours examining every little detail of their two matches and the trip generally. The subject then turned to Jim explaining his concerns about San Diego State. "San Diego is a team that is very steady, because they execute well in all phases of the game. Their wins are mostly the result of their opponent's errors."

Kristy offered, "You know, even though we're undefeated, I think we made too many errors. Simple things like serving, passing, and back row defense to put it bluntly. I think our hitting and blocking in most every match was why we've won."

"Stats show that our block was very effective, as was our hitting. It also shows that we missed way too many serves," Chris said. "Passing was another area that was sketchy."

"Ok. Kristy, I'd like you and Mark to plan this afternoon's practice, with an emphasis on serving and passing. I don't want our team to become complacent in those areas, thinking they can just hit and block their way to winning matches. The possibility of our team becoming dominant could well rest on improvement in those two areas," Jim said.

For lunch, Jim stopped at Tater's Café, trying to check out which places in town he would frequent the most. It was open from six am to three pm, seven days a week, which would cover breakfast and lunch. He was learning that not having a home anymore, required thinking about a lot of things people take for granted.

The afternoon's practice was just what Jim asked for. The first hour kept everyone busy with serving drills and the second hour was all passing. Surprisingly, both drills tired the players out more than the coaches expected. It was too early in the season to have the players do something fun to get them going again, so Jim gathered the players together and said, "Ladies, I thought you were in better shape. You all look pretty tired, so I'm going to call it a day. Make sure you get to bed at a decent hour from now on."

After attending to a few details in his office, Jim headed for Liz's house. A couple of blocks from the University Jim noticed that a black SUV was following him. At first, he thought it was just a bad driver, but it was still behind him as he passed the last building in town. When he sped up, the SUV sped up. Jim thought to himself that this could not be happening again. On a stretch of highway that had a few curves, he slowed down a bit trying to see who was in the car. On the second curve, the afternoon sun provided a good view of the passengers and Jim's suspicions were true. Just to be sure, he decided to head up into the coast range and, if he was followed, lose the SUV. There was no way he wanted to be followed to Liz's house.

It didn't take too long before Jim was free of being followed, so he descended back into the valley by another route. When he got to Liz's house, he drove around to the back and parked inside the barn, being careful that his car could not be seen.

The first thing Liz said when Jim came in thru the kitchen door was, "That's interesting. Why did you put your car in the barn?"

"I wish I didn't need to tell you this, but I think I'm being followed by more thugs. A least half the way from Dallas to here, they were right behind me. I got a look at them in the review mirror and decided to lose them up in the coast range. I don't want them wandering around trying to spot my car, so that's the reason it's in the barn," he said.

The next morning Jim left a note for Liz and departed before breakfast. He rolled past the University parking lot looking for the black SUV. Thankfully, the lot was almost empty at this early hour, so he decided to look for the Deputy Sheriff that he talked with the night he learned his house was a goner.

When Jim arrived at the Dallas City Police department, which also housed the Polk County Sheriff's office, he went in and said, "Good morning, I'm Jim Sams and I'd like to speak with Deputy Sheriff Rafferty."

"Good morning to you as well, I'm Officer Wingard. I'll see if he is free," said the Officer at the front desk. A few minutes passed and he told Jim he could see Rafferty right away. "Just follow the corridor to office seventy-four, which is on the right."

The door was open, so Jim walked in and said, "Hello Deputy Rafferty. Do you remember me from the house fire the other night?"

"Yes. How are you doing?" Rafferty asked.

"About as well as can be expected. I lost about everything I owned, but my insurance should cover everything. I've been thinking that the fire was not an accident. It doesn't make sense to me that my house could be so engulfed in flames if the firemen arrived within minutes of being told there was a fire," Jim said.

"You know, I've been thinking the same thing. I'm about to call the CID to see if they'd be able to look into this fire."

"What's the CID and what do they do?" Jim asked.

Detective Rafferty said, "They're a department of the State Police that investigates arson events. They can usually determine what caused the fire initially, why it took so long to extinguish, and in some cases, who set it."

"Who is it that gets this 'CID' involved?" Jim asked.

"I can get the ball rolling from our end. They will send out a team almost immediately and work until they find out everything about the fire. Then, if they're able to confirm arson, they will pass it along to the state police or, if needed, to the FBI," Rafferty said.

"The FBI for a house fire in Dallas, Oregon? Seems like overkill," Jim said. "It's just surprising. It won't bother me at all if the FBI needs to get involved."

"Yea, sometimes. But I think this fire needs to be inspected. I'll keep you informed," Rafferty said.

"I'd appreciate that. Thanks."

Jim headed over to the University and went directly to Henry Talbot's office and asked, "Is the boss in yet?'

His secretary pushed a button on her phone and asked, "Do you have time to speak with Coach Sams?"

"Yes. Send him in," Talbot said. "Hello Jim, how's the relocation coming?"

"That's why I'm here to see you this morning. Is your offer to find me a place to stay on campus still an option, at least thru volleyball season?" Jim asked.

"I'm sure we can do that. What made you change your mind?"

"Once I cleared my mind and settled down about losing my house, I concluded that I could get a lot more done If I stayed on campus. That way I can spend more time developing Coach King and working with the new players on our team. Also, we are going to do a lot of traveling this season, and not needing to drive south twenty miles after being who knows where in this country, will be a lot easier on me. Everything is just more convenient."

"I understand. I should be able to find a nice place for you on campus by this afternoon. Give me a call shortly before your practice this afternoon and I'll let you know where you'll be staying. Ok?" said Talbot.

"That's great," Jim said.

12
BAD NEWS

Jim went to lunch early, having missed breakfast this morning, so he headed back to Tater's Café to get a better idea of their limited menu. As he was preparing to order his phone buzzed.

"Mr. Sams? This is Deputy Rafferty. I'm calling to let you know that the CID arson inspectors will be at the site of your burned house early tomorrow morning. They will cordon off everything and prevent anyone, other than their forensic team, from entering beyond the tapeline."

"That didn't take much time. Any idea when they'll be able to find out what caused the fire?" Jim asked.

"I'm thinking they will be done by next Monday. House fires normally aren't very complicated."

"Ok. Do I call you or will you call me?"

"You'd better call me. I may get busy and forget to contact you," Deputy Rafferty said.

"Sounds good. Thanks for taking care of this," Jim said.

After eating a big lunch, Jim called Liz, "Hey, sorry to leave so early this morning, but I wanted to take care of a few things before it got too crazy here. Did you get my note?"

"Yes. I know you have a lot on your mind right now. No problem," she said.

"Well, I've changed my mind about staying at your house, at least until I find out who was following me. If it turns out to be the next wave of thugs, there's no way I want them to know where you live."

"I was really looking forward to seeing you all the time, but I understand. I think it's the right thing to do," she said.

"Thanks for understanding. I need to get going now, so I'll call you later tonight. I love you," Jim said.

During the hours before the beginning of practice, Jim spent an hour looking at video tape of their next opponent, San Diego State. A reporter from the Polk County Itemizer-Observer walked into Jim's office and ask, "Hello coach Sams. Would you have a few minutes to talk with me?"

"Maybe. Who are you?" Jim asked.

"I'm Anthony Valentina, but everyone calls me Tony. I'm the new sports reporter for the Polk County I & O newspaper."

"What would you like to talk about?"

"I'd like to do a piece on you and Cascade's volleyball team. I'm also interested in finding out about your house burning down while you were away, if that would be possible?" Tony responded.

"Well, me and the volleyball team are possible. The house thing is impossible?"

"I was really interested in the 'house thing' as you put it. Is there some problem?" questioned Tony.

"No. There's no problem because I don't know what happened. If you drop the subject, I'd be happy to talk about our volleyball team. If I ever see one word in your newspaper about my house burning down, I'll never talk with you about anything again. Ever! Clear?"

"Absolutely!" Tony said.

The interview was better than Jim thought it would be and as Tony was leaving, Jim received a call from Director Talbot. "Jim. I've arranged for you to stay in the Cramer House. It's located behind our building and bit to the south."

"Good, that's great. Thank you, Henry," Jim said.

He was happy about being in a house instead of a dorm and its location would let him keep an eye on the athletic department's parking lot.

The afternoon's practice was a lot better than he'd anticipated. Both passing and serving were substantially improved. The players worked hard and followed directions from Mark and Kristy.

When the workout was done Jim asked his assistants, "What did you two do to get this type of improvement from the kids?"

Mark answered, "It was just a simple change in what you'd asked for yesterday. We had them work on passing first and serving second. Both drills tired them out again, but they were fresh for passing."

Kristy added, "If you remember, we've been winning almost all of our matches in three games. I think what you told them about getting to bed earlier will help as we go deeper into our schedule. I doubt if it had any effect on today's workout."

"Good point Kristy and a nice move by both of you switching the sequence of drills for today." Jim said.

After checking his office to see if anything needed his attention following practice, he went to check out the Cramer House. It had furniture, a television, appliances in the kitchen, towels and toilet paper in the bathroom and a queen size bed in the bedroom. There was no food in the place, which ment he would be eating at a restaurant in town this evening.

He decided to treat himself and selected the Washington Street

Steakhouse and Pub, more for the food than the ambiance. After polishing off an Angus sirloin, he topped the meal off with their famous cheesecake.

When he got back to the Cramer House, He was too full to do any volleyball work, so he turned the television on, without sound, and called Liz. "I hope it's not too late to call."

"Not at all. How have things been going today?" she asked.

"Pretty well. Talbot arranged for a house for me. I had a visit from a sports reporter from the Polk County I & O newspaper. And the Deputy Sheriff got the CID to investigate what caused the fire at my house,"

"That sounds like a full day. When will someone tell you what caused the fire?" she asked.

"The deputy said they should be done by Monday. I just hope they can confirm the reason for it burning down, and not just that they're done investigating. I want to know the reason why it happened," Jim said.

"That would be nice. If I know anything about you by now, I know you will not stop pressing until you know for sure," Liz said.

"Yea, you may be right. I do tend to need all the facts with things that affect us or my family," he said. "I guess it's a good thing that it's volleyball season now or I would be a lot worse. How are you doing?"

"It's only been a day without you here, but I'm worried I could become very lonely if you don't find out what happened soon," she said.

"I feel the same way. Why don't you come to the match Saturday night and spend the night here with me?" Jim asked.

"That sounds good. What time do you start playing?"

"Play begins at seven pm, but the warmup begins at six. That's when I would like you to be here. Ok?"

"Yes. I'll see you then. I love you," she said.

Jim decided to hold full practices on both Thursday and Friday, which was something he seldom did. The decision was based on his players having all day Saturday to rest up before the match in the evening. San Diego State played exactly the way Jim described. Cascade lost the first game, won the second, lost the third and won the fourth. It all came down to the final game, which was supposed to be played to fifteen points. That game was a back-and-forth affair and went all the way to a final score of twenty-three to twenty-one, in favor or Cascade. A tremendous roar from the packed house went up when the final point was scored.

It's never easy for coaches to get out of the gym at the end of a volleyball match, particularly when they win. Cascade's ADs, coaches, players from other sports and fans always want to celebrate and compliment the team and coaches. Now there was the press that had to be considered, win, or lose. It was close to eleven pm by the time Jim and Liz left the gym. Jim found Kristy and asked her to tell the team that they had Monday off.

Liz was waiting for Jim to finish talking with friends and fans. When he spotted her, he asked, "Are you hungry?"

"Not really. Let's just go to your place and celebrate."

"Sounds good. Don't expect too much, it's kind of rough," Jim said as they left the gym.

It was ten o'clock the next morning before either one of them opened their eyes. Jim said, "Since there is absolutely no food in this house yet, I know of a great little place in town to get breakfast. What do you say?"

"Sounds good. I'm really hungry this morning for some reason." Liz said.

Jim took a quick look through the front window to check out the parking lot. He wanted to be sure the black SUV, that followed him the other day, was nowhere to be seen.

When they arrived at Tater's, Liz suggested, "Can we eat outside? There's a couple of empty tables and it's a lovely morning."

"Yes, that's a great idea," Jim said. He ordered an omelet and a glass of milk and Liz ordered eggs benedict and tea. They spent the better part of an hour enjoying their meals and the fresh air. Jim asked, "I've got to go grocery shopping and then get some new clothes. I've been living out of the suitcase I took to New Orleans. Would you mind coming with me?"

"Not at all, this could be fun," she said, with a big smile.

Having bought everything he needed, he cruised past the parking lot in front of the Cramer House. There were just a few cars parked near the Athletic Department building, but he did see the black SUV in the far corner of the lot. Knowing they could see both buildings from their vantage point, Jim kept driving. He headed to the Dallas Police Department and asked the officer at the front desk, "Hello officer, is officer Wingard working today?"

"No, he's off on Sundays, I'm Officer Nowlin."

"Is there someone I can talk with about a suspicious vehicle following my every move?"

"What's the problem?" Nowlin asked.

"I was hoping an officer could confront a couple of guys driving a certain black SUV and try to make them stop following me."

"We don't have any officers on duty here at the station today since it's Sunday. I can call a patrolman and have him meet you somewhere. Will that work for you?"

"Yes. That would be good. I'd like to see him as soon as possible on the north side of the University, next to the fountain. Should I go there and wait for him?" Jim asked.

"It would be best if you let him get there first. That way, if there's any confusion on where to meet, you would be better able to track him down," said Officer Nowlin. "You should wait here until I contact him, and he responds that he is in place."

"Perfect. I can't thank you enough," Jim said.

Thirty-five minutes passed and Jim walked over to check with the desk, "Does it normally take this long to get an officer in position to meet?"

"No. This is not at all normal. I would say you can go take a look. Call back and let me know if he's there or not. He could be someplace nearby waiting for you," Nowlin said.

Jim and Liz could see the police car as they pulled onto the cement surrounding the fountain. There was no sign of life, except that the officer's vehicle's passenger door was open. Jim parked well away from the police car and, as he began to approach it, he could see what looked like bullet holes in the back and driver side windows. He approached the open door carefully and saw that no one was in the cruiser. He quickly turned around and looked to see if he was in danger. What he saw was the harshest thing imaginable. The patrolman was float-ing face down in the fountain. Blood was slowly seeping out of two bullet holes in the back of his head. He ran back to his car and told Liz to get down out of sight. Jim called the Police Station and quickly described the scene to the Desk Officer. Within three minutes, Jim and Liz could hear sirens blaring in the distance.

Soon there were three police cars, a Deputy Sheriff's car, and a State Police car surrounding the perimeter of the fountain. Close behind them an ambulance arrived that had 'EMT-Paramedic' written on its sides, which distinguished it from other ambulances. The police officers removed their colleague from the water and placed him on the grass where the medical examiner pronounced him dead.

The officers began to search the area for evidence related to this tragedy and another small group of officers talked to each other. Finally, one of them from the group approached Jim's vehicle, and said "May I have your name please?"

"Certainly, I'm Jim Sams."

"And what's the woman's name?"

"This is Liz Barnett"

"Tell me what you two were doing here," the officer asked in a rather rude voice.

"I was sent out here by the Desk Officer at the Dallas Police Department. We were to meet an officer here. I suggest you call the Desk Officer to obtain any more information," Jim said.

"I'll do that. But I want both of you out of the car. Now!"

"Yes sir," Jim said, as he and Liz got out.

"Stand in front of the car and don't move until I tell you to move!" said the officer.

A State Policeman joined the officer questioning Jim, and then they both searched the car thoroughly. When they were done, they told Jim he and Liz could get back in their car. The officer stood outside Jim's window and called in to his Station. After about five minutes, he turned to Jim and said, "Mr. Sams and Ms. Barnett, thank you for being so cooperative. I hope you will forgive my rudeness in ordering you around, but me and all of the police you see here just lost a great comrade."

"Yes, we understand. We're sorry for your loss. Can we go now?" Jim asked.

Heading back to the Cramer House, Jim decided to get things unloaded and to follow Liz on her way back to her house. That way he could be sure that the black SUV did not follow.

13
WHY

It was smooth sailing to Liz's house, with never a sign of the black SUV. "Well, I'm happy that there were no thugs following us. I think it's best if you stay away from Dallas until the police figure out who killed that police officer," Jim said. "I think if something ever happened to you, my world would end."

"That's so nice of you to say Jim. But you need to know that if anything ever happened to you, my world would also end."

"Looks like both of us need to be extra cautious," Jim said. "Do you have anything in the house to protect yourself with, besides Queeny?"

"All I can think of is kitchen knives. I've never looked through the things in the attic, but I think Dan may have had a gun hidden somewhere up there," she said.

"Would you mind going up into the attic with me while I look around?" he asked.

"Ok, but I warn you, the place is a mess. I've avoided it because of too many memories."

"That's just why I asked you to come up with me. I don't want to look through anything that would bring back those unpleasant memories," he explained.

They spent over an hour looking in trunks and boxes, many of which lacked any identification about what was inside. Jim opened a medium size wood box that contained an assortment of pistols. He was not as knowledgeable about handguns as he was about fishing rods, but he figured out what Liz would need to protect herself. He selected a SIG Sauer P365 XL Romeo Aero Elite, with a 3.7" barrel and a twelve-round clip for Liz. For himself, he found a SIG Sauer P229 Equinox Elite Compact, 9mm Luger, 3.9" barrel length, with Day/Night sights, and a fifteen-round clip, all kept in a dual combination gun case. A Styrofoam box contained numerous boxes of ammunition and cleaning supplies.

Liz carried the pistols downstairs and Jim carried a couple of boxes with cartridges for both guns. "Do you mind if I try to find a rifle or shotgun up there?" he asked Liz.

"Really? You don't think that a pistol will do the job?" she asked.

"I'm kind of concerned about someone breaking into the house in the middle of the night. With a shotgun you don't need to be too precise. You just point and shoot. I don't know how accurate I'd be waking up with only a handgun."

"Yea, I see what you mean. Go ahead and look," she said.

Jim came down twenty minutes later, carrying a strange looking rifle. Liz asked, "What is that?"

"I have no idea what it is. It just looks like a bulky shotgun from the prohibition era. The paperwork in the box described it as a full-auto AA12 Sledgehammer shotgun. The price receipt said three-thousand two-hundred fifty dollars. It can hold up to thirty-two rounds in a drum magazine. I need to go back upstairs and carry down the ammo for this thing."

"Jim, I had no idea that all this was up there," Liz said.

"Don't let it worry you Liz. It's something from the past that happens to be just what we need now to protect ourselves. That policeman in the fountain had a gun and he was still killed. At least this way we may be able to protect ourselves," he said, trying to calm Liz down. "Now that we have these weapons, and that I don't need to be back to work until Tuesday morning, I think we need to head up into the mountains tomorrow and practice a little. Are you alright with that?" he asked.

"Yes. I think we should do that, but I don't know a thing about guns," she said.

"I don't know a lot either, but we both graduated from college, so I know we can figure out what we need to work on. Let's grab a bite to eat and call it a night."

Monday morning, after a light breakfast, Jim and Liz went up into the coast range mountains, to an old rock quarry, and practiced shooting for about half an hour. Seeing that they were both hitting the targets more often than not, Jim said, "What do you think? Should we stop, or rest a bit and have another go at it?"

"I'm done. I don't think my ear drums can take it anymore. You can shoot some more if you want, but I'll wait in the car," she said.

"Sorry about your ears hurting. Guns do make a lot of noise, don't they? I've had enough too. I think I've got the hang of it. I don't need to mess with the Sledgehammer now. I'd like to get h72 down back up to Dallas before late afternoon and see if the forensic crew has any information about what started the fire at my house."

"That's fine. I'll fix something for lunch, and you can be on your way. Do you think the police will have any information yet on who killed the man in the fountain?" Liz asked.

"I doubt that they have anything yet." Jim said.

Jim pulled into Dallas just after two pm and stopped at his burnt lot, hoping to be able to speak with the forensic team. The yellow 'no trespassing' tape was still up, but there was no sign of activity. He dialed Detective Rafferty, but it went straight to a recording. His next option was to head to the Dallas police station and find out if they had any information about the dead officer.

"Good afternoon, Officer. Any news on why the policeman was killed yesterday, or who may have killed him?" asked Jim.

"None. It's only been about twenty-four hours since he was killed. Why are you so anxious to find out?" asked the desk Officer.

"I'm kind of worried that whoever killed him, may be trying to kill me as well."

"I doubt it. You just need to let us figure things out and then we'll let you know the what, and the why."

"Yea. I'm just concerned. That's all. Thanks," Jim said.

Jim dialed Detective Rafferty's number from his car, and again, it went to a recording. He was beginning to feel that he was completely out of the loop on these two problems. He wondered how he could protect himself if he didn't know why his house burned or why the police officer was killed. He thought about calling Agent Wallace to see if he could get some answers, and then remembered that the FBI would not get involved in intrastate crimes.

Jim looked at his phone to see if it was too early to think about supper. He decided to visit Abby's Legendary's Pizza and ordered a small Abby's Special and salad to go. He was making a habit of driving by the athletic department and checking out the parking lot before parking at the Cramer House. A few cars were in the lot, but no black SUV, which was good news to Jim.

He parked and carried in the food from Abby's and both guns. His next thought was about where to stash the guns. He vacillated between the living room and the bedroom, knowing that the hiding place needed to be easy to get to at a moment's notice. He decided on putting the handgun in the nightstand next to his bed and the Sledgehammer just behind the bed's headboard, with the barrel down and the stock end up. The house was so small, he knew it would take just a few moments to get to the bedroom from anywhere in the house.

Jim put away all the clothes he'd purchased and straightened up his bedroom. He checked all the windows and both the front and back doors and found that they needed to be beefed up. The ACE hardware store in Dallas had everything he needed to increase the safety of the house and it also offered a variety of warning devices that would broadcast any unwanted entry. It was supper time when he finished installing everything and felt the house was now secure. He ate a cold pizza, salad, a warm cup of tomato soup, and finished off the meal with some fresh blue berries. After eating, his thoughts wandered back to the security of the Camry House. He decided to get a visual record of anyone that tried to break in, so before calling it a night he went online and ordered two 'Ring'   doorbells.

He spent a restless night and awoke from a confusing dream at six am. The first thing he did was look out the front window to see if the black SUV was in the parking lot. An idea popped into his head, and he used his phone to take a couple of photos of the cars that were in the lot.

Following a long, hot shower, in a very small bathroom, he headed to Tater's. Two eggs, over easy, hashbrowns and two pieces of wheat toast prepared him for the day's work.

In his office, the phone rang while he was completing his expense report for the matches in Louisiana.

"Hello, is this Jim Sams?" asked a familiar voice.

"Yes. Who's calling?" Jim asked.

"This is Agent Wallace."

"Oh yea. Sorry. I didn't recognize your voice. What's up?" Jim asked, hoping for some good news.

"Well, it's a long story. We have received information from the Utah Field Agency, regarding a fire recently at your former residence."

"That's strange. How did the Utah FBI get information about my house burning down?"

"That's what the 'long story' is. The Field Agency in Portland, Oregon received the results of an arson investigation by the Oregon CID. The investigation was at your burnt house, and a piece of evidence regarding what started the fire there, matched evidence of what started two fires in Twin Falls, Idaho. Those fires in Twin Falls are being investigated by the Salt Lake City Field Agency, as part of a much larger investigation." Wallace said.

"What larger investigation are they conducting," asked Jim.

"I'm sure you understand that I'm not at liberty to discuss any of that investigation with you."

"Sorry." Jim said. "Will I be told what happened at my house. Who did it? What started the fire? Why did the whole house burn to the ground?"

"That I can discuss with you. First, there were two points of ignition. One in the kitchen and one in the front room. Gasoline was used to start those locations. The thing that was most destructive and what made it so hard to extinguish, was that the fire was oxyacetylene. Evidence of bottles of oxyacetylene were found in every room of the house and the garage. Once the gasoline flames heat the place up, the high temperature ignites the oxyacetylene, which can reach temperatures in excess of a thousand degrees fahrenheit. And water does not extinguish oxyacetylene flames."

"So now what?" Jim asked.

"It looks like we have three house fires, that were all destroyed the same way, and with the same ingredients. The FBI will now try to connect the three fires, and concurrently, we'll be looking for the perpetrators," Wallace said.

"Am I cleared to begin building on my lot," asked Jim.

"It's all yours my friend. We have no further interest. Thanks for your help," said Wallace.

Jim thought for a minute that investigating all three fires might somehow, ultimately involve him. He realized that scenario was nothing to worry about now. His team and the black SUV were where he needed to focus. Making one highly successful and getting rid of the other would now be his top priority.

He advised his insurance agent that he was now cleared by the authorities to begin construction of his new home. "Good," the agent said, "Our inspector has completed his inspection and determined that your home was a total loss."

Jim chuckled and said, "I don't think his job was too tough on this one."

"I agree. From our end, you can begin construction at any time. You will be required to retain all receipts, drafts, blueprints, city required inspections as construction advances, a copy of electrical inspection from state, a list of all contractors, certificate of insurance during the time you are building, a copy of the Right of Occupancy from the city, approval from the state, and anything else that has to do with building your house. You and I will sit down, when you've completed construction and replaced all the different items that you lost in the fire, so we can issue a new Homeowner's policy."

"When do I give all of this stuff to you?" Jim asked.

"You should get everything turned in as soon as you can. Some items, have progressive completion dates. Just mail or bring in everything you get as soon as you get it. If there's something that's not complete when you give it to me, I'll tell you how to handle it."

"Ok. Don't get upset if I'm late on some things. I'll have a lot on my plate trying to get the house built, especially while I'm coaching my team, and then during the time I'm away recruiting," Jim said.

"I'm not worried. I know you'll be able to handle everything," concluded the agent.

Cascades next opponent was TCU, coached by his friend Jaydon Wilson, and Jim needed to prepare his coaches and team for that competition. Jim new that Jaydon was a good coach and would be able to compete in the match with the talent he inherited.

He called Chris and said, "Chris, I want you, Mark, and Kristy to be in my office in half an hour. Please make sure they both know."

"Consider it done," Chris said.

Fifteen minutes before the meeting Jim got up and walked around the second floor and looked out the windows onto the parking lot. So far today, there was no sign of the black SUV. He wondered if he'd seen the end of that car and the people inside. Just to be sure, he found a window that looked down on the Cramer House and checked for the SUV there. The whole parking area by the house was empty. His mood improved as he returned to his office.

"Hello Jim. How's everything?" Mark asked.

"Not bad at all. I've just received the go ahead on building a new house on the same lot as my previous house. Talbot arranged for me to stay in the Cramer House, just behind this building, until my house is completed. And, we have a match against TCU at home this weekend.

Their coach is a friend of mine, and he just got the head coaching position. When I first approached him about playing us, he was a bit apprehensive. There is not much talent now at TCU, but I'm sure he will have his players ready to play. I want each of you to motivate our players to play hard and not let up at any time during this match."

14
DANGER LURKS

Jim enjoyed the match with TCU a lot more than Jaydon. His players were not quite Division I athletes, and they struggled most of the match. When he and Jaydon shook hands at the end of the match, Jim tried to be as gracious as possible. "Don't worry, I know you will turn this program around. It will take some time, but I know you can do it."

"I sure hope so. I've never been with any collegiate team, at any level, that got stomped like this team tonight," Jaydon said.

"Is there anything you need before you head back to Texas?" asked Jim.

"No thanks. After the team showers, we'll head for the airport and be home around midnight. I'll definitely refrain from talking about tonight's match with the team. I think it just needs to sink in with these players. Thanks for a nice welcome and everything you had ready for us. I was impressed," Jaydon said.

"I look forward to the return match at your place after you have time to field the type of team you envision. I wish you all the best."

Before leaving the gym, Jim asked Mark to let the team know they had Monday off.

"That's getting to be a habit," Mark said.

"I agree, but I don't want them to ever feel that volleyball is all they do. Particularly while we're in season," Jim said. "I want them to look forward to practicing and enjoy coming to the gym."

Jim woke up Sunday morning at six-thirty and decided to drive down to Liz's house. He showered, ate a light breakfast, and went out to his car. As he was leaving his small parking lot, he glanced in his rear-view mirror and saw the black SUV at the far end of the lot next to the athletic building.

"Why," he asked himself out loud. "Every time I think they're never to be seen again, they appear."

He pointed his car towards the Cascade Mountains, on the east side of the Willamette Valley, knowing he could elude them without too much effort. Staying well away from Liz's house was his goal anytime he was followed. Before he got too far ahead of the SUV, he slowed down, trying to see who was in the vehicle. The SUV reacted to Jim's slowing down and speeding up, which made it hard to get a good look through their windshield. At one point he was able to see two, big scary guys in the front seats and what looked like two more guys, in the back seats.

Up in the mountains, he knew he could stay so far ahead of them that they would never know when he descended back into the valley. As he drove across the valley and on to Liz's house, he began thinking about Liz moving further south, maybe to Creswell. That small community had four ways to get out of town; south, west, north, and east. But it was a small town and probably everyone knew everyone else who lived there. Cottage Grove might be a better option. The town was much larger, and it too had four ways to leave town, two of which led into the mountains.

It was a bit after nine when he pulled into Liz's barn. The back deck door into the house was locked, so Jim went around to the front. The front door was also locked. Finally, he knocked a couple of times and waited for Liz to answer. No response. He began to call for Queeny knowing that dog could hear anything around the house. Absolutely no response. Now he began to worry. He went back to the rear deck and dialed Liz on his phone.

"Hello," she answered, without sounding sleepy.

"Liz, this is Jim. I'm sitting on the back deck. I knocked here and on the front door. Didn't you hear any of that?"

"I have great hearing, but I can't hear you from the grocery store," she said.

"Oh. I thought you would be home. My bad," he said. "How much longer will you be shopping?"

"Give me twenty minutes. I'm anxious to see you," she said.

Even though it was Sunday, Jim used the time waiting for Liz to call the Dallas Police Department. "Hello, this is Jim Sams. Are you the officer that usually works the front desk?"

"No. This is Officer Wingard. Officer Nowlin is out sick today," said Officer Wingard. "What can I help you with?"

"I'm calling to find out if you guys have figured out who killed the police officer that was killed the other day in the fountain on the campus of Cascade University."

"We are getting close to making an arrest. That's all the information I can give you right now," said Wingard.

"That sounds like your department has identified someone," Jim pushed.

"Like I said, we're close to arresting someone. Will there be anything else?" asked Wingard.

"No thanks. I appreciate what you've told me. Sorry to push."

Fifteen minutes later, Liz pulled up. Jim helped bring in the groceries and after hugs and kisses, he said, "I'm beginning to think that living here is too dangerous for you. There are now four big guys in the black SUV that try to follow me whenever I leave the house. From what I can tell by looking at them in my rearview mirror, they could be Mexican, or from somewhere in Central or South America. They are relentless. They have all the time in the world to find out where we live, and to plan how to eliminate us. The Dallas police won't tell me who killed the cop we discovered in the fountain. At this point, I think it's best if you relocate further south."

"Do you mean to stay with one of your daughters again?" Liz asked.

"No, I don't think that would be a good idea. In addition to me, these guys are smart enough to try and kill anyone associated with me. I was thinking of getting a rental for you in Cottage Grove, or even Roseburg for a few months."

"Does that mean I wouldn't be able to see you very often?" she asked.

"I will try my best to see you as much as I can. It may be a little hard during the volleyball season, but I know that we will see a great deal of each other once the season is over."

"Let me think about it for a while. Right now, I'd much rather be with you all the time. We do have the guns for protection," she said.

"Liz, I'd like to be with you all the time too. I think it would be smarter to get you completely away from these animals. Four of them with guns, against two of us, gives them the advantage. Plus, they would have the element of surprise on their side," he said, trying to reason with her.

"When do we do this?" she asked.

"I'm free tomorrow. How about we drive down to Cottage Grove and look around, and then continue on to Roseburg. If we don't find anything we like in either town, we'll go to plan B," Jim said.

"And what is plan B?" Liz asked, in a not so happy manner.

"Plan B is you come live with me in Cramer House until I get the new house built. We'll just need to be super cautious," Jim said.

"I don't care for plan A or plan B. Why not just stay in my house?"

"I would love that, but I know that each time I'd come to see you, I'd need to get away from the guys who follow my every move. Odds are they'd figure things out sooner or later," Jim said. "How about we drive down to Cottage Grove and Roseburg tomorrow, just to look around? Then we'll keep checking with the Dallas Police to see if they've figured out who killed the officer in the fountain. I think that when they solve that crime, we'll be able to get around-the- clock protection while we're in Cramer house. What do you say?" he asked.

"I like that better," Liz said. "It's time for lunch. Are you hungry?"

"I'm hungry for lunch and for you," he said, with a twinkle in his eye.

The next morning it was raining hard when they got on the road, and it was raining harder when they arrived in Cottage Grove. Jim decided to continue on to Roseburg, hoping the rain would let up when they arrived.

Liz opened the map app on her phone and suggested that they get off of Interstate Five at Winchester and take the north bank road into the city. The rain had stopped, and blue sky was beginning to show through the clouds. It took about twenty-five minutes to reach the northern outskirts of the city of Roseburg and they saw a lot of nice homes during their detour.

"How do you plan to look at all the neighborhoods here?" Liz asked Jim.

"I want to find a place that is located where there are three or four exit roads, should we need to leave on a moment's notice. I've learned that the easiest way to elude the people who've been following me is to head into the mountains. But I'd like to be able to get out on Interstate five as well."

After looking at all the contingent neighborhoods, they found a real estate office and went inside. "Hello folks, can I help you?" asked a nicely dressed young lady.

"Yes. My name is Frank, and this is my wife, Scarlet. We're interested in renting a house or condo located near the Templin Beach Park," Jim said.

"Nice to meet you. My name is Lauren. Give me a minute while I check to see if we have any listings in that area. I'm sorry to tell you that there is nothing available in that area or for any of the neighborhoods west or east of the river until you get way up the North Umpqua Highway."

"I guess we'll just have to look a bit more. Thanks for your help," Jim said. They headed up the North Umpqua Highway and turned on to the north bank road. "Didn't we see a couple of 'For Sale' signs up this way?" he asked Liz.

"I don't remember. I was too busy looking at the countryside," she said.

About half a mile north, Jim spotted the home he'd seen that had a 'For Sale' sign out by the road. He crossed the cattle guard and before they reached the house, the front door opened.

He parked the car, and both he and Liz got out and approached the house. "Hello. We saw the for sale sign over by the road. Are you the owner?" Jim asked.

"I am. My children want me to sell this place. They think I'm too old to live here all alone."

"Are you working with a real estate company or are you selling it yourself?" Jim asked.

"I'm selling it myself. I can't see any need for those blood suck-
ing salespeople."

"My name is Jim, and this is my wife, Elizabeth. We'd like to talk
to you about buying," Jim said.

"Ok. Now's as good a time as any. Come on in," the lady said.
Once everyone was inside and seated, she asked, "What do you want
to know."

"First off, we'd like to know the asking price for the house
and property."

"This old house sits on fifteen acres and I'm asking two hundred
seventy thousand for the whole shebang," she said.

"That sounds reasonable. I also want to know how you get your
water and electricity," Jim asked.

"Water for the house comes from a well my husband put in for-
ty-seven years ago. We didn't want to be drinking water from that
filthy river. But we had a pump that brought water up from the river
to irrigate with. Electricity comes into the house, underground, from
those telephone poles out by the road," she said. "Any other questions?"

"Do you own the house?" Jim asked.

"You bet your sweet ass I do. Bob and I got it paid off twenty-nine
years ago. We loved living here. He passed away six years ago and
since then, I've gradually lost interest," she said as she began to tear up.

Liz got up and sat down next to the lady and said, "There now,
there's no need to cry. It sounds like you have done quite well out
here. Maybe being with other people is what would be best for you
now. I have a suggestion that might work for you."

As she dried her eyes, the lady asked, "What's your suggestion?"

"Maybe Jim and I could rent this from you for a while and you can
move in with your children. Or maybe try living in a retirement home,
just to see if you'd like it or not. If you like either option, we will live

here and pay you rent. That way, you will still own everything. If you don't like living somewhere else, we will move out and you can come back and live here. We'll let you think about this and check back with you in a few days," Liz said.

"That sounds pretty good young lady. Let me give you my phone number so you can call me, and I'll let you know in four days. By the way, my name is Betty, Betty Brown, everyone calls me BB."

"Thanks BB, for talking with us today. We'll wait for your call Friday, four days from today. It's been a pleasure to visit with you," Liz said.

As Jim and Liz drove away, Jim said, "That was a great thing you did back there. I'm sure you made BB feel better. This must have been the first time she's had to face the reality of moving out of her house. And you gave her a way to return if she decided she didn't like living somewhere else. Plus, we don't need to go through the hassle of trying to buy her place. The house was livable, from the little we saw, but it would take lots of work."

"You don't mind what I said?" Liz questioned.

"Not at all. How you comforted her and what you suggested were priceless. I couldn't be prouder of you. Time to head back to your house. I'll stay with you tonight and leave early tomorrow morning for Dallas," he said.

15
TOO MANY THINGS

Rising early allowed Jim to drive up to Dallas without rushing, and it gave him time to think. He felt that he had more things than usual on his mind to think about and he worried that he might not take care of all the details. Liz, his family, his job, building a new house, moving Liz to Roseburg, and the scary thugs, circulated endlessly in his head, and he was having trouble falling asleep at night. The only time his mind relaxed in the evening was when he slept with Liz.

The one thing that kept popping up in his mind, was the policeman in the fountain. Jim, Liz, and the desk officer at the Dallas Police Station were the only ones who knew the meeting place and time. There was only one way the thugs could have known when the officer would've been there. Jim considered confronting Officer Nowlin, but instead he called Agent Wallace.

"This is agent Wallace."

"Hello, this is Jim Sams. I need to talk with you about a homicide here in Dallas. You're the only one that I trust. Have you got a few minutes to talk?" Jim asked.

"Hey, Jim. Certainly. What's on your mind?"

"A few days ago, my girlfriend and I went into the police department here in Dallas, to ask if they could find out why a black SUV was following my every move. This was on a Sunday, and the regular desk officer was not working. We spoke with an officer named Nowlin, who said he filled in on Sundays. This Nowlin guy told us we should meet with a patrol officer to discuss the problem. We agreed to meet with the officer at a fountain on the north campus of Cascade University. Nowlin told us we should wait for the officer to call in and let us know he was at the fountain. After thirty minutes or so, I asked Nowlin if we shouldn't get over to the fountain instead of waiting in the station. He told us to go ahead. When my girlfriend and I arrived, we found the officer's patrol car shot up and then discovered the officer face down in the fountain. I called back to the police station and told them what I'd found. Minutes later we were surrounded by Dallas Police, Deputy Sheriffs, and State Police. They interrogated us and, after me telling them that we were sent to the fountain by the desk officer at the Dallas Police Department, they let us go. I got to thinking about how everything happened and decided to call you."

"Sounds like a mess, but why call me?" asked Wallace.

"Because I think the guys in the black SUV, that have been following me, are the same ones that may have killed Trish Kingery. And, I think the desk officer, Nowlin, told the SUV guys where we were to meet the officer, so they could kill both of us. I think Nowlin's dirty. So, if it is him and the SUV guys, that's crime in Oregon, connected to crime in Idaho. What do you think?" Jim asked.

"You may have something. I'm going to need a couple of days to finish up things I'm working on here before I can't get away. How does Thursday sound?" Wallace asked.

"I'll look for you on Thursday. Thanks," Jim said.

The conversation with Wallace made Jim feel better as he headed to his office. He knew he was behind on recruiting at this point, so he decided to spend the next two days trying to contact both of the players he was recruiting. His goal was to convince them that Cascade University was the school that would be best for them. He needed to wait until the players got home, from school and volleyball practice before he could call, which gave him time to look for sub-contractors he would need to build his new house. He spent time creating a list of trades that would be needed and jotted down their phone numbers. What he quickly realized was that most of the builders were busy until after the normal work hour, and only a few of the businesses he called answered. Everyone he spoke with told him it would be months before they could commit to his job.

Frustrated, Jim visited with two others in his building, that had their homes built, trying to get contact information so he could call them. He learned that both of the builders had retired.

The only thing left to do, was to go to practice. He entered the gym and greeted his assistants, spending a bit of time making small talk with them, before Kristy and Mark began warmups. Jim moved off to the side of the gym where Chris was sitting and asked, "How's the search for housing going? Have you guys got a realtor yet?" he asked.

Chris said, "We do, but we're not real impressed with him. Mark is leaning more towards building instead of buying at this point. It won't be long before we need to move out of the apartment that the school provided for us. It looks like we'll need to rent for a while. Either way, buying or building will take time."

"Yea, your right. I thought building would be pretty easy, time wise, but I've just started looking for subcontractors and they're all busy. Looks like months before anyone I select can begin," Jim said.

"Would you mind telling Mark? I think he'll listen to you more than me," Chris said.

"Sure. No problem," Jim responded.

After warmups concluded, Jim called the team together and said,

"Ladies, our performance so far has been excellent. This weekend's matches, like the rest of our schedule, will be challenging. I know you have the ability to defeat any team we meet, but don't take anything for granted. The first part of practice today will be playing against one another, without any attacks. It will be all roll shots to the middle of the court, shots to the corners, isolating the opponent's setter for their first contact, and blocking by both teams. We will play short games to eight. The second part of practice will be games where you attack from anywhere in the court, with no dinking or soft shots, also to eight points. Any questions? Oh, I forgot to tell you, Sally and Iliana will choose teams. There will be a lot of movement on the court so be careful not to run into anyone."

Anyone watching practice, that didn't know what was happening, would have been completely confused. However, the players did their best to follow instructions, and they were all having fun.

When practice ended Jim went back to Cramer House, looked around for the black SUV without spotting it, and made himself some dinner. At seven o'clock he made his first recruiting call to Carol Mattingly. She was a six foot three, left-handed outside hitter from Fargo, North Dakota, that played for the best club team in the state. "Hello, this is Coach Sams from Cascade University. I apologize for calling so late. Would Carol be available to talk for a few minutes?" Jim asked.

"Hello coach. This is Carol. I can talk to you as long as you like," she said.

"That's nice of you to say, but people tell me I tend to talk too much. You are my number one recruit this year and I hope you will be able to make a visit to Cascade University to meet our team, see our campus, and the state of Oregon."

"I'm very interested in visiting your school and checking everything out. But I've talked things over with my mom and she wants me to go to a school near here."

"Carol, that's a very common reaction by parents. Most have a difficult time dealing with the fact that their child is growing up. What they don't consider is that their little girl has a great opportunity to experience new places, to get a free education, and to prepare for life on their own," Jim said. "The decision has to be your own. Your mom is not going to lose you. You will return home during the summers and maybe your mom could visit you out here."

"Coach, I understand all that, but she's a single mom and there are no relatives here for her to be with if I leave," Carol said.

"What do you mean by no relatives?"

"Dad died when I was in middle school. She was an only child, and both of her parents have passed on. She has a few friends, but no relatives."

"I see. That does make it a tough situation. How about it if I come and do a home visit with both of you?" Jim asked.

"That's a good idea. I think she'd enjoy meeting you. Me too. When can you visit?" Carol asked.

"I'll look at the recruiting rules and let you know in a day or two. You're still in your volleyball season, right?"

"Yes, I can send you an email with our schedule if you like."

"Please do that. I'd like to visit North Dakota. Also, if you don't mind, send me anything you have about your high school grades, activities, work experience, interests, that sort of thing.

I guarantee you a full athletic scholarship, but there may be a chance to get you more support from other bursaries."

"Coach, what was that last word you just said?" Carol asked.

"It means grants. It's a good thing."

"Oh. I'll get everything you asked for in a couple of days. Thanks so much for calling me tonight. Goodbye," she said.

"It was my pleasure, Carol. Goodbye." Jim concluded.

His second call for the night was to Cloe Stratford, a libero from Lees Summit, Missouri. "Hello, this is Coach Sams from Cascade University. I apologize for calling so late. Would Cloe be available to talk for a few minutes?" Jim asked.

"Hello coach, I'm Cloe's mom, Linda. Cloe's at practice now and should be home in about half an hour."

"I'm reluctant to call that late at night. Sometimes a conversation can go on for a couple of hours. What's the best time to call?" Jim asked

"That's a good question. She's so busy with her volleyball, the school play, the marching band, and other coaches calling. There's usually time just after four in the afternoon, before dinner. She's told her father and me that her previous club coach is now coaching at your school. Cloe just loved playing for him and hoped she would hear from him about playing at your school," Linda said.

"That's exactly why I called. Coach King has told me all about your daughter. I'll have him call her so both of you can speak with him. How does that sound?"

"Sounds good. I know she'll be thrilled to talk with him. Thank you."

The next person he called was Liz. "Hello Jim," she said."

"It's so nice to hear your voice. How's everything? Are you doing, ok?" Jim asked.

"I'm fine, except for missing you. What have you been up to?"

"A lot. I've contacted an FBI agent, who will arrive in a couple of days, to look into the death of the police officer we found in the fountain. I'm working on finding subcontractors to build the new house, Chris has asked me to talk to Mark about them finding a rental or building their own home, we're working the team pretty hard trying to get them ready for this coming weekend's matches, and I've been on the phone tonight with two great recruits," Jim said. "When it rains, it pours, is a spot-on axiom."

"Sounds like you have your hands full. Do I need to make an appointment to see you?" she asked, playfully.

"Well, I've got you penciled in for tomorrow, all day. How does that sound?" Jim asked.

"That sounds perfect. The longer I know you, the more I miss you when we're apart."

"I'll spend the time driving down to see you figuring out what we'll do all day. I'd like you to think about what you'd like to do as well. Between the two of us, we should put together a great agenda," he said.

What was becoming a normal, early morning habit, was to check the parking lot for the black SUV. Jim peeked out the front window and saw that the lot was empty except, for a crystal white XC90 Volvo station wagon parked next to the athletic building. After a quick breakfast, he walked around to the far side of the athletic building and went in to check all the offices on each level.

It seemed he was the only one in the building this early. He walked down to the ground floor and looked straight through a window at the Volvo's front license plate. It was a Utah plate that had words below the numbers that said 'Honors Veterans'. On the left side of the numbers were five colored ribbons that indicated the Combat Theater and Marine & Navy Combat Action Ribbons. Now he was completely puzzled.

16
BABY STEPS

Jim left the athletic building and walked out to the parking lot and looked through the Volvo's windows. He could see a woman in the driver side seat, sleeping, with the seat fully reclined. She was nicely dressed, and Jim noticed that there was a Samsung phone resting on the center console between the front seats. Not wanting to wake her, he walked back to Cramer house and watched the lot until other cars begam to arrive.

With the lot about a quarter filled, he saw the woman in the Volvo sit up and look around. She then opened the car door and walked around a bit, stopping occasionally to stretch. Jim decided to walk out to the parking lot and confront her. However, when he reached the car there was no sign of her anywhere. Jim went into the athletic building and looked all around for the woman without seeing her.

As Jim was heading to his office, he glanced into the office of the Associate Athletic Director and saw the woman from the Volvo sitting in a chair facing Robert Paige. Deciding not to interrupt, he continued to his office, and sent Paige a text asking if the person in his office was a friend? A few minutes later Paige texted Jim, telling him to come meet her.

"Coach, this is Malika, an old friend of mine," Robert said. "She's here in Dallas to meet you."

Jim reached out his hand and said, "Hello Malika, nice to meet you."

Paige said, "She is with the FBI's Human Trafficking unit out of Portland."

"Ok. Why do you need to talk to me? Is there something I can help you with?" Jim Questioned.

Malika asked, "Jim, can we talk privately somewhere?"

"Sure. I think it would be best if we talked outside. Is that alright with you?" Jim asked.

"That's fine. Robert, I need to get back to Portland after Jim and I talk. It's been nice seeing you again," she said.

Page got up and hugged her saying, "Same here Malika. See you next time."

Jim said, "Let's go out the north side of the building. There's a nice patio there where we can be comfortable and have privacy."

After looking around and being seated, Jim asked, "What is it that we need to talk about?"

"Our office in Salt Lake City has asked me to see if we can get some more information, from you, regarding the death of a former collegiate volleyball player, that you coached, and her mother."

"Alright, ask your questions."

"Do you have any information on who was responsible for their deaths?"

"The first I heard about them being killed, was from a female friend of theirs that I'd met one time when I was at their house for dinner. The woman's name was Trish Kingery. Another FBI agent in Utah recently informed me that Trish had been killed a short time ago. I have no idea who killed either of the other women."

"Who was that FBI agent and why would he tell you about this Trish person being killed?" Malika asked.

"The FBI agents name is Wallace, and he told me he got my phone number from a piece of paper that survived the car fire that Trish was found dead in." Jim went on and explained how the piece of paper led Wallace to call him.

"Would that be Dominic Wallace by any chance?" Malika asked.

"I don't know his first name. The few times we've talked, it's been short and to the point. In fact, he's going to be here tomorrow afternoon," Jim answered.

"Jim, this may come as a shock to you, but Dominic Wallace is not an FBI agent. He is based in Salt Lake City and is part of a large human trafficking cartel based in Columbia. His real name is Ricardo Adriano. The Salt Lake Field Agency has been watching this Wallace person for almost two years as he masquerades as an agent. He's as dirty as they come."

"You're sure? How do you know all of this?" Jim asked.

"Because I'm an FBI Agent with over thirteen years' experience. I'm now with the FBI's Human Trafficking, unit out of Portland, and I've been in that position for six years. You can contact the Portland Field Agency if you want. Would you like their phone number?"

"No, that's not necessary. I would like to see your badge though."

With that, Malika reached behind her and took the badge off her belt and handed it to him.

"Thanks." Jim said. "Your last name is Ochoa?"

"Yes. Why do you need to know that?" she asked.

"I've found out recently that a lot of people are not who they claim to be. Times have changed. I hope you understand my suspicion," Jim said, with raised eyebrows. "So, what am I supposed to do when Wallace arrives tomorrow afternoon?"

"Just act normal when you see him. Let him dominate any conversation you have with him early on. I'll have half a dozen agents with me, scattered around, that will protect you at all times."

"Malika, I want you to know that when I talked with him a few days ago, I told him about a cop in the Dallas police department that I felt was dirty. Last Sunday my girlfriend and I were to meet a patrol officer on the campus of Cascade University to ask for protection from some very scary guys who followed me everywhere I went. When we arrived at the meeting spot, we found the officer face down in a large fountain. I didn't know who to trust around here so, I called Wallace and told him the story. That's when he volunteered to come meet with me tomorrow."

"And now, you should know that he's not coming to help you. Don't worry, we will make sure nothing happens to either of you. Just be sure that you meet him in some large area that doesn't have too many people around. Actually, the parking lot on the other side of this building would be ideal," she said.

"I'm reluctant to meet him in that parking lot, because that's where I usually see the scary guys in the black SUV. I think we need to meet someplace off campus. How about a vacant lot that once held my house that burned down. There's plenty of room for a meeting, without being too obvious," Jim said. "I can take you by it on your way back to Portland if you like."

"Ok. I'll follow you and have a look," she said.

Malika agreed with Jim meeting Wallace at the house lot. She told Jim she may have a couple of agents dressed like contractors, walking around during their meeting, plus more agents scattered about in the neighborhood, which Jim approved.

Jim immediately left for Liz's house, knowing it would be a short visit. This time he went directly west into the coast range to see if he was going to be followed. After half an hour, there was no sign of the black SUV, so he dropped back into the valley and kept checking for the SUV. True to his new routine when visiting Liz, Jim put his car in the barn.

He walked up onto the back deck and noticed wet footprints. He carefully opened the kitchen door and followed the prints that stopped next to the carpet in the living room. He could hear some noise upstairs and went up, still not saying anything. Jim first checked Liz's bedroom and then opened the door to the bathroom, which was fogged up. Not wanting to scare her, he moved back to the hallway door and softly called to Liz.

"Is that you Jim?" she said.

"Yes. Why are you taking a shower at this time of day?" he asked, while crossing the bedroom and entering the bathroom.

Liz pulled the shower curtain back just enough to see out and said, "I was out in the hot tub earlier waiting for you. I waited a long time and thought I might as well take a shower and get the chlorine off. Now that you're here, get naked and join me."

"You don't have to ask twice," Jim said.

They spent the next half hour, washing, hugging, and caressing each other. Jim finally said, "It's time to move to the bedroom."

Neither of them stopped to dry off before they got on the bed and made love. They both woke up at four-forty in the afternoon, still holding each other in their arms. "Liz, are you awake?" Jim asked.

"A little bit. What time is it?" she asked.

"It's almost time for dinner. Do you want to sleep some more?" he asked.

"No. I'd better get up. You must be hungry, and I know Queeny's ready to eat."

Liz fixed a big pot of spaghetti sauce, some noodles and toasted a few sourdough rolls. She put a slightly chilled bottle of Pinot Noir on the table and called Jim, "Dinner's ready. Do you want to eat in the dining room or in front of the tv?"

"I'm in favor of the dining room. That way I can enjoy you and the dinner at the same time," he said, smiling.

It was dark outside when they finished dinner, and Liz said, "Let's go outside on the back deck and look at the stars. What do you say?"

"Can we finish the bottle of wine out there." Jim asked.

"You can do whatever you want out there. Why don't you arrange the deck chairs, while I clean up the kitchen?"

Outside, Jim moved a small wooden porch swing where they had a great view of the night sky, and he put a small table in front of the swing. He went back into the house and helped Liz clean up the kitchen. For the balance of the evening, they snuggled and looked up at the night sky.

Liz was the first to wake up the next morning, even though Jim usually got up early so he could get back to Dallas. She'd been wanting to surprise him for a long time, and this looked like the perfect time. Jim was sleeping on his back, so Liz softly pulled back the covers and laid down on the bed next to him, with her head towards his feet. She got up on one elbow, leaned down and took Jim's limp penis in her mouth. She sucked softly, moving her tongue from side to side, being careful not to put her teeth on what was now beginning to expand. Jim was smiling as he slowly woke up and realized what was happening.

"Oh, Liz. That feels so good. I could lay here all morning," Jim said.

Liz looked up at Jim and smiled the best she could, with his penis still in her mouth. When she was sure that it was as big as it usually gets, she cupped his testicles in her hand, leaned down and slipped one into her warm mouth. She moved her body over his legs so she could use her other hand to stroke his hard, warm penis. Fifteen minutes after she started her 'surprise' he filled her mouth with a considerable amount of sperm.

"Wow Jim! That was more semen than I could swallow. You always surprise me. I've got to go clean up," Liz said.

Jim followed her into the bathroom and wiped away what remained on his penis and legs. He asked, "How would you like to get back in bead and let me surprise you?"

"Do you think you could do that after what you just squirted down my throat?" she asked, smiling in a teasing way.

"You just get back in bed and toss the covers on the floor. I'll show you what I can do," he responded, smiling.

Liz was getting more excited as she stripped away the bed covers and laid down. "Ok lover boy, show me what you've got."

Jim walked into the bedroom and knelt down on the floor at the end of the bed. He slowly slithered up onto the bed and grasped Liz's ankles, lifting, and spreading her legs as he moved forward. He released her ankles before his head was close to her vagina and the first thing that touched her there was his tongue. He allowed the saliva that accumulated in his mouth to drip down onto those beautiful lips. Jim sat back on his knees for a moment while he grabbed a pillow and slipped it under her bottom. Then he worked his tongue all around her vaginal opening and focused on her clitoris. As she began to arch her back, Jim mounted her and used long, slow strokes while penetrating her. He then alternated between licking her clit and mounting her.

Liz experienced a long, loud orgasm that had her body quivering. Jim laid down next to her and held her in his arms until she settled down. She asked, "Where did that come from? Why did you wait so long? That was absolutely the best thing I've ever felt!

"That makes me happy. I've wanted to wait until the right time, and this morning was the right time!" he said.

They laid in each other's arms for another hour before getting up and going down to the kitchen for breakfast. As always, Queeny was happy to see them, and she let them know that she needed to go outside.

Just before noon, Jim told Liz he needed to get back to Dallas, so he could be there to greet the FBI agent driving in from Twin Falls, Idaho. "I'm not sure what day next week I'll be able to come back, but I'll be thinking about this morning while I'm gone."

He hugged Liz tight for a long time before going down the back deck steps and out to the barn. Jim arrived in Dallas just before one-thirty in the afternoon. Since there had been no call from Agent Wallace, he decided to swing by the lot where his house used to be. He got out of his car and took a short walk up and down the streets near his lot, looking for Malika.

He walked back to the lot and was about to get in his car when he heard Malika say, "Jim. Over here, by the fir tree."

Jim looked in the direction of her voice and saw her next to the tree, dressed in camouflage from head to toe. He walked over to her and asked, "How long have you been here?"

"The other agents and I have been here since shortly before sunup. No sign of Wallace yet. Why don't you sit in your car until he calls you. When he gets here, greet him, and begin to walk towards the middle of the lot. Just let him do most of the talking. You should also be ready to run or hit the ground when we make our move to nab him."

"I understand. I'm going to move my car up near the intersection so I can see him coming from either direction."

17
EDUCATION

Before too long Jim's phone range, "Is this Jim Sams?" the voice asked.

"Yes, are you Agent Wallace?" Jim asked.

"Affirmative. I'm in the parking lot of what looks like an athletic building. Is this where you wanted to meet?" Wallace asked.

"No. I don't want anyone inside that building to see us together. They'll have too many questions the next time I'm there," Jim said.

"Where do you want to meet?" Wallace asked.

Jim gave Wallace directions to his vacant lot. He was getting anxious as he waited because not many cars used these streets at this time of day. Out of nowhere a black SUV pulled up behind Jim and Wallace stepped out of the car and onto the sidewalk. Jim waited a couple of minutes to see if there were any others that would get out of the car. Satisfied that Wallace was alone, he walked over next to him, extended his hand, and said, "How was your trip from Idaho?"

"Nothing to it. Just stay between the lines and keep heading west," Wallace replied.

"Well, I picked this place to talk because it's away from the University and the Dallas Police Department. I knew we could have privacy here, and we could talk about how you're going to approach the Police Chief," Jim said, as he walked slowly out to the middle of the lot.

Wallace turned to face Jim and reached inside the upper left portion of his suit coat. Jim stepped back sharply and waited to see what Wallace was doing. He was ready to run or drop to the ground if it was a pistol. When Wallace's hand came out of his coat, he was holding a pack of cigarettes. Jim tried not to smile and alert Wallace that he was startled about what he might have had in his hand.

Wallace said, as he lit up a cigarette, "I should probably just visit the police department and ask for the chief. Whenever I do something like that, everyone in the place is on high alert and they do anything I ask for."

"That sounds good to me. Do you want me to come with you?" Jim asked.

"I don't think that's such a good idea at this point. If they see you with me, they'll put two and two together. Then it would be like pulling nails to get any information out of them," Wallace contended.

As they both turned towards their cars, they saw three men in camouflage, walking towards them, with guns drawn. Wallace turned abruptly, and started to run towards the trees, when he saw five more men and a woman, all in camouflage and all armed, walking right at him. He stopped in his tracks, laced his fingers up behind his head and dropped to his knees. When he was surrounded, he almost shouted, "I'm an FBI Agent. You're all making a big mistake. Think about what you're doing. You'll all spend years in jail!"

Malika said, "Hello Ricardo, how's everything with you? Have you been enjoying yourself? I sure hope so, because you are about to hate the rest of your days on this planet."

"Malika, you bitch! Was it necessary to bring the army with you?" Ricardo said in a caustic tone.

"No. Not at all. Getting my hands on you was much easier than I anticipated. These are just eight, well rounded friends of mine, who are also FBI agents. You know, the ones that don't steel, lie, or kill innocent people like you do."

Jim could not keep from laughing to himself, listening to Malika put Adriano down. When everyone left, he walked back to the black SUV, hoping to find out if it was the car that followed him everywhere. He noticed the new car smell and saw that the keys were still in the ignition. He punched the start button on the key so he could check the odometer, which had only eight hundred forty-three miles on it. Next, he opened the large door at the back of the SUV, curious about what he might find. "Bingo", he said out loud. Laying under two jackets, was a scoped, 308 Winchester. Jim picked it up and checked to see if it was loaded, which it was. Then he opened the breach and looked down the barrel to see if it had been fired lately. It was as clean as a whistle. This was not the SUV that followed Jim.

Jim drove to Abby's Legendary Pizza to celebrate what just happened. While he ate, he thought about what information Malika would draw out of Wallace. He called Malika and asked, "Hey Malika, this is Jim Sams. What's going to happen to the black SUV that Adriano arrived in?"

"Two of our agents will pick it up later this afternoon. Thanks for helping today. I'd like to talk to you in my office in Portland, so I can ask you about the two women and the Kingery woman that were all found dead. What's a good day for you to come up?" she asked.

"How about next Tuesday morning, say around ten?" Jim asked.

"Give me a moment to check my calendar," Malika said. "That works for me. I'll see you then."

Jim went back to the Cramer House and parked his car on the side of the house. He walked over to the athletic building and went up to his office and asked Kristy and Mark join him.

Once his two assistants arrived, the first thing he asked was, "Have you two got todays practice worked out?

Kristy nodded and said, "Yes. We're all set."

"Good. You know how I've been asking you two to set up the practices recently?" he said. 'It turns out that I'm going to be busy before practice every day, so I want you two to prepare each day's work out. Do you think you can handle that?"

Kristy looked at Mark, who nodded in agreement, and said, "Ok, we can either lay out practice each day, after asking what you want to work on, or we can give you our work out and you can make notes, cross things out, or add things. What would you prefer?"

"Actually, I think melding the two together works best for me. If I don't give you anything before hand, you do what you think needs to be worked on. If I like what you have, we'll go with that, or, I'll pencil in what needs to be changed. That way it will take just a few minutes for me to approve or mark up what you have. We'll try this for a week or two and see how it works. How does that sound to you two? Oh, one more thing. I want you to give the players Mondays off if we've played a match on Saturday or Sunday. If for some reason we need to practice on Monday, I'll tell you."

Mark said, "Works for me"

Kristy agreed and asked, "Anything else on your mind?"

"Yes. Our match this Saturday will be with Portland State, and again, the Portland Alumni Association will host. Mark, this is an annual event with a very nice reception in the Benson Hotel for our players and alumni. We are staying in the Benson Hotel Friday night, so it's up early, a light breakfast, the reception, lounging in the hotel lobby to visit with friends and family, and then back up to their room by 3:00 p. m. No friends or family in the players' hotel rooms at any time." Jim said.

Practices the balance of the week were crisp and competitive. On Thursday Jim brought the team together after practice and said, "We will not work out on Friday. I want everyone at the bus by five forty-five. We will depart at six p.m. headed to Portland. After dinner at the Benson Hotel, you will go up to your rooms. Lights out at eleven. Breakfast Saturday morning is at eight a.m., and you are to be at the Alumni Association Reception at ten a.m. You new players need to ask the players that attended this function last year to learn what you can and cannot do during the time after the reception until we leave for Portland State."

At the reception, Jim ushered his team into the Benson Hotel ballroom first ahead of the coaching staff. The players received a big round of applause as they entered, followed by a larger round of applause for the coaches. The crowd inside the ballroom was larger than last season's and the refreshments looked delicious. After all the speeches about the team and coaching staff concluded, the players and coaches were approached by fans, former players, and financial supporters of Dallas University.

The team left the hotel for the playing site right on time. Mark conducted the warmup beginning at six p.m. and the match began at exactly seven. The first two games were closer than Jim expected, but Cascade won. For the third game, Jim decided to change the lineup with all different players, except for Iliana, the setter. He wanted to see what the reaction would be from the team and his staff for doing such a thing. To his surprise, and everyone else's, this group won easily by a score of fifteen to twenty-five, which Jim was hoping would happen. He felt it would send a message to the players who'd been starting regularly.

Once the team was on the bus for the ride back to Dallas, Kristy stopped Jim before getting on themselves and asked, "Coach, what was your thinking behind changing the usual starting lineup for the third game?"

"I know I took a chance there, but I really wanted to see what our subs were capable of. Actually, they played much better than our starters. I know it will send a strong message to every player on the team, and it will give us more options for who's on the court at any one time," he said.

For the first half of the ride back to Dallas, the team was very happy and talking a lot with one another. The second half of the trip was much quieter. Jim knew he had two days off, so he woke up at five o'clock Sunday morning and left for Liz's house.

He arrived in less than an hour and needed to wake Liz up to get inside. "Jim, is something wrong?" Liz asked as she opened the door.

"No, not at all. I just woke up early this morning and decided to come here, thinking we could have two full days with nothing to do," he said. He took her in his arms and asked, "Unless you have something in mind."

"Actually, going back to bed to sleep some more is what I'd like to do. Ok?" she said.

"Back to bed it its. Let's go."

Liz awoke at nine-thirty and slipped out of bed to let Queeny out. She prepared breakfast for herself and Jim. Just before letting her dog back in the house, Jim walked into the kitchen.

"How did you sleep Liz?" he asked.

"I slept very well. It's so nice to have your warm body to snuggle up against. Were you able to get some more rest?"

"Yea. I was so anxious to get here I wasn't sure I could get back to sleep. Looks like that's one of the things I needed. The last few days have been really busy, with the Alumni Association Reception and the match at Portland State. Listen to this. We were leading two to nothing in games, and I did a really strange thing before the third game of the match. I changed all but the setter for that game. It was a spur of the moment decision, but it turned out great. The third game was a blowout with almost all second-string players. I'm sure every player will now work a lot harder when they're in a game, knowing that they can be replaced at any time."

"That's actually one of the things I like about you. Sometimes you're very regimented and other times you just try stuff without too much preparation." Liz said.

"That could be true. But, you know, I think about a lot of things, off and on, that are not part of the moment. Then sometime later, maybe even years later, a thought pops back into my mind that is of the moment. Do you understand what I'm trying to explain?" Jim asked.

"Sort of. Whatever you do, or did before, keep doing. I think you're a very smart man and a very caring man. I think we are a great couple and I've grown a lot since being with you. I don't ever want you to stop what you're doing, or like to do," Liz said as she hugged him.

"How would you like to take a ride down to the Umpqua River? I'd like to see if the salmon are running, and we can have lunch at the Steamboat Inn. I know you will like this place that sits above, and right next to the Umpqua. I'm pretty sure it's another part of Oregon you've not yet seen."

"Sounds good to me," Liz said. "We'll need to take Queeny. I don't want to leave her at home."

Jim stopped at a few places on the Umpqua river to see if he could hook a fresh king salmon before lunch time. About the only thing he hooked was a tree branch that was stuck under water between to boulders. He was not happy that the tree branch will have one of his best lures forever. Losing his lure signaled him that it was lunch time. He and Liz drove upstream for fifteen minutes and pulled into a parking spot in front of the Inn.

"This place is pretty small," Liz said as she was getting out of the car. "Are you sure we should eat here?"

"Patience my love. This place is the real deal for lunch. I'll ask you again when we return to the car," Jim teased.

Finished with lunch and approaching the car, Liz said, "This may be the last time I question anything you say or do. I could not eat another bite if you paid me a million dollars!"

"So, I take it that you liked it?" Jim asked.

"Like, is not the appropriate term. I liked it more than eating at Kings Estates Winery!"

"Another idea just popped into my head. How about I fish at a couple of places up the river and then we will head up to Crater Lake and see if we can get a room for the night in the lodge?" he asked.

"You know, I like those ideas that keep popping into your head. I think the next time you seem to be quiet, I'm going to ask, 'what's Poppin'?"

Salmon fishing in the upper Umpqua was no better than it was earlier down the river. At least he didn't lose any lures this time. The ride up to Crater Lake offered a variety of landscapes, with beautiful forests of fir trees, areas of old, dead trees killed by lava flows, and other areas of thinning pine forests due to the higher elevation. As they got closer to their destination, snow was becoming heavier and accumulating on the narrow asphalt road. Finally, they reached a point where they could not continue without chains on their tires.

"Well, it looks like spending the night at the Crater Lake lodge is impossible now. We're still seven miles from the lodge and there's no way I'm going to try to drive through all that snow on this road," Jim said. "We have two options. Drive back to your house or find a motel up in Crescent. What's your choice?" he asked Liz.

"If you think we can drive back to my house without encountering snow, I'd prefer that. I know I like my bed better than those in a motel. Do you mind?" she asked.

"Home it is. I'm sure we can make it in less than three hours," Jim said.

The drive took just over three hours when they pulled into Liz's driveway and the first order of business was to let Queeny out. "Liz, I have no idea how dogs can go so long without making a mess in the car," Jim commented.

"I learned a long time ago that whenever she would be cooped up in the house for a long time, that I would cut back on food and water. Not to punish her, but to slow down her digestive system. It must work because she's never left any surprises in my car or the house," Liz said.

Sunday was spent being lazy. They enjoyed a late breakfast, watched some tv, and showed a lot of attention to Queeny. Liz cooked a nice evening meal of mashed sweet potatoes, sweet corn, baked chicken thighs, and a salad. It brought back pleasant memories of how life was when his wife, Annie, was alive. After dinner and dessert, they watched a couple of hours of tv, which was really boring. Jim turned off the television and began to snuggle up to Liz, which she gladly accepted.

18
WHAT NOW

Jim was up earlier than normal Tuesday morning so he could be at Malika's office on time. Surprisingly there was very little traffic on the road heading north, including Salem and northeast Portland. He parked at the FBI building on northeast Cascades Pkwy and walked into the exterior entry building. He approached the desk and said, "Good morning. I'm Jim Sams and I'm here to speak with Agent Malika Ochoa. She told me to check in upon arrival, so here I am."

The nice-looking lady at the counter said, "Good morning, Mr. Sams. Agent Ochoa is expecting you. Please attach this pass to your left lapel and keep it on during your entire visit. Her office is on the third floor of the building behind us. Check the office directory on the wall next to the elevator door. Once you reach the third floor, you can find her office number. Please exit this building and walk across to the door in that building. I hope you enjoy your visit."

"Ok, thanks," Jim said. Following instructions, he found Malika's office and opened the door. "Good morning. I'm Jim Sams and I have an appointment with Ms. Ochoa for ten."

The receptionist told Jim that it would be another fifteen minutes before she was available and asked him if she could get him a cup of coffee or tea. He accepted her offer and asked for coffee.

A full twenty minutes later Malika opened her door and welcomed Jim. "How's everything with you this morning Jim?"

"Things are going well. It would be nice if they keep going that way. What is it that you need to talk with me about?" Jim asked.

The Salt Lake City agency wants me to ask you about the three women you knew that were all killed and then incinerated, one in a car and two in a house."

"You do know that I went through this with Wallace or Adriano, right?" he asked.

"Yes. I'm aware that you spoke with him. But that's not to say he relayed accurate information to the Salt Lake City agency. They want you to explain all you know about the three women."

"No Problem," Jim said.

He spent most of the next half hour repeating everything he'd said to Adriano about Helen Peterson, Lilly Pederson, and Trish Kingery. It was not easy to maintain continuity due to the various ways questions were asked, but in the end, what Jim told them was accepted.

Malika finished a call with the Salt Lake office and thanked Jim. He thought he was done and asked, "Is that all? Can I get back down to Dallas now?"

"Actually, I've got a bit more information for you, and an important question. It won't take too long. And you don't need to give me an answer to the question until you have time to consider it. Ok?"

"Yea, what are you going to tell me?" Jim asked.

"The scary guys, as you described them, took their orders from a man named Lester. So did two detectives that were with the Corvallis Police Department, which I understand harassed you quite a bit in the recent past," Malika said.

"Yes, that's correct. Attorneys for Cascade University pretty much shut those two down," Jim said. "Is that all?" he asked.

"No. This Lester person is the head of a Salt Lake City human trafficking ring, controlled by a Columbian Cartel. The FBI has been watching the Salt Lake operation for at least four years and the Cartel for five years."

"And is watching all that the FBI does?" Jim asked.

"Jim, by now you should know that we gather every last detail of a case. Getting all the facts, firsthand, is why you're here today," she said in a rather displeased tone.

"Yes. I apologize for that stupid remark," Jim said. "Keep going, please."

"This investigation will lead to a number of arrests in the near future, both in Salt Lake City and nationally. My boss wants to know if you'd be willing to work with us, while we attempt to take this Lester person into custody?" Malika asked.

"Actually, right off the top of my head, I don't ever want to deal with any of those people that you mentioned in Salt Lake City. But I would like to know what you mean by working with you, which I assume is the FBI?"

"Yes, it is the FBI that you'd be working with. We know that you have an important job coaching volleyball at Cascade University. But you would always be protected by FBI agents in everything you do and wherever you go," she said.

"When would I get protection, and would it be everywhere I go or when I'm at home every night, or at a volleyball match in another city, or out recruiting players for my program, or when I visit my lady friend or my daughters. Or even if I were to just float down the McKenzie River fly fishing," he asked, trying to get all the facts.

"I guarantee you'll be protected around the clock, every day, everywhere you go, by at least four FBI agents. You'll never be alone." Malika stressed.

"Can I tell my lady friend and my family about the FBI protection," he asked.

"We'd prefer that you not tell anyone. However, if not saying anything to your lady friend is a deal breaker, it would be alright to let her know. But just her. And she is not to tell anyone else," Malika said.

"I'd like to take some time to consider what you've asked and give you my answer in a few days?" Jim asked

"That's fine with us. How about your answer this coming Friday?" Malika asked.

"Ok. I'll give you my answer this Friday. Do I call you or text you," Jim asked, just to be sure.

"I need a phone call. No texts, ever! Security is the thing. I look forward to your call."

Jim exited the FBI building and headed for his office. His head was going a mile a minute thinking about all that just occurred. His main concern was that, if he agreed to work with the FBI, would he, Liz, his daughters, and their families really be safe? He understood that eliminating the Salt Lake City human traffickers, particularly Lester, and as many of the other human traffickers nationwide, would make our country vastly safer.

Back in Dallas, Jim parked in the lot next to Cramer House and walked over to the athletic building, looking everywhere in the larger parking lot. Satisfied that there was no sign of a black SUV, he felt he may enjoy having around the clock protection from FBI agents. He wondered to himself what this level of protection would cost our taxpayers? Even though he felt he needed to think about every little detail of what Malika asked, he realized that he needed to do his job as a coach, especially for this team. Once inside the athletic building his mind automatically shifted to volleyball.

Kristy was in her office as Jim past by and he asked her to come to his office. When she appeared at his door he said, "Come on in. Bring me up to date on anything I need to know. Things like player problems or problems with a player. You're evaluation thus far with our two new staff members. Is there any news from up top about the team getting Mondays off? Does anyone on this floor dislike me or talk about me behind my back," he asked with a big smile.

"The answers to your questions are as follows. No, not that I've heard, both of them are doing fine and they are a great addition to the staff, no one has asked anything about Monday's off, and no and no," she said, with a big grin.

"Ok. Now that we have that out of the way, what do you have planned for practice today?" Jim asked," Jim said.

"Our normal warm up, pepper, ten-foot line work. Then I've put in working on little things like wiping tight sets off the blocker's hands, recovering balls that are hit into the net, and bump sets by players other that the setter," Kristy explained.

"I like all of that. I want you to add, delivery of a free ball to the opponent's area one. When our player delivering the ball is in front of our ten-foot line, I want it high and deep on the opponent's side. If our player delivering the ball is behind the ten-foot line, and under control, I want it low and fast to area one. If our player delivering the ball is anywhere behind the ten- foot line and is not in control trying to just hit the opponent's side of the court, put it anywhere. Does that make sense to you?" Jim asked.

"Yes. I can fashion a drill for that. No problem. The balance of the practice is our normal work, unless you have something else," she said.

"Going forward, I'd like you to mix up the starting lineups each day, so that the players don't become complacent with who starts a game. That's about it for now," Jim concluded.

After Kristy left his office, Jim watch film of their next opponent, the University of Tennessee.

He had little respect for the head volleyball coach and wanted to be sure he would know what Cascade would be up against in this match. As usual, most of their players were tall and athletic looking. But the tape he was watching showed that they struggled with passing and blocking. One player stood out as their 'big gun', and Jim looked up her bio according to their

Sports Information Department. She was a six-one, outside hitter with a .289 hitting average, which was nothing outstanding, but a player to stop. Jim made a mental note to put his best blockers opposite her.

Practices the rest of the week went well. A light work out on Thursday made sure the players would not use too much energy, and that there would be almost no chance of injuries. "Ladies, you are on the bus to the Salem airport at noon tomorrow. This match against Tennessee will be a true test of our ability. They are a mature team, they have height, and their starting six have been together for at least two seasons. I'm sure they will be ready to play us," Jim said.

Jim kept himself busy around his office Friday morning until ten o'clock. He dialed Malika's phone number and waited. The connection went to voice mail, asking to leave a message, which was frustrating to Jim. He decided to rewatch the film of Tennessee just to be sure he hadn't missed anything.

Halfway through the first game, his phone wrang. "Coach Sams, may I help you?" he answered.

"This is Malika. Are you calling to give me your decision?" she asked.

"Yes. How on earth could you know that?" he said, trying to be funny.

"You'd be surprised at some of the calls I get. So, tell me, what's your decision. Please. It's very important on how we move forward with our plan."

"I've decided to fulfill my patriotic duty. I pretty much hate these people and I'd like to see them all behind bars. My only concern is that my family, my lady friend, and I don't get hurt. I'd also like to know that if players on my volleyball team, and everyone in the Athletic Department will be safe. That's all. If you think you guys can do that, I'm in!" Jim said.

"You have my personal word that each and everyone you've mentioned will be safe. I've got nineteen of our top agents who will be distributed amongst each group. Three will be assigned to you, so that one will be able to sleep, and two will be with you. They each carry a concealed firearm at all times. When your team is practicing, traveling, or competing, three more agents are assigned to them, just as I described about your agents. Finally, the same thing applies to your lady friend, each of your daughters' families, and four agents will be inside the athletic building at all times. What do you think about that?" Malika asked.

"I like it. Thank you. Now, what's next? When does everyone meet the agents assigned to them?" Jim asked.

"Six agents will be going with you to Tennessee and be with you and your team every minute while you're away, and until you come back. After returning to the university, the team members will only be protected while they are practicing. However, the agents protecting the team will roam around campus from sunup until practice starts, and after practice ends, they go back to roaming until midnight. So, you will meet the first group of six at noon today, before you depart for the airport at Salem. I've checked with Page to be sure there is room on the company plane. He approved that in a heartbeat. Your lady friend, daughters and their family, and people in the athletic building will all meet the other agents tomorrow," she concluded.

"I'm impressed. Now, are you going to inform me when any attempt by the FBI to apprehend those criminals from Salt Lake City are in Dallas or near my family, or lady friend?" Jim asked.

"You may be warned if something might go down around you or your team. The same goes for your family and lady friend. But the problem is that we can't always warn those we protect before an action to apprehend has begun," she answered.

"So, what are any of us being protected supposed to do when a spur of the moment action begins?" he asked.

"All I can say is to take cover immediately. Please believe me when I say that we will do all we can to keep everyone safe. I highly doubt that an action will take place without anyone that we protect being warned. I can't remember anytime our agents in Oregon started an action without warning those they protected," she said, trying to reassure Jim.

19
THREATS

Team members, support staff, and coaches were ready at eleven forty-five to board the two vans for the trip to the Salem airport. Noticeably absent were the six FBI agents. At noon, straight up, he told everyone to board the vans. He pulled Mark aside and explained that six FBI agents would be traveling with the team, to and from Tennessee, three in each van.

"Tell the player nearest the side door to be ready to open it. When three men get in your van, ask each of them to give their names, so the players will know that much about these men. Then, instruct the players that they are not to talk to the men and the men are not to speak to the players."

Jim was sitting in the driver's seat of his van, and Mark was just getting into the driver's seat of the other van, when three men approached each van's side door. Jim asked the player sitting near the door to open it so the three men could board. Needless to say, most everyone wondered who these people were and why they were in each van. "Ladies, these gentlemen will be with us for the entire trip to and from Tennessee. Do not speak with any of them and they are not to speak with you."

The drive to the Salem airport, and the flight to Knoxville was quiet. Jim realized that he would need to make some sort of explanation to his staff and the players upon arrival in Tennessee.

"Alright, everyone gather around. I know you're all curious about the men that accompanied us to the airport today. As mentioned, when they boarded the vans, these men will be with us for the entire trip. Their duty is to make sure that each of us from Cascade University will be safe. The reason for their protection is that there have been threats directed at the volleyball team, our staff, and the coaches. They are dressed to blend in with our group. They may not look like it, but they are highly trained FBI agents that can handle any threat that might arise. I ask that you play well tomorrow afternoon. You each need to forget about these guys and focus on playing. Do you think you can do that?" he asked.

All the players and staff responded with a rather quiet 'yes'. "Hey! I'm serious. I told you why they're here because they will be with us from now until the FBI ends the threat. Oh, and another thing. Back home, you will see these men and a few others like them in the athletic building and around campus when you are not practicing. When you are practicing or we're hosting a home match, they will be with us from start to finish. You will get used to them before long. Just make sure you focus on playing volleyball tomorrow to start with. Finally, following the match, and after you shower, we're all back on the plane and heading to Dallas tonight. I'm having dinner catered so we can eat on the flight. Are there any questions?" he asked.

One of the players asked, "Will we be able to visit with friends or family after the match?"

Jim was beginning to lose his patience, so he paused a bit to respond. "After the match, you are to go directly to the visitor locker room, clean up, gather your belongings, and wait outside the locker room door for all your teammates to finish. During that waiting time you can visit with family and friends, but no strangers. When everyone is out of the locker room, we all head for the plane."

Everyone was in the hotel breakfast room at eight a.m. as mandated. Since the match with Tennessee was scheduled to start at one p.m., Jim told Mark, "I'd like you take all the players on a short run, beginning at ten a.m. and concluding at ten-twenty a.m. After the run make sure they all stay in their rooms until eleven-thirty, when we're due to get on the bus to the playing site."

"No problem. Will the FBI guys be running with us?" Mark asked.

"Oops, I forgot about that. I'll let them know so they'll run with you and the players," Jim said.

Everyone followed Jim's instructions to be on the bus and getting to the playing site on time. The team was quiet, but Jim knew that was nothing to worry about before an important match. Tennessee looked good during their warmup period. Knowing the players were tall did not surprise him as much as how high they jumped. That particular fact did not appear in the player information sheets. That one fact caused him to start the same six players that finished the third match at Portland State.

The first game of the match was close and hard fought, but Tennessee prevailed. After submitting the roster for the next game, Jim gathered those players together and asked, "What did you learn from watching the last game?"

Iliana said, "Their number seven is a chair. We should be able to serve her off the court. Their setter will force the one from almost anywhere."

"Excellent. Did any of the rest of you notice that?" Jim asked.

Two other players raised their hands.

"Do the rest of you understand what Iliana said?"

They all said yes.

"Did any of you see who was their primary strong hitter? Did they tend to set the back slide, or the back row middle?"

Various other players offered accurate comments on each of Jim's questions.

"Ok, I'm glad you were so attentive. Now, go out there and show everyone how we are going to beat this team!"

The second and third game were easily won by Cascade. The team got way behind in the fourth game, but Jim did not sub in any players. After his team's second time out, they took the court and gradually worked their way back to twenty-four all. The game continued with one team up by a point and serving for the game, then the other team would battle back and be serving for the game.

With the score tied thirty all, one of the Tennessee blockers got caught up in the net and came down on her right ankle. She had to leave the game with a bad sprain. Her replacement looked like a carbon copy, tall and athletic looking, but Jim knew this player had been watching for over an hour and a half and was not ready to play.

The matched wore on for a bit when the Cascade setter, playing front row, went up to jump set and dumped the ball over the net behind her head. Jim smiled at her and gave the hand signal for her to do it again. Cascade served and the Tennessee setter made a great set, which put her hitter up against only one blocker. The hitter crushed the kill and somehow Cascade's libero dug the ball high and tight to the net, which Iliana dumped again, behind her head, for the point that won the match. Excited subs for Cascade rushed the playing floor and jumped and screamed with joy. Needless to say, the Tennessee fans were quiet, which Jim thought was tough on their players, who had played well.

The players followed the instructions Jim had stipulated and headed for the locker room. He waited outside the locker room door with three of the FBI agents, who were keeping an eye out for anything unusual. Jim took a moment and said, "I want to thank you fellows and the other agents as well, for doing such a good job keeping the players and my staff safe. It is much appreciated."

Their response was a slight smile and a head nod.

Jim got up early Sunday morning and departed Dallas, headed to Liz's house. He was followed by the three FBI agents Malika mentioned, in a separate vehicle. When he pulled into Liz's yard, there was another car with no one in it, parked in front of the house. He went around to the barn and both he and the agents parked in the barn. He asked, "Are any of you guys familiar with the car in front of the house?"

They each shook their head, no.

"Ok men, it looks like it's time to show your stuff. My lady friend is about five foot six and has blond hair. Be extra careful not to harm her. Just find out if it's the FBI agents who will be watching after her or if we have some Salt Lake City thugs here."

Jim waited and watched thru a crack in the barn siding as the agents spread out to make sure Liz was safe. They must have been spotted as they approached the house from three different directions, because the door to the back deck opened and Liz said hello to the one agent standing in the yard. Upon seeing that, Jim chuckled to himself while also realizing that she could have been in a vulnerable position if these FBI agents had been the bad guys. "Liz," Jim called out as he left the barn. "Are there any FBI agents inside the house right now," he asked.

"Yes, Jim. There are three of the most curious men I've ever met," she said.

"Did they tell you they were FBI agents and that they are here to protect you?" he asked.

"Yes. They were very polite. We were trying to decide if they would spend the nights inside or outside the house."

"Which did you decide on?"

"I've not decided yet. I wanted to talk with you first. Now that you're here, what do you think?" Liz asked.

"I think it's best if they're inside. Is that ok with you?"

"If it's ok with you, it's ok with me," she said.

Jim, Liz, and the FBI agents that protect Jim, all went into the house. Jim introduced himself to Liz's agents and advised them that they should spend the nights inside. "After you three look around this house from top to bottom, I suggest all of you agents station yourselves outside."

With all the agents finally outside, Jim asked, "Liz, I'd like to drive down to my daughters houses and make sure the FBI agents are in place. I'd like you to go with me. What do you think?"

"Certainly, I'll go with you. That's a given. Remember me telling you that I need to be with you every minute from here on?" she said.

"I do remember, I apologize. Let's go."

"I've got one final, important question for you. What are we going to do with Queeny?"

"We'll take her with us," he said.

Jim advised all the agents that he and Liz would be driving south to check on his daughters. "So, I guess all of you will be following me."

The caravan stopped first at Jim's youngest daughter's house. Sarah was on the front lawn talking to a policeman. Jim could see that she was crying as she spoke with the officer, which concerned Jim greatly. He got out of his car and hurried over to comfort her. "Sarah, take it easy. Tell me why you're crying and talking to this officer?" he asked.

"Sir, please step back and let her finish speaking with me," the officer said.

"Officer this is my daughter. I'll speak with her whenever I want. Also, do you see those cars over there? Those are all FBI agents, and they will take over now."

Two of the FBI agents walked over and had a brief conversation with the policeman. The rest of the agents surrounded the house and went inside to look around.

Jim asked, "Sarah please tell me why you were crying?"

"Dad, I got a call from the school about half an hour ago, telling me that Brad did not show up for school today. He usually walks by himself every day. I don't know what to do. I'm so glad you're here. I need you to help me find my son," Sarah said, while still crying.

Jim glanced at his car and motioned for Liz to come. "Go back in your house with Liz and her dog Queeny and settle down. Three of these FBI agents will stay inside with you and the rest of us will try to find Brad. Ok?" Jim said.

He gathered the FBI agents together and asked, "Look, I don't know which of you is in charge, but I want three agents to protect Sarah. The rest of you need to help me find my grandson. Can you do that for me?"

One of the older agents said, "Mr. Sams, we are here to protect you and your family. We need to start looking for the child now. We have three cars available to cover all the streets between here and the school. Three agents will cover your daughter in the house and they each have dedicated phones so that no one can hear us talking. If someone has kidnapped your grandson, they will more than likely call to negotiate his return. Money is usually what they're after."

"I don't think its kidnappers we're dealing with," Jim said. "What I've noticed in the past is that the thugs from Salt Lake City drive black SUV's and they're not after money. They're here after me and my loved ones. They are ruthless. I think we need to be looking for a black SUV, and we will need to cover more area than just from here to the school," Jim said.

"Sounds like a good plan. Let's get started," the older agent said.

Jim said, "Give me a minute to call my other daughter and find out if she and her family are safe." Jim dialed Erin's number and spoke with her for five or six minutes. "Ok. Agents are at her house now and her children have skipped school today. Let's get started looking for my grandson."

The FBI agents and Jim drove up and down every street in town and there was no sign of a black SUV. Jim got a call from Liz saying, "Jim there is an SUV out front and five men with guns just got out. You need to get back here as fast as you can."

He told the others in the three cars helping him what Liz just said. He was surprised when the agents turned on their flashers and sped back to Sarah's house. All three vehicles arrived and found two thugs on the ground, bleeding from the head, with three others shooting into the house. The agents with Jim made short work of those thugs. Jim rushed into the house to see if anyone was hurt. Liz and Sarah were scared, but ok. They were attending to one of the agents that sustained a shoulder wound. Jim looked around the room and saw Queeny lying on the floor near a window, bleeding and not moving.

He walked over to the dog and asked, "Liz. Have you seen Queeny over here? It looks like she's been shot. It doesn't look good," he said. He kneeled down and put his hand on the dogs side, just behind her front leg. He then opened her mouth to see if she was breathing. "She's dead," he said softly.

Jim stood up and asked the agents, "Can anyone of you examine the seriousness of the shoulder wound in your comrades shoulder?"

The older agent said, "Charlie, take a look at Chuck's shoulder and get him to a hospital as soon as possible, if needed." He then turned to Jim and said, "We need to check the black SUV that these idiots were driving to see if your grandson is somewhere inside the vehicle."

Jim and four agents descended on the SUV and searched it up one side and down the other, finding nothing. Jim asked everyone to be silent. "Do you hear that?" he said softly. He stuck his head inside the back seat door and said in a loud voice, "Brad, this is grandpa. Can you hear me?"

"Grandpa, I'm smashed behind the back seat. Can you hear me?" Brad said as loud as he could.

"Ok men, let's remove the back seat and backrest as carefully as possible."

Five minutes later, Brad was in Jim's arms, as they both hugged each other. Jim was tearing up as he comforted Sarah's only child, who was bruised and scratched up on his face and arms. "You're ok now young man. You're in a lot better shape than those idiots who kidnapped you and stuck you behind the backrest. That was a terrible place for anyone to be. These FBI agents killed every one of the bad guys. Let's go see your mom."

Brad ran over to the porch, where Sarah and Liz were standing, and hugged his mother. "Oh baby, are you ok?" Sarah asked.

"I'm ok mom. Are you and aunty Liz ok. I heard a lot of shooting and thought you would get shot," Brad said.

"We're fine, thanks to all these gentlemen. We were so worried about you." Sarah said.

"Grandpa told me that these guys killed all the bad guys. I'll probably have bad dreams if we stay here tonight. Can we sleep somewhere else?" Brad asked.

Liz said, as Jim walked up, "Sarah, I think Jim wants to go to Erin's house to check on them as soon as we can. I think that might be a good place to spend a night or two, to let things settle down. What do you think Jim."

'I know it would make me much happier if it's ok with Erin and Roy. I'll give them a call right now."

When Jim was done calling Erin, Liz walked up to Jim and put her arms around his waist saying, "Queeny's gone. My dog got shot. It's terrible. She was such a sweetheart," she said, as tears flowed down her cheeks.

Jim pulled her closer to his body and said, "It's not right. That dog would not hurt a flea. There's no justification for her being killed."

20
TOO CLOSE

"Erin said she's sure Roy will be ok with having her sister's family spend a couple of days with them," Jim said. "So, Sarah, why don't you put some things together that you'll be needing while you're at your sister's house, and we'll all follow you guys down to Erin's as soon as Stan gets home."

The caravan of cars arrived at Erin's house around six p.m., and there were hugs everywhere, except for the FBI agents. Jim and Liz stayed for a short time and then headed north to Dallas and the Cramer house.

Jim stopped at Sarah's house and buried Queeny at the far end of the back yard. The rest of the trip north was silent.

The Cascade volleyball team was getting better as the season wore on, having lost only one match to the University of Oregon. Jim felt he needed to lighten the intensity of daily workouts and asked Kristy to explain Doctor Dodgeball to Mark and insert it in practice. As always, it was a big hit with the players, especially those new to the team.

Saturday's match with the University of Nevada, Reno was important to Jim because three recruits, for the class two years in the future, were coming to watch Cascade play. They'd asked Jim If they could all visit at the same time and he was not surprised, because they all played for the same club team out of Reno.

The recruits arrived at the Salem airport late Friday night and Kristy picked them up in the baggage claim area. "Ladies, I'm coach Winslow. I trust you all had a good trip?" she said.

The tallest of the three, Tora, answered, "Actually it was kind of dull. It was too dark to look out the window and not enough time to get a snack."

"Wait a minute," Linda, the next tallest recruit, said, "I could see out the window just fine. The mountains were gorgeous, and the moon shined off of the lakes we flew over. I enjoyed looking out the window more than eating a peanut butter cracker."

The third recruit just smiled and shook her head. Kristy figured that she must be a setter.

Kristy thought to herself that the tall one must be spoiled, the second one must be a negotiator, and the quiet one must be smart. "Let's get in the van and head for Dallas. Who knows, we may find a nice place to eat. How does that sound?" The players looked at each other and agreed in unison.

Kristy pulled into the 'Word of Mouth' Neighborhood Bistro, knowing that the place had many options for the recruits to choose from. She was not wrong. An hour later, she paid a bill of fifty-seven dollars, without the tip. With the tip the bill was sixty-four dollars. She thought to herself, as she was getting everyone back in the van, that these three better be really good.

Jim met Kristy and the recruits in the parking lot when they arrived at the Cascade University dorm building where the recruits would be housed. "Ladies, Welcome. I hope you had a good trip. Have you had a chance to eat?" he asked, looking at Kristy.

"Yes. We ate in Salem at the 'Word of Mouth' Neighborhood Bistro. Here's the receipt," Kristy said, smiling,

"Ok. Kristy, their hosts are waiting inside the athletic building. "I'll see all of you tomorrow morning at breakfast. Enjoy yourself."

Jim walked back to the Cramer House and found the door wide open, which stopped him in his tracks. He backed up about twenty yards and motioned for the one FBI agent who was with him to check things out. The agent entered the house, turned on the lights in every room, and called for Jim to come inside.

"Liz is nowhere in the house, but as you can see by the furniture being tipped over, it looks like there was a struggle. Do you smell gunpower?" the agent asked.

"Yes, now that you mentioned it. I wonder where my other two agents are?" Jim asked.

"Follow me. Stay close behind me and we'll circle around the outside of the house," the agent instructed.

As they approached the back corner of the house, they found one agent lying on the ground with multiple gunshot wounds in his body, and two in his head. Knowing he was dead, they continued their search and found the other agent on the far side of the house. He was lying face down in the grass, with wounds in his upper back and his head.

"Now what do we do," Jim asked the agent. "It looks to me like Liz has been taken."

"The first thing I'm going to do is call the sheriff and an ambulance to take these two agents to the morgue, then I'll call Malika Ochoa," the agent said. He placed the first call and waited for his boss to answer on the second call.

"Hello. This better be important. Why are you calling me so late at night?" she asked, in a rather unpleasant tone.

"Ms. Ochoa, this is agent Cox. I'm with Mr. Sams at the Cramer

House. His friend, Liz, is missing. The other two agents who were in my detail were found dead outside the house. There is no sign of a gun battle. Mr. Sams and I were nearby and did not hear any gunshots."

"So, am I to understand that you split your protection detail?" Malika asked.

"Yes. We were away from the Cramer House, while Mr. Sams met the arrival of three recruits. I felt that the other two agents were adequate, and that we could respond at the first sign of trouble," the agent said.

"Bad choice by you. I want you to stay with Sams, inside the house and to notify the agents protecting the athletic building to send two agents to cover the outside of the Cramer House. I'll send three more agents in the morning. Understand?" she asked.

"Understood. Thank you," the agent said, not looking too confident. He turned and asked Jim, "Did you hear what we were talking about?"

"Yes. But don't you think we should be looking for Liz?" Jim asked.

"I understand your concern, but it's overcast and pitch dark outside. It would be impossible to find her in the dark. If they are after you, they will contact you and use her as bait to get to you," agent Cox said.

"Yea, that makes sense. It's just that I'm really worried about how they'll treat her. I have a suggestion. Rather that deplete the agents protecting the Athletic Department, why don't you and I get out of this place and spend the night in the athletic building?"

"I like that idea. I'm already in trouble with Ochoa, so why not?" agent Cox said.

After a restless night by both men, they were up at sunrise, dressed and headed for Tater's Café. They returned to the athletic building and learned that the three new agents had arrived.

Agent Cox called one agent from each squad and informed them of the loss of two agents last night. "Additionally, Mr. Sams' lady friend has gone missing. Sams, me and two of you, that have just arrived, are headed out to try and locate where the culprits have taken Ms. Barnett. If this plays out like I think, we'll be hearing from them shortly. When we do hear from them, I want all of you who are securing the athletic building to get to where they are as fast as you can. This encounter is shoot to kill – but not if Ms. Barnett is compromised! Understood?"

The whole group of agents nodded their heads in agreement.

"What we need to do first this morning is to go over to the Cramer House and look for anything that may give us information about last night's encounter," agent Cox said.

Agent Cox, Jim, and several other agents combed the ground around the Cramer House and found dozens of green tipped, 62-grain M855 spent cartridge shells. "So, our adversaries are using AR-15 rifles with devastating ammunition, which tells us to be super careful going forward," Cox said. "That's enough searching in the grass. Now, spread out and see if there are any signs of tire tracks in the dirt or on the cement leading out of here."

There were several tire tracks on the cement, close to the dirt, but only one track went off into the mud. "This looks like the only track of importance. Do any of you men recognize the tire's tread marks?" Cox questioned.

"Sir. That's a tread design built for going off road, and it's not manufactured in the US. I would say it's a Toyota Land Cruiser. There's a lot of mud splattered around, so if we are able to spot a Land Cruiser, we should also look at the tire sidewalls and up in the wheel wells," one of the newly arrived agents said.

With that, Cox broke the group up into three men each, with Jim riding in Cox's car, and they headed out to scour Dallas. They'd looked in every nook and cranny by noon and found nothing. Jim suggested eating at Oscar's delicatessen, and everyone agreed. Oscars was not too busy when the group of FBI agents pulled into different parking spaces. Jim said, "I'll go in and ask if they can seat all of us together."

Once everyone was seated, Ellora brought a handful of menus to the group. "Hey, coach Sams, are you coaching men's volleyball now?" she asked, with a laugh.

"What makes you think that. These are a bunch of middle-aged men. I doubt if they could beat a middle school girls' team. The one thing I know is that they are really hungry," Jim said, teasing.

After everyone was done looking at the menu, Ellora returned to the group and started with Jim, asking what he wanted. "You know, I've had a craving for enchiladas lately." Some of the other men spoke up saying they'd like that too.

Ellora said, "Now wait a minute. We've only got two serving of enchiladas left. How do you want to decide who gets them?"

Jim said, "I was the one that suggested enchiladas, so I should get one order. What about you agent Cox? You're in command of this group. Do you like Mexican food?"

"Not really. I have more of an interest in Italian food. One of the other guys can have the last order." Cox said.

While Ellora was waiting for someone to ask for the last order, Jim asked, "Isn't that strange for you to run out of enchiladas so early during the noon rush?"

"Yea, I couldn't believe it. But six Mexican dudes came in and ordered all but two orders of them enchiladas. Good for us, but not good for you guys," Ellora said.

"Uh, Ellora, did you see what kind of vehicle they were driving?" Jim asked.

"Damn right I saw their SUV! They almost drove it into my side windows. I gave them hell for being so careless," she said.

"What color was the SUV. Do you remember?" Jim asked.

"How could I forget the color. It was inches away from those windows behind you. That SUV looked like a shiny penny, a real piece of crap. While they ate, I looked at the car and at them, and wondered what a grubby bunch of bums was doing in a pimp car like that!" Ellora said, as she rolled her eyes.

"Agent Cox, what do you say about forgetting lunch and getting back on the road right now?" Jim asked.

"Jim, I know it's hard to be patient. Let's just have lunch and then we can spend the rest of the day out beyond the city limits. Hungry men are not good scouts."

"Ok. The rest of you need to order and eat so we can get going," Jim said.

Lunch took a little over forty minutes and everyone was back on various roads out beyond the Dallas city limits. After three hours with no luck, Cox decided to check all the streets within the Dallas city limits. Just under an hour before sunset Jim called it a day.

"Agent Cox, it looks like we will need to expand our search. We're not getting anywhere just driving around. Do you think the FBI will let us use a helicopter? That would really speed things up," Jim asked.

"I'll call Malika when we get back to Cascade's campus and see if she will sit still for using a helicopter," Cox said.

When all of the agents had made their way back to the athletic building, agent Cox advised them that they'd continue their search at daylight tomorrow morning. Jim, Cox and two more agents walked over to the Cramer house to get ready for dinner and Jim's phone rang.

"Hello, this is Coach Sams, may I help you?" he answered.

"Jim! This is Liz. A bunch of Columbians broke into the house night before last, tied me up and put me in their SUV."

"Senior Sams," interrupted one of the thugs. "This is Leandro. We have your bitch and if you ever want to see her in one piece again, you will meet me tonight on the Dallas Golf course off of Orrs Corner Road at two-thirty tomorrow morning."

"Where on the golf course do you want me to meet you?" Jim asked, as he held the phone away from his ear so Cox could hear.

"We will be in the middle of the fifteenth fairway. If you are more that fifteen minutes late, you will never see her alive again" Leandro said.

"I'll be there," Jim said, and cut the call off.

"Did you hear all of that?" he asked Cox.

"Yes. I heard. Are you familiar with the fifteenth fairway at this golf course," Cox asked.

"Yes, I've played there many times. The fifteenth fairway is a par five and it's wide. On the east side of the fifteenth is a barbed wire fence with a hay field on the other side that's already been harvested. There are a lot of those round hay bales scattered around the field. On the west side of the fairway are some trees scattered here and there. There is an outhouse off to the east side of the tee. Otherwise, it's wide open," Jim explained.

"Let me contact Malika and ask about the copter," Cox said. "Malika, this is agent Cox. I've got information to give you and I need to ask you an important question."

"Agent Cox is there any reason you can't call me earlier in the day?" asked Malika.

"Yes mam. We were busy most of today. This call is important, so please listen. From daybreak to just a few minutes ago, we've been out trying to locate a large, bronze colored SUV. That car is carrying six Columbians and Coach Sams' lady friend," Cox said. "We just got a phone call from some guy who called himself Leandro, and he said he had Liz. He's stipulated the place where he wants to meet Coach Sams and the time to make a trade."

"Ok. Tell me more," Malika said, in a more interested tone.

"This Leandro person wants to meet in the middle of the fifthteenth fairway of the Dallas Golf course at two-thirty tomorrow morning. Basically, later tonight. I think we need a helicopter to back us up. I've checked the weather and there will be no moon until four am," asked Cox.

"A helicopter! Are you nuts. Do you know how much that will cost the department?" she asked.

"A lot less than the loss of life on our side, and Coach Sams, and Liz!" Cox responded.

21
BAD GOLF

"Yea, I see what you mean. Let me get back to you. Give me about thirty minutes," Malika said.

"Ok, Coach. She's looking for the helicopter right now. She said it will take her about half an hour to get things set up," Cox said, loud enough for the other agents to hear.

"If we are going to confront these bastards on the golf course to-night, we need to eat dinner and then talk about how we get Liz back without any of us getting killed," Jim said.

Jim and all of the agents in Dallas ate dinner in the campus dining hall. Just before the men finished eating, Cox's phone buzzed. "Agent Cox speaking," he said.

"This is Malika. I've got some bad news and some really good news. The helicopter was a no go. But I'm sending you six agents, four to enforce your numbers, and two expert drone handlers. These are not run-of-the-mill drones. These are military drones, and they have protective armament, night vision, and are armed with concussion bombs. They tell me the concussion bombs will knock down and stun anyone within a ten-foot radius on impact. I've also sent fifteen night vision goggles for your men. The four agents coming your way are FBI snipers and will be armed with the latest M27 Infantry Automatic Rifle. Is there anything else you think you need?" she asked.

"Ms. Ochoa, you're already sending so much. Thank you, it's really appreciated, but there are two more things I think we could use. First would be something bullet proof, that one of our men could wear, while impersonating Coach Sams, when meeting this Leandro guy to make the exchange for Liz. The final thing we could use would be four army Belgian Malinois dogs, if you can get them on such notice," Cox said.

"Ok. You do know that if we can get the dogs, their handlers must also come. I'll see what I can do," she said, sounding a little annoyed. "I'll make sure you have everyone and everything you've asked for in Dallas by midnight."

After Cox advised the group of what Malika said, Jim asked, "Do you think we should sneak out to the fifteenth fairway and check things out?"

"I'd bet you a year's salary that some of the thugs are out there right now. If any of us were spotted sneaking around we'd be dead before we realized what hit us, and you could kiss Liz's ass goodbye," Cox said, in no uncertain terms. "We are going to wait here for the arrival of everything and everyone that Malika said she'd send. Once I have a chance to talk with the drone agents, we'll have them send the drones out to the golf course and check things out for us," Cox said. "Are you ok with that?"

"Yes. Nice thinking," Jim said, with an embarrassing look on his face.

Jim sat in the Cramer House living room with Cox and stared out the window, looking at the parking lot of the athletic building. A million things were going around in his head. The thought of Liz being captured by those guys driving the pimp SUV was all he could do to keep from screaming out his frustration. The more he thought, the closer he was to crying. He finally, gained control of his emotions and began to think about how to get Liz back without her being injured or killed.

"Agent Cox, I'm trying to think about how we can get Liz back, without her being hurt, and capturing or killing her captors. Actually, I'm struggling to think of a plan. What about you?

Have you got anything yet?" Jim asked.

"I do. That's part of our training. Sometimes a plan works perfectly and sometimes it doesn't, and that's when a lot of those on our side suffer," Cox said. "Here's what I've got in mind. The first thing is to discuss with those two drone experts how close they need to be to the fifteenth fairway. I think they can be a mile away, which will not expose their presence to the kidnappers.

If they can work from that distance, we'll send them and their equipment out, and one agent to protect them. I'll tell the guys working the drones to cover every square inch of the fifteenth fairway and about twenty yards on all asides of the fairway. I will have them look for where vehicles are positioned, both those who have Liz and any other security vehicles. Once we get the images, we can then determine where our guys will be placed. I definitely want the four FBI snipers to be in a semi-circle facing the direction where the exchange will take place. The snipers are to take out Leonardo and whomever else surrounds Liz, including any nearby in the brush or tree line. The balance of the agents we have will maneuver as close to the fifteenth fairway as they can, knowing there will be other thugs hiding in whatever cover they can find. My hope is that the drone guys can pick out each of the six kidnappers that we think are here," Cox concluded.

"That's a good plan. I wish there was a way we could signal Liz to drop to the ground, face down when the fireworks begin," Jim said.

"At this point, I doubt that we can do that. We'll just hope and pray that she gets down on her own," Cox said, looking into Jim's eyes.

At ten-fifty-five four FBI SUVs pulled into the lot next to the athletic department building. Jim, Cox and the all the other agents walked over to greet the newcomers. A big surprise was the four Belgian Malinois dogs and their handlers. Cox directed everyone to get into the athletic building so he could explain the night's plan.

When Cox felt everyone was up to speed, he called the four snipers and Jim aside. "I'm pretty sure the head man, a guy named Leonardo, will use Liz as a shield. I think there will be a couple of other thugs with him who will try to protect Leonardo when the shooting starts. I want each of you to communicate who your target is and to make sure the first shot kills the scum you're taking out. Agent Hays will be dressed in a lightweight, bulletproof hoodie and pants made by IIIA and, after your first shots are fired, he will move forward and cover Liz while they run back to the car they arrived in. By that time, the other thugs will be shooting from their position on or around the fairway. There are six thugs, so each of you need to be aware of how many of them the snipers get and how many are left. The agents controlling the drones will be watching the entire area and will alert us if any of the thugs have made a break. Whoever is closest to a runner, listen to the drone operator and he will guide you to the guy's position. Once we're sure we've eliminated all of them, we'll signal each of you to see if any of you've been hit.

If all goes well, they are dead, Liz is fine, and each of us has not been hurt. I'm sure that the local sheriff and police will respond to our location, hopefully after the shooting has stopped. Do not confront or try to tell them who you are or what you're doing out here. Just drop to your knees and lift your arms up over your head. I will deal with each officer that arrives on site.

Do any of you not understand or have questions?" Cox concluded. Everyone nodded their head in the affirmative.

With that the agents handling the drones and one dog handler loaded their SUV and headed out to a position about a mile south of the golf course. They backed up into a group of trees that had an opening facing north and put one drone up about five hundred feet in the night air.

Before moving the drone north to the golf course, they moved it around for about ten minutes to check the clarity of the picture. Next, they increased the altitude to a thousand feet and again checked the clarity, which was still good. The agent controlling this drone asked the other agent, "Do you want to check the armed drone for clarity at different heights?"

"Yes. I think we better do that, knowing how strict agent Cox is," the second controller said.

The agent handling the Belgian Malinois dog was constantly checking out the area around the drone controllers, to make sure the area was void of anyone else.

When each drone checked out satisfactory, they looked around their position and then moved up to the Dallas Golf Course. They recorded every square inch of the fifteenth fairway and its surroundings, twice. Once at five hundred feet and then at one thousand feet.

Agent Cox contacted them and asked, "Is what you've sent me, everything I need to see?"

"Yes. Actually, we've increased the area out beyond the fifteenth fairway from twenty yards up to a half-mile on all four sides," one drone agent said.

"Ok, that's good. However, I'm having trouble spotting anybody on or around the fairway. No vehicles and no human movement. Why is that?" he asked.

"That's because there are no cars there and no people there yet. It's close to half an hour before their arrival time. We will be monitoring all movement in and around the fifteenth fairway from now on. Aren't you going to try to be here before they arrive?" the agent asked.

"Affirmative. We are moving out of the Cascade University parking lot as we speak. One of you keep your eye on and around the fairway, and the other one of you start watching us so we can be alerted if they arrive before we get situated around the golf course. Agent Hays will be alone driving one of our SUVs to the exchange spot in the middle of the fairway. I had a couple of agents put an X on the top of that vehicle, so the armored drone doesn't strike it. Do you understand everything we just talked about?" Cox asked.

"Yes sir. Good luck agent Cox," the drone agent said.

"Thanks son, same to you," Cox responded.

The FBI agents were all in place at one-fifty, ten minutes before the exchange was to take place. Right on time, the pimp SUV drove along the tree line side of the fairway and unloaded four thugs before turning out to meet the FBI's SUV head on, at a distance of about thirty feet. The driver opened his door and then opened the back seat door behind the driver's side. A tall, Columbian man got out and pulled Liz out, placing her directly in front of him. The other thug positioned himself a short distance behind, Leandro and to the side by about five yards, holding a pistol in his right hand. The three of them began to walk towards agent Hayes until they were all about fifteen feet apart. Cox could see that there was what could be a major problem, when he realized that Liz was stark naked, doing her best to keep herself covered with her arms.

"Hey Sams. You see I've got your woman here! I thought you would like to see that she is not hurt," Leonardo said, laughing, as two shots wrang out.

Both Columbians were killed instantly with a single shot to their heads. Hays rushed forward and forced Liz to the ground, lying on top of her and asking, "I'm agent Hays, with the FBI. Are you ok? Have they hurt you in any way?" he asked.

"I'm fine. They pretty much left me alone until tonight when they told me we were going to see Jim. That's when they stripped me," she said, in a fairly weak voice.

"Stay down as flat as you can. I'll take off my hoodie so you can put it on," Hays said.

While a gun battle raged, Jim could do nothing but watch Liz laying on the ground between the two SUVs, with an agent on top of her. As quick as it started, it was all over. Cox asked the drone agents, "Tell me why everything has stopped?"

"Agent Cox, we've located all six thugs the moment they arrived, and they've all been killed. It's now safe to move to the remains and check in person if they are all dead," said the drone agent.

"Not so fast. We were lucky when we arrived and were able to get in place. I want the whole fairway to be checked out with a metal detector before anyone moves," agent Cox said.

It took a little over thirty minutes to locate the metal detector and check the entire fifteenth fairway for underground explosives. Before making their way to the main entry onto the golf course, Cox called the Dallas Coroner's office to come and gather the six thugs and take them in for processing. Before long, they could hear sirens blaring. Six police officers, and not coroners, got out of their cars and pointed their weapons at the FBI agents, telling them to put their hands up.

Cox, and the agents with him, did as instructed and he said, "Gentlemen, we are FBI agents. If you allow me to reach into my pocket, I'll show you my credentials."

"You just stand still and don't move a muscle. Bobby, go over to him and get his credentials out of his pocket so he doesn't try something cute," the Sargent said.

"Sarge, it's just as he explained," Bobby said.

"Bobby, bring that over to me. It's probably fake. FBI agents don't wander around in the middle of the night. Check the other two and that guy with the detector," the Sargent said, in a know-it-all tone.

"Sarge, they all have FBI credentials. I think they are FBI agents," Bobby said.

"Well, ok," he said, looking at Cox. "Tell me what you're doing out here at this time of night."

"We're out here at this time of night to rescue a woman who'd been kidnaped by six Latin men, which we did. They were all armed and thought they could kill us and then the woman and her friend. Two are laying in the middle of the fairway, and four are laying in the brush by the trees on the north side of the fairway, all dead. That's all you need to know. Agent Jeffers, round up every other agent and get them over here so these officers can see the size of this operation," Cox said. "Also get the three agents who worked the drones up here."

Twenty minutes later, there were fourteen FBI agents, and four Belgian Malinois dogs, surrounding the police officers. "Geeze, you guys had a small army just to apprehend a few Mexicans," the Sargent said.

They were not Mexicans. They were Columbian, and we don't like to lose!" Cox said.

"Ok, Sargent? We are going to gather our equipment and get out of here."

Cox walked back to the FBI SUV parked in the middle of the fifteenth fairway and drove Jim and Liz back to the Cramer House. Before they got out of the SUV, Cox asked Liz if he could talk to her in the morning about her abduction and what the thugs were talking about before they came to make the trade for Jim.

Jim and Liz entered the Cramer House and went directly into the bathroom. "Liz, I'm so sorry that those basterds took you as a hostage. If Cox would have let me shoot that Leandro bastard, I would have emptied the gun into him. I know you must have been terrified. Did any of them touch you physically?" he asked.

"No. Not at all. They kept me in a dark room at a rundown house up in the coast range. The food was unbelievably bad, and the toilet was an antique disaster. I can't wait to shower. Do you want to join me?" she asked.

"Not right now. I want you to get cleaned up, so you feel better. I'm so pissed at these Columbians right now that I can't think straight. I feel like I've let you down and broken your trust in me. When you got out of their vehicle and I saw that you were naked, all I could think is that they'd raped you. I damn near rushed the transfer point," he said, as he was close to tears.

"Hey. Jim. Take it easy. I'm ok now. I'm here with you, safe and sound. Somehow, I knew you would get me out of that situation. I know you will always come through for me," she said, giving him a tight hug. "Let me get cleaned up and then we can get some sleep. Ok?"

"Yes. Thank you so much for not despising me. You and I are going to be next to each other at all times, no matter where we go or what we're doing," he said, looking at her for validation.

"That works for me. I love you, Jim. I always will," she said smiling as she stepped into the shower.

22
MOVING UP

Jim was awake at first light. When fully aware, he propped himself up on his elbow and looked at Liz a long time. All of his thoughts ended with him thinking that a real angel was lying next to him. How could anyone on this earth defile such a perfect woman? He laid back down and began to think about what he would've done to the Columbians if she had been killed, or even hurt in some way.

He checked the time and realized that he needed to get to the cafeteria so he could eat with his staff and players. "Good morning everyone. Are you all awake and ready to go. Tora, Linda, Aofi, how was your night?" Jim asked.

Zofi spoke for the other two, saying "It was really nice, thanks to Kristy and the girls on the team. They were so nice to us, and we felt more than welcome. We wish we could skip our senior year of high school and join your team next fall."

"It would be great to have you on the team that soon. However, if that were to happen, your parents and a lot of other people back home would not be real happy. Kristy, have you had a chance to introduce Coach King and Chris?"

"Coach Sams, Chris and I met these three future Cascade University volleyball players this morning. I'm sure they will make a great addition to our team," Mark said.

"Ok. As you all know, the match begins at six this evening. I want all of you to be on the court for warmups at five sharp. If you need to see the trainers, do that early so you can begin warmups with everyone else," Jim said.

He looked at the three young recruits, and said with a big smile on his face, "I don't know who you'll be rooting for this evening, but it makes no difference to me which side you choose. In fact, I'd expect you to be pulling for URN. It's also ok with me if you know someone on their team that you would like to visit with. We have seats for the three of you right behind the player seats, for both sides of the court. The one thing that I will not allow is sitting next to and fraternizing with any young men. Are you clear on that?" he asked. Each of the three recruits shook their head in the affirmative, while showing slight smiles.

"This evening is an important match. I want each of you to take it easy physically, during the day. From the minute you step on the court for warmups this evening, I want it to be all business. Understood?" This time a loud verbal response was from all of his players, and the three recruits, which Jim sensed as a positive sign that the three recruits would be on his team a couple years from now.

He left the team and his staff and walked over to Liz. "Sorry I take so long talking to my team on match days," he said.

"That's no problem. I'm used to it by now. In fact, I enjoy how you treat your players and staff. I'm sure it makes them feel important," she said.

'Hey, I just remembered that I've got something to show you. How dumb of me to forget," Jim said.

"You've got to be kidding. Don't you think there's been enough to think about recently?" Liz said.

"Yes. But I've been known to be able to deal with two or three things at the same time."

"I'm sure glad you had only a couple of things on your brain yesterday!" Liz said. "So, tell me what you're going to show me."

"What I'm going to show you is better seen than explained. We'll let Cox know that we are going to take a little ride in fifteen minutes," Jim said, with a big smile on his face.

Jim and Liz waited in his car until Cox and the other agents were ready to go. The trip took less than ten minutes and Liz shouted her surprise out loud when she saw what was happening. Jim parked next to the lot where his old house had burned to the ground.

"When did this start?" Liz asked, as she looked at the framing and cement slab that now occupied the lot. "You told me you were having trouble finding a contractor."

Just then, Cox walked up and knocked on Jim's car window. "Why are we stopping here?' He asked Jim.

"I once owned a nice home on this lot. As you might be able to guess, a couple of thugs from Salt Lake City burnt it to the ground. I jumped through a lot of hoops, working with other FBI agents, and my insurance man, before I could rebuild. I was just explaining to Liz what's now happening on the lot," Jim told Cox.

"I'm glad you came over here today. If we'd known about this from the beginning, we could have investigated the background of every one that will be connected with building your new home. That investigation will begin today," Cox said.

"Please, get in the back seat and listen as I tell Liz how this came to be. One day, a few weeks ago, I was having breakfast at Tater's, and there was this guy sitting there alone, so I started to talk with him. His name is Charlie. I'd never seen him anywhere in town before, and I wondered if he was just moving through or if he was going to make Dallas his home. Turn's out he and his wife had just bought a nice little house on the south side of town. They were both retired, and he'd been a building contractor. He was looking for something to keep himself busy. He was easy to talk to, and one thing led to the next. So now, I have a super qualified building contractor, managing a small crew of carpenters, electricians, and plumbers, building my new house," Jim said.

"That was a very fortunate meeting between you, who was looking for a building contractor, and him, who just happened to be a building contractor. You really didn't think that this might have been too easy? That this guy might be working for the scum from Salt Lake City?" Cox asked, in a disappointed tone.

"Agent Cox, you're right. I was shortsighted and, in a hurry to get this house built. I completely overlooked the obvious, as you just pointed out. How long will it take for you guys to check on him, and all of the other craftsmen, to see if they are the real thing or thugs from Salt Lake City?"

"I'll start immediately. If all these people are really journeymen house builders, we'll know by the end of today. If they are part of the filth from Salt Lake City, they'll be arrested this afternoon, I'll guarantee it!" Cox said. "Both of us need to drive back to the Cramer House, so we don't scare any of them away. I will communicate with Malika and ask to have her people do all the leg work to find out who these workers are. Let's get moving."

As they were driving back to Cramer house, Jim said, "I can't believe I was so stupid to not check these guys out right from the start. The more I think about it, the more it makes me feel like an idiot!" he said.

"Not really, you just learned a good lesson at this point in your life. Just like when you decided to ask me if I wanted to have dinner with you sometime. Remember?" Liz asked, smiling.

"Yes. I remember everything about that afternoon. One of the best questions I've ever asked!" Jim said, looking straight at Liz.

As Jim and Liz pulled into the athletic building parking lot, Jim looked over at the Cramer House and saw that agent Coxes' SUV was parked next to a white SUV. "Liz, do you see what I see at the Cramer House?" he asked.

"Yes. I see two SUVs; one I recognize and one I don't recognize. I'm for going over and seeing whose there."

"Have you got your gun with you?" Jim said, with a twinkle in his eye.

Jim and Liz walked into the Cramer House and found Cox talking with Malika. "Hello, Malika. What brings you our way?" Jim said, while shaking her hand.

"Good news and bad news, again," Malika said. The good news is that you secured Liz and that she's suffered no physical harm. How are you doing today, Liz?" Malika asked.

"I'm fine. Better than I thought I would be after being held for that long. Those guys fit the definition of being 'the scum of the earth'. Usually, I'd be all upset if someone was killed instead of captured. But these guys deserved exactly what they got. Your agents were perfect, and I think your resources ensured that I would make it. Agent Cox should get a medal if you were to ask me. He is a great leader," Liz said.

"Ok. That brings me to the bad news. Agent Cox is being promoted to take my job here in Oregon. He's to become the head of Oregon's FBI's Human Trafficking Unit based in Portland. I know he will do a great job. That's not bad news for him or any of you. The bad news is for me. I'm being dismissed immediately from the FBI here in Oregon for having given you guys everything you asked for in this last incident," she said with a straight face.

"No! That can't be right. No way is that fair! Everything you got for us made sure Liz would be safe and that no agents would be hurt. Let me talk to your boss," Jim said.

"Well, ok. I'll give you his phone number on one condition," she said, projecting a hang dog look.

"Just tell me the one condition and the number, and I will fix everything right now," Jim said, in a very positive tone.

"Actually, I'm only being moved from the Oregon Human Trafficking Unit. I will now be the new Assistant Director of Salt Lake City's FBI Human Trafficking Unit. This is a solid upgrade for me, a woman, in charge of more than three hundred agents. I don't think you should call anyone down there. I think I'll be alright!" she said with a big smile on her face.

There were hugs all around. Liz opened a bottle of whisky and, everyone but Jim, raised their glasses to congratulate Malika for being promoted to such an important position within the FBI.

"I hate to shut down this happy gathering, but it's time for us to get over to the gym for tonight's match against the University of Nevada, Reno," Jim said.

Before Malika left for Portland, she asked for a moment with Jim. "When your season comes to an end, we'd like you to relocate to

Salt Lake City for a short period. The Director of the Salt Lake City Department wants you to be there when we begin to dismantle the Columbian contingent in that part of the United States. Do me a favor and think about this and get back to me sometime in the next two weeks. Ok?" she asked.

"I can tell you right now that I'm not at all interested. It's that simple" Jim said.

"Are you forgetting how easily those thugs have been coming here trying to eliminate you and any others that you care for?" Malika said, with a stern look on her face.

"I've not forgot. I'm not a man of violence by nature, and I have no idea why you need me in Salt Lake City?"

"The Director of the FBI operation in Salt Lake City is a very intelligent man. He has access to all kinds of information, and he has a great memory. Just between you and me, you don't want to get on his bad side. From the little he shared with me about all that was going on in the Dallas area, and the greater Willamette Valley with these thugs, the more I would encourage you to move temporarily to Salt Lake City, as he has asked me to tell you," Malika said.

"Ok. Now I feel that I'm being induced to move to Salt Lake City. Between you and me, what would be his response if I were to refuse the offer?" Jim asked.

"Between you and me, you really don't want to know. He's aware of most everything you've been doing from the time you found that woman on the banks of the Willamette, down near Harrisburg, to your perfectly camouflaged trip to Budapest, and the trip to the Arenberg Convent, and finally the flawless driving accident with a log truck on the McKenzie Highway! Believe me when I say he knows everything about what you've been up to," Malika said, with a sinister smile.

"Well now. It looks like I better spend some time in Salt Lake City after all!" Jim said. "My lady friend, Liz, knows nothing about all you've alluded to. Have you, or will you be telling her anything about what you just told to me? Ever?" Jim asked.

"Not a word to another soul. Your family or friends, anyone at the college or your staff, police or sheriffs in Dallas, anyone in the volleyball coaching profession or businesses you use the services of, will ever be aware of anything you've done on your own or for us," Malika said.

"You know, Malika, I believe you and everything you just told me. I'm still worried that sometime, somehow, someone, will become aware of why I'm helping the FBI in Salt Lake City. If the University were to learn of this, they would refuse to give me my pension and all the other perks that I receive. Losing those, would destroy my relationship with Liz and my family, and it would ruin me profession-ally, and financially. Can the FBI guarantee me, in writing, that if our little secret gets out, I will be compensated financially, equivalent to the dollar amount I would have received when I retired?" Jim asked.

"I don't know if anything that you've just questioned has been addressed by the Director," Let me speak with him and I'll get back to you," Malika said.

"I can tell you right now, that if you get a positive response about the financial end of what we just talked about, I'm in!" said Jim. "I just want this whole issue, from Harrisburg to having FBI agents cover me and my family's every move, to go away. I didn't ask to be involved in any of it.

The thugs from Salt Lake City were behind everything that made me respond the way I did."

"I'll try to get an answer as soon as possible and I'll let you know when I know," Malika said.

Jim's mind went directly to tonight's match between Cascade and the University of Nevada, Reno. Liz was waiting for Jim in his car and the agents were lined up behind them in their vehicles, all ready to head for the gym. Upon arrival at four twenty-five, Jim could see that all of his players were dressed and ready to go.

As the players and coaches began to take the floor to warm up, agent Cox pulled Jim aside and said, "Coach Sams, I have the results on your contractor and the subs that are on your building site as of now. They are all legit and can continue to work on your project. If any new craftsman joins your project, they must first get clearance from the FBI. Understood?" he asked.

"Yes. There will be no problem from me in that area. Thanks for checking." Jim responded.

As his players went through the warmup, and began to hit, Jim could see the three recruits watching with their mouths wide open and their eyes focused on every hitter. Kristy walked up and asked Jim, "What do you think. Are our girls ready?"

"Absolutely. I've been observing the recruits watch our players hit and two things are obvious.

First, if they've not seen UNR hit like this, we may be in for an easy match. Second, maybe they themselves don't hit like this? We shall see," Jim said, smiling a bit.

The match results were just as Jim suspected. Cascade won three zip, in a bit over an hour and fifteen minutes. Jim made sure that each of his players saw court time.

Just before he and Liz departed the gym, he reminded Kristy and Mark to monitor the recruits activity tonight and to get them headed home on time tomorrow.

23
SALT LAKE CITY

Only three regular matches remained for Cascade's volleyball team. But Jim began to feel that they seemed to be stressing out a bit too much. He wondered if he should bring Professor Martin in to talk to the players again this season.

On Sunday afternoon he called Kristy and said, "I get the feeling that too much stress has found its way onto our team. Would you mind contacting Professor Martin Monday morning and see if she would be willing to talk with the players on our team again. I think she'd be willing to do that, but I want only one session this time."

"Sure. I'd enjoy talking to Sandra. What time and day should I ask for," Kristy asked.

"So, you're calling her Sandra now? Are you two friendly enough that she doesn't mind you using her first name?" Jim asked.

"No, not at all. We've become friends ever since the last time she talked to our team. She's a great person," Kristy said.

"That's good. Relationships like that never hurt. I'm glad that she's open to helping us. You two can pick whatever day and time works best all around. I also want to meet with you and Mark first thing Monday morning. Ok?" Jim asked.

"We'll both be there bright and early. See you then."

Jim joined Liz in the living room of Cramer House and said, "I apologize for not showing you more attention. Especially after all you've just been through. Is there anything you'd like to do for the rest of the day?" he asked.

"I think I just want to sit here with you and have you hold me. The reality of what I've been through while those Columbian slobs had me locked up is beginning to sink in. I feel as if I might have been killed. Why do you think they kidnapped me?" she asked.

"They must have thought that getting you would be the easiest way to get to me. You need to remember that a lot of them came to Dallas trying hard to find a time and place when they could grab me. They even had that jerk at the Dallas Police Department trying to set us up. This group of scums probably knew a gazillion ways to nab somebody and use them for whatever purpose they had in mind," Jim said, trying to settle her down.

The balance of Sunday was spent on the couch with Jim holding Liz tight to his side, and both of them under a large, warm blanket. Even though they tried to watch some football on television, Liz was now relaxed enough for her to fall asleep for a couple of hours. After dark, Jim slipped out from under the blanket, without waking Liz, and prepared dinner.

His choice for dinner was clam chowder, that he'd thawed out earlier that morning, and a slider salmon sandwich. He added some oyster crackers to finish the meal off. It was just enough food to make you feel good without feeling like you'd overeaten. He brought the food into the living room and put it on two TV trays, and gently woke Liz up.

She moved a little without waking up at hearing his voice. But once she smelled the food, she sat up and was ready to eat. "You're always full of surprises. This looks so good! Thank you for making this and for letting me sleep," she said, before taking the first bite.

Following a good night's sleep and a substantial breakfast, Jim and Liz stopped at his lot to update Charlie about some changes he wanted. "Charlie, how's everything going?" Jim asked.

"So far, so good. What's up with you?" Charlie asked.

"First, I want you to meet Liz. We've been together for some time now, and since we live together, I wanted her to see what's going on over here," Jim said. "I've been thinking about some more things that I'd like to have in this place. Maybe you should write this stuff down. I think the list may be too long for memory."

Once Charlie was ready to write everything down that Jim was going to tell him, he nodded his head.

"Here's what I want. Sister all the two by four studs with six-inch studs. Put a moisture barrier annealed to bullet proof sheathing. I want all walls, both exterior and interior to be insulated with closed cell spray foam. I want bullet proof doors, and windows. I want an Interior mechanical room inside the house, not in the garage, plus an air exchanger, an interior water supply, and natural gas shut off. I also want an overhead sprinkler system in every room. Next, a 10kw generator and an air conditioning unit, both inside the garage with their exhaust vented to the exterior. Finally, I want all wall studs fastened to the base plates and roof rafters by steel tie downs," Jim said with a smile.

Charlie tightened his jaw a bit and looked up at the sky as he said, "I really doubt if we can complete the house at the price you originally quoted, and by the time you've given us to complete everything."

"I know it will drive the costs up and take longer to complete. But, if I'm going to live here for the rest of my life, I want to be well protected from whatever mother nature or mankind can throw my way. Sounds crazy, I know, but that's what I want," Jim said. "Do you think you can handle that?"

"Oh, I'm sure I can do it. I would like to be able to take a few days off every now and then, or maybe take my wife on a little vacation from time to time. If such an arrangement works for you, it'll work for me," Charlie said, with an agreeable smile.

Jim reached out to shake Charlie's hand and said, "Done. Are you able to find two or three samples of each item I'm asking for?" Jim asked.

"I've done that sort of thing my whole working life. It will take some time, but I'll get it done. I usually start looking for the things that need to be put in place first, then work through the rest of the stuff in sequence." Charlie said. "Do you want me to have things delivered to the project once you tell me your first choice?"

"Absolutely! That's just great. I'm going to be really busy out of town, maybe for the next few months. Call me anytime you have a question or need anything. If I don't answer right away, I'll return your call as soon as possible. Charlie, I can't tell you how much I appreciate everything you're doing for me," Jim said as he shook Charlies hand again.

As the Cascade's regular volleyball season came to an end, Jim's team had a twenty-nine and one, won-loss record. Now they'd need to wait a few days to see what their seed would be in the NCAA National Championships.

Jim answered the phone and listened to Malika ask, "Jim, is your volleyball season over yet?"

"Yes. We played our last regular season match this past Saturday. Why do you ask?" said Jim.

Malika said, "Because things are heating up in Salt Lake and I need you there as soon as possible."

"I'm sure that I told you that we would be playing in the NCAA Championships after the regular season. We won't know the time and place of our first matches for another few days," Jim said. "We will be playing matches every week until we win it all or until we get beat. I'm afraid I have no idea how long that will be. I do know that the last match of the Championship will be December Seventeenth."

"I'm happy for you and your team, but we need you here before that," Malika said.

"Why," Jim asked.

"Things here have accelerated faster than I'd assumed. Could you make it up here for a few days each week while your team is practicing? The Director is getting impatient. He wants to meet you and bring you up to speed on what he has in mind for you," she asked.

"I might be able to spend two or three days a week down there. Say a Sunday, Monday, and Tuesday. What do you think about those days?" he asked Malika.

She asked, "Why those particular days?"

"Because NCAA Championship matches are played on Thursdays and Saturdays, and they are played in different venues each week up to the finals. Locations and time are stipulated. We have no say where or when we compete," Jim said.

"Well, that will have to do. Let me know as soon as you know the details of each contest. Thanks," she said.

"Malika. There is one more thing. Liz will be going with me wherever I go and whenever I go. I'm not going to go through another time when we are apart, ever, until we're rid of the Columbians," he said. "Do you understand, and will that arrangement work for you needing me in Salt Lake City?"

"Yes. I've already cleared it with the Director. You two will receive plane tickets to and from Salt Lake, and you will have secure housing in the city," Malika said.

"Sounds good. I'll see you when I see you. Goodbye," Jim said.

Jim thought for a few minutes about how he would handle what

Malika just asked for. The first thing he needed to do was talk to his athletic director. He walked down the hall to Associate Athletic Director Robert Paige's office and asked his secretary, "Would Paige have a moment to talk?"

"Hello coach. Congratulations on a nice season. Let me check," she said." Ok, you can go right in."

"Thanks," Jim said. When he opened the door, he saw Paige sitting at his desk talking with the Athletic Director. "Hello Henry, Robert. I've got a couple of questions. Do you two have a few minutes?" Jim asked, more surprised than he wanted to be.

"Sure," Henry said. "We both want to congratulate you on an outstanding season. What does it look like for the playoffs?"

"We're waiting for the brackets to be announced in a couple of days. Once that happens, I'll inform all involved with transportation and housing. With our won-loss record we should play all our matches at one location, until the finals. Those matches will be played in Atlanta. We're going to be doing a lot of flying in the next few weeks. I hope we can use the University's plane for most of the trips," Jim asked with a smile.

"Absolutely, Talbot responded, "It's about time that one of the best teams in the history of sports at Cascade University is treated first class."

"Thank you, Henry. I'm sure the players will appreciate it more than you can imagine!" Jim said. "I have another issue to ask you about. I don't know why, but for most of this last year, a group of Columbians, based in Salt Lake City, have been trying to do me in. They have tried to hurt me and members of my family. I have no idea why. All I know is that they kidnapped one of my grandsons and attacked my daughter's house. They also took my lady friend, Liz, and tried to negotiate switching her for me. Both of them are safe and now back in their homes."

Jim looked at Paige and asked, "Does Henry know about Malika and what she's arranged to protect me and my loved ones?"

Before Paige could answer, Henry said, "Yes, Jim. I'm aware of the FBI protection for you, this building, your friend, your staff, and our volleyball players. It would be kind of hard to not know when we have four or five FBI agents in this building twenty-four hours a day."

"I was hoping to not make it a big deal here, but Malika insisted. Did you get to meet her when she was here?" Jim asked Talbot.

"Yes, Robert introduced her to me. She has a very important position in the Oregon branch of the FBI."

Jim said, "Had! She's been promoted and will now work as the Assistant Director of the Human Trafficking Unit in Salt Lake City. That's a huge promotion for that young lady. However, she has asked me to be in Salt Lake City on Sundays, Mondays, and Tuesdays. I asked why and she explained that the Director is moving really fast to find, arrest, and convict all of the Columbians working in human trafficking in that part of the United State. Which means that after our season concludes, he wants me there full time until they find and arrest every one of the thugs in the Columbian Cartel. I don't need to stay while they're being convicted and deported."

"They seem to need you more than we do after your season ends," Henry said. He looked at Paige and asked, "What do you think Robert? Can we do without him for a few months?"

"I think we can, considering all he's had to do this season. His team has improved tremendously, he's hired two outstanding assistants for the volleyball program, and he continues to recruit excellent athletes,"

Paige said. "We might be able to put him on sabbatical, that way he can still get paid. I doubt if the FBI is going to cover his salary."

"I Think that's a good idea, and it solves any dispute by other coaches in the department," Henry agreed. "Jim, when do you start your full time in Salt Lake City?"

"The day after we lose our last match or, win the tournament. It could be at any time. I'll stay in close contact with anyone in the department that impacts our coming and going during the Championship. After that, my first assistant Kristy Winslow, will be able to handle most everything I would normally do. If she has questions about anything to do with the volleyball program, I'll have her call me first. Believe me, I intend to keep an eye on this program at all times," Jim said. "Finally, Malika informed me that the FBI will fly Liz and I to and from Salt Lake City, while I'm still coaching our team in the Championship. After that, until they don't need me anymore, they will continue to fly us around, when needed. She also said they will provide our housing for the entire time we're there."

24
FIRST THINGS FIRST

Cascade University won the first two matches of the Championships, played in San Diego, against teams that were markedly less skilled than Cascade. The next two matches were played in San Antonio, which Cascade won, by playing very aggressively against two good teams. The championship rounds are played on a Thursday-Saturday format and will be played in Atlanta. Jim returned home after the first two and second two matches to talk with his team and travel with them to their final contests. Before boarding the Cascade plane headed for Atlanta, Jim asked Kristy, "How did the kids practice this week? Do you think they can win these next two?"

"They were all business during practice this week. This is a super confident team and I know they think they can win," Kristy said.

"Was Tuesday's workout demanding?" he asked.

"Yes, Mark pushed the kids hard. I was wondering what he was trying to do," she said.

"Did you ask him?" Jim questioned.

"No, not really. I just tried to hurry that portion of the workout. None of the kids complained, in fact, I think they enjoyed it," she said.

"Are you two getting any questions or complaints about the same players starting every match?" Jim asked.

"Not at all. We've been able to get some playing time for a lot of the players that don't start. We may not be able to sub in too many for the final two matches," she said.

"No matter what happens in the next two matches, win, or lose, we need to be super positive with the players They have done a great job playing and supporting each other. In volleyball, support is a rarity by women players," Jim said smiling.

The flight to Atlanta started out smooth as silk. However, after passing the southern Rocky Mountains things began to get rough. Fortunately, they stopped in Houston to take on more fuel. Once in the air again, at altitude and headed towards the southeast coast, they encountered even more turbulence. The coaches checked their players for any signs of air sickness and found all of them doing well.

When the plane landed, Jim had his players wait for all the other passengers to deplane first. "I want to take a couple of minutes to talk about these next two matches. First, I believe there will be a lot of press and journalist waiting to get what's called 'sound bites'. A little is ok, a lot is not ok! When you do speak with the media, be kind to our opponents and don't reveal anything at all about our team or players. We are here to play our best, eat, sleep, practice, learn and enjoy the thrill of competition. I have years of volleyball experience, and I know what I'm talking about when I tell you that we can win the Championship! You are also going to play in a large building, and there will be a lot of noise during each game. I'm proud of each of you and I wish you all the best. Now, Let's get off this plane and see what Georgia Tech and the outside world has in store for us!"

Cascade ate early so their stomachs would be empty for their match. Jim was impressed by the height of Florida State's players and how hard they hit from most anywhere on the court. He knew that his block and defense would be the deciding factor. The first game began, and Florida State won easily, which disappointed Jim. Each team switched sides for the second game, and, during the pause, Jim got Kristy and Mark together to discuss what to do next. "Alright, that didn't feel good. Each of you give me your ideas on what to do for the second game."

Mark started with, "I think we were in the worst rotation we could've been in. Their block destroyed our hitters and their hitters never got blocked or dug. I think we need to move the rotation ahead two spots."

Kristy suggested, "I agree Mark, but I think we need to move the rotation back two spots."

"Ok, we'll try one of those. Let's talk with the starters for a couple of minutes," Jim said.

Having made the changes that Mark suggested did not result in a win for the second game, but Cascade played much better and lost by a score of twenty-nine to twenty-seven.

Again, he talked with his assistant coaches. "Well, this time we're going to try Kristy's rotation, and I have an idea which may help," Jim said with a smile on his face and a quick raise of his eyebrows.

Cascades players struck gold for the third and fourth games, winning both by the score of twenty-five to eighteen. There was a lot of discussion on the Florida State bench between games. All Jim said to his players was, "Ladies, if they've changed their line-up for this last game, be ready to respond. By this time, every one of you should know each of the other player's tendencies and you will need to adapt if a stranger is in front of you when you're at the net. Ok, let's go win the match and show them what Cascade University's volleyball is all about."

And show them they did. Cascade got off to an eight to two lead when they reached the side-change, knowing that the fifth game of the match is always played to fifteen points, or to the team exceeding that by two points.

Florida State was not ready to lay down and take a bad loss. They chipped away until the score was thirteen all. Jim had another idea flash into his head and, without thinking about it, he called on a player that had not played much all season. He called the player to go in and serve saying, "Sally, use you're jump, cut serve from our back left corner. Don't stress out. I would not put you in if I wasn't confident you could do this!"

Sure enough, Sally went in, without showing any sign of stress, and her first serve was hit sideways to the right sideline. It was all the setter could do to put the ball up high, completely across to the other side of the court and at least twelve feet off of the net. The hitter gave it her best shot and hit it out by ten feet over the back line. The people in the stands rooting for Florida State just sat still in their seats and hardly made a sound.

Sally's next serve, which could win the match for Cascade, was like a sidewinder rocket as it cut sharply on the opponent's side and landed exactly on the back line in the left corner. A huge cry of happiness came from Cascade's subs as they rushed onto the court, and all piled in a large circle with the starters. Little was happening on Florida States side as the players in the game waited by the net to congratulate Cascade's players.

Jim, his coaching staff, and players milled around on the court visiting with a few parents and fans. To many in Cascade's group, it was taking time for what had just happened to sink in. After Jim located and hugged Liz, he immediately called Henry, back at the University. "Hello, is this Henry?" Jim asked the first person who answer the phone.

"Jim, you bet this is Henry! That was just about the best volleyball match I've ever seen! You and your staff have done an outstanding job this season. Everyone here, and I mean everyone, which includes all of our head coaches and their assistants, plus all of the support staff in the athletic building, watched the entire match. Congratulations to you and the great staff you've put together!"

"Thank you for your kind words. I do think we have an excellent volleyball staff. We seem to be able to discuss what to do next at crunch time without anyone disagreeing. It's a really nice feeling. Please thank everyone there for watching us today. We play in two days at the same time. It will be either Penn State or Stanford depending on who wins the late match tonight."

"Will do Jim. Everyone here is pulling for our team to win it all. Again, you have our congratulations," Henry said.

Jim returned to Liz and his coaching staff. "Everyone back home watched our match and was excited about winning. He looked at Mark and asked, "How long do you think before the team is ready to eat?"

Mark said, "It won't be too long before the next match starts. How about letting the players get something to nibble on during the next match and then we can go out to eat later?"

"Ok Kristy, what do you think of Marks suggestions?" Jim asked, smiling.

"Well, he did pretty good tonight. We should give him another chance to see if it was just dumb luck earlier," she said with a big smile on her face.

"Ok Mark, you're in charge of taking our players to the concession stand and letting them graze a bit on something that won't fill them up before dinner. Please be back by the time the match starts. Also, have certain position players sit with other players like them. Delicately, let them know that they can visit with their friends and families for most of tomorrow," Jim said.

"Kristy, hopefully this next match will give us the chance to discover weaknesses in both teams. We're going to be playing one of two teams that have been through this rodeo many times before," Jim said.

"Coach, who do you think will win, Stanford or Penn State?" she asked.

"If I were a betting man, I'd put my money on Penn State."

"Why?" Kristy asked.

"Penn State's head coach has been in that position for over thirty years. He is the one person who knows all and sees all. I would never bet against his teams. On the other hand, Stanford's coach is good at what he does, but he's never had the talent before, that he has now. It will be up to his players to have confidence in him. Would you like to make a small bet?" Jim asked.

Liz, who was with Jim all the time now said, "Kristy, you don't want to bet against anything Jim tells you. He's either the smartest or luckiest man I've ever known. If you should bet against him, don't put up one red cent."

"Ok. Enough of this you two. Let's hit the concession stand before the next match begins," he said.

Jim was looking forward to the late match, which would determine the other team in the final match of the Championship. He was feeling great about his team making it all the way to the ultimate contest of the seasons. Once the first game started, Jim had to wake himself up about how pleased he was and start keeping notes on both team's tendencies. The match was a real battle between two great teams. Stanford won the first game without too much effort.

The Penn State coach completed his team's line up for second game and then he stood up to speak to his team. All of his players gathered around him and not one of them took their eyes off their coach. He talked to his team in a very measured way and glanced about so each player would concentrate.

Penn State won the second game with a five-point margin. Now it was the Stanford's coach that needed to make adjustments. His approach was to address his team and in a casual way. As he and his players teased a lot, it was apparent that the coach wanted to lower whatever pressure that each player might have. His assistant coach turned in the lineup for the third game, which gave the head coach more time to keep his players relaxed.

Penn State ended up winning the final two games of the contest, which gave them a three to one score. Jim looked at Kristy and Mark, and said, "What did I tell you two. That guy is going to be a tough nut to crack. His players don't look overwhelming, but they are trained well, and they do as they're told when it comes to what the coaches say. Penn States coaches never yell at their players or embarrass them. I've learned a lot from him over the years."

On Friday, their day off, besides an afternoon practice, Jim split his team into two groups. One went with Jim and the second group went with Kristy and Mark. Jim wondered how that group would fare. Both groups spent time looking around Atlanta and were especially interested in shopping. They all met for a light lunch before the afternoon's work out. When they were finished eating, Jim said, "Ok everyone. Let's get back to the hotel and rest a bit. Be sure to bring nice clothes to change into for tonight's dinner."

The afternoon's practice went well, and each coach kept remarking to one another how good the players looked at the end of a long season. It took thirty-five minutes for the last player to board the bus going to the evening's meal. With all the Friday night traffic, it took forty-five minutes to reach their destination, the Canoe Restaurant, located on the banks of the Chattahoochee River. Jim watched as everyone in the group walked slowly from the bus to the restaurant and beyond to look at the river.

During the evening's meal a wide variety of food was ordered and consumed, with lots of sharing. The coaches enjoyed watching their athletes having a good time. When the Canoe wait staff cleared what was left of dinner, they presented each person with a dessert menu. The only thing on that menu that they bragged about was the Brioche French Toast. One waiter suggested that he bring a few samples to the table so the players could sample it before ordering.

Jim interrupted the waiter and said, "I'd prefer that you bring only two orders to the table. I think that will be enough for these young ladies to see if they want a whole order." Surprisingly, only eight players ordered desert and not one ordered the Brioche French Toast.

Before heading back to the hotel, Jim outlined the activity for tomorrow. "Breakfast will be in the hotel from seven to ten in the morning. There will be a twenty-minute run with Coach King beginning at eleven. Lunch is at one in the afternoon, at the hotel, and we will have a short discussion period before taking the court to warm up. Any questions."

Jim called Malika when he found a quiet place in the hotel's outdoor garden. "Malika, this is Jim Sams," he said. "I'm sorry to call you so late this evening, but our last match will conclude no later than ten, tomorrow evening. I plan on sending everyone but Liz and me back to Dallas. Will that work with your group, flying us from here to Salt Lake City, or do you want me to return to Dallas with the team?"

"Let's see. Tomorrow's Saturday, and I think that it would be a waste of your time to fly to Oregon on Sunday and then turn around to fly back to Salt Lake. I'll have one of our mid-size planes waiting for you at the Georgia State airport on Sunday morning. When you get off the plane in Salt Lake City, I'll have an agent take you to where you'll stay while working with us. The agent will have another car at the hotel, which you and Liz will use," Malika said. "See you first thing in the morning Monday at my office."

Jim was still thinking about the day's activities when he and Liz got in bed. He was talking a mile a minute about how his team played Thursday and what they needed to do Saturday. Liz just laid there watching Jim and listening to how excited he was. She thought that it was nice that he could focus on his team for a while, instead of worrying about everything else that was going on in his life. After the better part of an hour, she finally asked, "Jim, are you ready to go to sleep now?"

"Yea, I guess it's pretty late. Would you mind if I snuggle up behind you and we'll call it a night?" he asked.

"We'll do whatever you want, coach," Liz said with a little giggle.

25
NEW TERRITORY

Saturday morning was bright and sunny outside. Both Jim and Liz enjoyed a nice, leisurely breakfast in their hotel room. Around ten-thirty, Jim called Kristy and asked, "How are things going this morning with you, Mark, and the team? Has everyone had breakfast?"

"Good morning coach," Kristy said. "Yes, everyone has had breakfast this morning. Mark's going to take the players on a twenty-minute run soon. I think he's getting to like running at that time in the morning. The players certainly don't mind running. Who knows, we may have some track talent on the volleyball team?"

"Sounds like it. What would you think about a movie for everyone after lunch today?"

"You know, you usually come up with interesting things to do to keep their mind off of tough opponents. This is not one of those 'things' today. I think they should just hang out at the hotel. I know a lot of them have brought schoolwork with them. They don't need 'things' that will take their mind completely off of tonight's match," she said.

"Yea, you're probably correct this time. I think Liz and I are going to take a look around Georgia State University and the city of Atlanta. I've been here once before, but I don't remember too much about what I did then. Liz needs to get away from just following me around on game days and have a few memories that don't include volleyball. So, I'll see you and the team around five-forty-five this afternoon in the gym, just before warmups," Jim said.

"Ok. I hope you and Liz have fun today. See you later coach." Kristy said.

Jim and Liz decided that the first place they wanted to visit would be the Zoo Atlanta. After that they wanted to visit the World of Coca-Cola and have a late lunch there. Saturday morning had less traffic than Jim expected, so they found the zoo with no problem. After getting their entry passes, Jim asked Liz, "Where should we start?"

"I've done a little thinking on the way here and I want to see the big cats first. You know, lions, tigers, leopards, and any other felines like that. I'd also enjoy looking at all the exotic birds. Then I want to locate the World of Coca-Cola exhibit and have lunch there, before checking out the history of Coca-Cola. What do you think?" Liz asked.

"Sounds like a good plan. Just remember, we need to be at the playing site no later than a quarter to six this afternoon," Jim cautioned.

They spent three hours at the zoo looking at all of the animals Liz was interested in, and a few more that Jim wanted to see. They then headed to the World of Coca-Cola and had a light lunch before looking at various exhibits. Jim checked the time and told Liz, "Time is running out. However, I would like to see one final display before we head to the gym," he said.

"That being?" asked Liz.

"The Vault where the legendary secret formula for Coca-Cola is secured, representing over a hundred and thirty-five years of history. I'd Just like to look at it. What do you say?" he asked.

"It's ok with me if you think you can get back to the gym without being late," she said in a serious tone.

At the conclusion of their sightseeing tour, Jim and Liz raced back to the gym and made it with four minutes to spare. Jim looked at Liz and they both started laughing. "Hey Kristy, how's everything going? Any problems with anything or anyone today?"

"Not at all. The team was great today. If anything, they've been more focused on winning than I've ever seen. How's your day been?"

"We've had a fun day. It felt great to unwind before this match. Ok, it looks like the floor is ours. Liz, I'll see you after the match. Wish us luck," he said as he kissed her on her cheek.

Cascades' warmup was smooth and impressive. Jim noticed two of Penn State's assistants taking notes as they watched Cascade. Shortly before Penn State took the floor for their own warmup, the two note takers handed their note pads to the head coach.

Jim thought to himself that he'd like to have seen those note pads and listened to the head coaches' response. While both teams were being introduced to everyone in the building, Kristy and Mark handed Jim their notes on Penn States own warmup. Jim responded, after looking at their note and said, "From the looks of these notes, this is going to be a real battle. Thanks!"

The first game was close and won by Penn State, which Jim had expected. Between games, Jim made a position adjustment to get better matchups. That maneuver resulted in Cascade winning the next two games. Jim spoke to his assistants before talking with his players, and said, "I'm almost positive that Penn State will now make changes to their own line up. Those last two games certainly worked in our favor. I think I'm going to make another adjustment to our lineup, hoping to mirror their changes, so we get the same lineup as the last two games. Any comments from you two?"

"Not at all. You're on a winning streak coach. Do it!" Kristy said.

Jim's changes failed to work. Penn State came out again in the same lineup as the other three games and won with ease. Jim thought to himself, that the other coach really knows what he's doing. Jim settled down before deciding which rotation to use in fifth and final game of the match. He learned a hard lesson from Penn States coach. That being 'never change what works'. He put the same lineup on the sheet of paper that won games two and three, and as he was giving it to the score keeper, he looked over at the Penn State coach and grinned.

Both teams realized that this game was for all the marbles and the level of play was first rate.

Jim was more than proud of how well his team was doing, when, at the score tied at seven all, his setter, Iliana, went down with what appeared to be a sprained ankle. The trainer was at her side in a flash, getting her calmed down and trying to determine how serious the injury was.

Kristy had the backup setter up and warming up with another bench player in case she had to take Ilana's place. The trainer put her arm around Iliana's shoulder and helped her gently walk off the court.

Jim looked at the trainer, giving her a look that questioned how bad it was, and the trainer responded, "She might be able to return once I get her taped up."

Jim motioned to Carol, the backup setter and said, "You've been watching Iliana this whole game, right?"

"Yes coach," she said.

"Ok then. Go in and give it your best shot. I'm sure you can do it," Jim said. "If you need to know what set to make or who to give the ball to, look over at me as soon as you need help."

The match continued with both teams siding out until the score reached eleven all. Kristy approached Jim and said, "Iliana says she's ok to go back in."

"Thanks" Jim said.

He called time out as soon as Penn State took a one-point advantage at twelve to eleven. It was hard for him to come to a decision on leaving Carol in or getting Iliana back in the game. While Kristy and Mark talked with the starters during the time out, Jim took Iliana aside and asked,

"Do you think your ankle is strong enough to finish this match?"

"Yes coach, I know I can do it. I've played with worse injury's," she said.

"Ok young lady, it's all yours," Jim said, smiling.

When the referee whistled for the teams to retake the floor, Jim subbed Iliana into the game.

Immediately, Cascade scored a point to make the score twelve all. Jim thought to himself 'now it's getting really interesting'. Jim knew that the final score could now go beyond the fifteen-point level. Iliana was playing as good as she was prior to the sprain, and she was making great decisions on who to set. Cascade again fell behind seventeen to eighteen when a referee called a touch on an attack by Penn State that clearly went over the blockers hands. No amount of questioning by Jim made any difference to the ref. The game continued on until the score was twenty to twenty-one, in Penn States favor. One of their players landed on the center line during an attack and tripped the Cascade blocker, causing her to fall off to the side and touch the net. The refs called a net on Cascade and that was it. Penn State won the match on two bad calls by the officials in what was otherwise a great match.

As the coaches approached one another during the traditional post-match handshake, the Penn State coach took Jim's hand and leaned in, saying, "You have a great young team. You just got robbed by the worst refs I've ever seen. I know we'll meet again in the future, and I hope we don't get these two again. I wish you all the best."

Jim was so upset, all he could say was, "Thank you. Your team played well." Now came the one thing that he hated to do most, and that was talking to his team after losing a match because of bad refereeing. When all the post-match speeches and awards were given out, and before his players went to their locker room, Jim ushered them over to a corner of the gym where he could talk to them without being heard by others.

"Ladies, that was the best match any team I've ever coached has played. I'm sure everyone watching will say the same thing for years to come. Penn State is, and has been for years, the ultimate Collegiate, NCAA Division One volleyball team in the nation. We took a loss because of two terrible, illegitimate calls made by the referees. Even after they had time to review each play and make the correct call. I guarantee none of you on this team will ever see those two referees again at one of our matches. I also know that this team will win many Championships going forward. You should never say that you lost this match. If anyone ever asks why we didn't win, just respond by saying we were beat by two horrible refs."

Jim looked at Kristy, just beyond his team sitting on the floor, and saw her slowly shaking her head from side to side. He realized what that ment, and said, "I just told you something that I want you to disregard. It's exactly what you should never say to anyone. As you can see, I can get too emotional at times. So, forget the last two sentences of what I said about losing a match and two horrible refs. That's what poor losers do. I apologize for even uttering things like that," he said.

"Ok then, hit the locker room, clean up, and head for the plane. You'll all be back at Cascade in the middle of the night. You will have Sunday completely to yourself, and then it's back to school. Kristy and Mark will notify each of you when the end of season banquet will be. It looks like I will be in and out at various times these next three months. If there is anything so urgent that you need to speak with me, Kristy will set up a call and we will talk to each other. I'm so proud of this team that words escape me at times. I truly want to thank everyone of you for all the hard work you put in this season," Jim concluded.

Jim and Liz got a ride to the hotel they were staying at in Atlanta from an FBI agent. At the hotel, the agent handed Jim an envelope and explained that information for the trip to Salt Lake City was inside, and that he would be parked outside in the morning for the trip to the airport.

"Well, Malika is always on the ball. Let's see," he said as he opened the envelope. "She has us leaving Atlanta at nine in the morning tomorrow, so we'll need to be up and ready to go by eight am. We'll arrive in Salt Lake City at ten, Utah time. She also wants both of us in her office by eight-thirty a.m. Monday so she can prep us for our meeting with the Director at ten sharp."

"I think this is going to be one, big pain in the rear, trying to sneak around at the beck and call of the FBI as they attempt to find all the Columbians in the area," Liz said as she crawled into bed.

"You're probably right but knowing how many agents they've had working on this for years, and all of the resources they have at their disposal, I think it will be very interesting. You and I just need to be super careful with whatever they ask us to do. OK?" Jim asked.

"We can pretend that you're Sherlock and I'm Watson. Maybe it will be fun," Liz said.

"What! I can't believe you just said that. After you experienced being kidnapped and held inside for three days, how can you say such a thing?" Jim said, in a serious tone.

"Jim. Get in bed. I was just kidding, it's late and I'm tired," Liz said.

They woke up at a quarter to eight and got ready to fly to Salt Lake City. The FBI agent made the short trip to the Atlanta Airport and let them off at the terminal for private aircraft. "Be sure you have everything you brought with you. When you're inside this terminal, you'll see three check-in counters. Yours is on the far left. Have a pleasant trip."

The flight from Atlanta to Salt Lake City was smooth until they reached the Rockies, and then it got a little bumpy. Once down in the valley, the landing was smooth. The clock in the terminal read eight o'clock. Liz and Jim grabbed their baggage and walked out into much dryer air than they'd been in for the last few days. There was an FBI car waiting to take them to the hotel that would be their home for a month or two. When they arrived at the hotel, the agent parked next to a light grey SUV and said, "The car next to us is what you'll be using while you're in Salt Lake."

Room key and car keys in hand, they were on their way to see Malika. It took only fifteen minutes to find her building, which ment they were outside her office door at exactly eight-thirty. Jim knocked on the door and heard, "Come in."

He opened the door and let Liz enter first. "Hello, Malika. I'm not sure if you've met Liz?" Jim asked.

"Only briefly. How was your trip to Salt Lake? I assume you were in the hotel we selected for you and that you're now driving the SUV we arranged for you."

"Yes, thank you. It's all very nice. So, we're all ears and anxious to hear what you and the Director have in store for us," Jim said.

"We will all meet him shortly and he will come right to the point of what he wants you to do. I know he has thought long and hard about what he has in store for you. I strongly ask that you don't flinch at whatever he says you'll be doing. You can ask for clarification if you are unsure of anything he talks about. I know from experience that he doesn't appreciate 'stupid'. He does have confidence in his agents and the plans they've developed. That's about it. Do you have any questions for me before we enter his office?"

"Nope. We're just curious at this point. Let's go," Jim said as he glanced at Liz.

26
TWICE

Malika knocked on the Director's office door and they all heard a loud voice say, 'come in'. "Good morning, Malika," Director Campbell said. "I see you have Jim Sams and his friend Liz Barnett," as he got up to shake their hands. "Please, grab some chairs and put them along the front of my desk, so we can talk."

"Jim, can I call you Jim?" the Director asked.

"Certainly, Director Campbell," Jim said, hoping he would reciprocate the familiar use of one's name.

"Liz, I would also like to be able to call you by your first name," the Director asked.

"That's fine with me," Liz replied.

"I want each of you to feel free to call me Wilson at any time, except whenever we're at a professional gathering or in a court room," he said.

"Thank you," Jim said.

"That's so nice of you. Thank you," Liz said.

"Enough of that. Malika, please show Liz around the offices on this floor, so I can talk about what I need Jim to take care of for us. Thank you. Liz I've enjoyed meeting you. I know we'll see you again," the Director said.

"Ok Jim, here is what I have in mind for you. First, you are aware of what this department's project will be regarding the Columbian Cartel that's using Salt Lake City and the north-south corridor thereof for human trafficking?" Wilson asked.

"My understanding is that you want to eliminate that group of the cartel, from their top person down to the last thug, working in this portion of the United States," Jim offered.

"Yes. That's it in a nutshell. You will not be involved in the pursuit and capture portion of our operation. That's much too dangerous for anyone that lacks appropriate training for that type of work. What I need from you is to locate and capture a man known as Lester and bring him to us alive. I know you were successful once. Do you feel you're up to something like that again?"

"I'd like to think I am. You probably know that I don't have anything with me that would allow me to protect myself or to look like I could capture one person by myself. In other words, I have no weapons. I'm certainly not going to knock him out with a volleyball," Jim said smiling.

"Funny," Wilson said, in a not so funny tone. "Let's think about how you could go about overpowering him. Are you skilled in any of the martial arts?"

"Not at all. Until I first discovered the woman on the bank of the Willamette River and had to deal with the detectives from Corvallis, I just tried to stay in shape by exercising," Jim said.

"This is not to sound funny, but do you know how to throw a boomerang," Wilson asked.

"No. I've never even seen a boomerang in person," Jim answered.

"Ok. Moving on. Before we get to firearms. Have you ever used a sling shot, or bolo?" the Director asked.

"Bolo no. I was pretty good with a sling shot when I was growing up. I had a paper route, on Sundays, and I would pull my wagon with papers stacked in the wagon and the sling shot tucked in the wagon next to the papers. My goal was to pick off the doves that would sit on the electric wires above the parkway. When I was done selling the papers, I would go home, pluck the birds, and cook the breast meat for lunch," Jim explained.

"Sounds like those two options are out. Have you ever set steel traps? The kind that are used to trap rabbits or hawks?" Wilson continued.

"Negative," Jim said.

"Ok. I'm done asking. How in the hell did you get him the first time?" Wilson said, with a slight smile.

"Sir, I had an assistant help me lure him up into a hotel room in Salt Lake City. I hid in a closet opposite the door to the bathroom. My assistant went to use the bathroom, allegedly to clean herself before they had sex. Lester got impatient and walked over to the bathroom door, and, when she opened the door, she was topless. He'd been drinking downstairs before they came up to the room and he was a bit unsteady. He tried to step towards her and that's when I came out of the closet and struck him on the side of the head with my salmon bat," Jim explained.

"You struck him on the side of his head with a what?" the Director asked.

"A salmon bat. It's a small wooden club, shaped like a baseball bat. Fishermen use them to knock out salmon after they get them it in their boat. I needed to use it on him a few times while I drove back to Dallas, Oregon," Jim explained. "When we arrived at my house in Dallas, I picked up the few tools I needed to get him hooked up to a cable that would drag him thru the blackberry vines, thereby rendering him dead," Jim said. "I'm not proud of what I attempted to do to him, but this guy had made life hell for one of my players and her mother. He was a lucky son-of-a-bitch because someone found him and freed him from the vines. I'll bet he was bleeding a lot by the time he was found."

"He was bleeding a lot. He was rescued by one of our agents. He just about blead to death in the short time he was in the vines. Do you think he would recognize you if he sees you here?" Wilson asked

"I'm not sure. I don't even know if I will recognize him when we face each other. I've been known to use disguises and I could do the same thing here," Jim said.

"That's a good idea. Now, I want you to train with a martial arts master for two weeks. All of the agents working under me work out three times a week unless they're busy on assignment. You'll feel pretty sore the first few days until you acclimate. Check with Malika on your way out and she will set things up for you at the gym. I want you to keep thinking about how you can capture Lester without seriously hurting him. He will be indicted and tried as soon as we get our hands on him. Once we have him in custody, you and Liz can return to Dallas. How does that sound?" Wilson asked.

"I'll give it my best shot. Thanks for not throwing me in jail for what I did to him before," Jim said as he stood up to leave.

"Even though I know it was a serious crime, I respect you for your effort to punish this ass hole," Wilson said, with his head down and waving goodbye with his hand.

Jim closed the door behind him and saw Liz sitting in a chair across the hall. "Have you been setting there all the time I was inside with the Director?"

"No, just for a short time. Malika showed me around for a while. She's one busy woman. How did you do in there?" she asked.

"You won't believe it, but they have me in a gym working out for the next two weeks, so I get stronger," he said.

"I'm going to like that. Having you in bed when you are all buffed up sounds exciting," Liz said, smiling again. "What's on for the rest of the day?"

"I need to see Malika before we go back to the hotel. She's supposed to set things up at the gym where I'll be working out. Then I'd like to explore Salt Lake City, so we get thoroughly familiar with it. Along the way we should find a nice place to have lunch. How does all that sound?" Jim said.

"Sounds good, let's go," Liz said.

The stop in Malika's office took only a few minutes, and then Jim and Liz were off to explore the main part of town. Jim began to remember all the places he'd been to when he and Trish were in the process of nabbing Lester. Those memories were not pleasant.

Liz pointed out a nice-looking lunch spot and asked Jim, "What do you think about that place?"

"Roots Café? Looks just like the place I want to eat today. Ok with you?" he teased.

They went in and sat down at a table in the back of the dining area. They each ordered different, great looking lunch plates and commented to each other how nice this little café felt.

A little more than halfway thru their lunch, Jim noticed a table with three Latin looking men. They kept to themselves and did not talk too much. Jim nudged Liz and said, "Look at the table closest to the front of the dining area. Looks to me like three Columbian thugs. I hope we don't run into Columbians everywhere we go in this town."

"Yes. I see what you mean. Should we finish our lunch and ske-daddle out of here?"

"I'd rather stay right where we are until they leave. That way, they should get on with their business and not pay us any attention. I think that if we leave before them, we'll need to walk right past their table and make them aware of us. OK?"

"Fine with me. Looks like I'll be having dessert," Liz said, smiling.

Back in the car, Jim and Liz continued to drive all around the center of the city, so much so that they finally realized that they'd been over the same streets a few times. Liz said, "I've got to use the bathroom. How long will it take to get to our hotel from here?"

"We're just three blocks away from our hotel. Can you make it to there," Jim asked.

"That's no problem," she answered.

When they were both in their hotel living room, Liz went straight into the bathroom and Jim sat down in a chair facing the street below. Liz returned to the living room, feeling relieved, and asked Jim if he was tired and wanted to take a nap?

"That sounds good, but I think I'll need something to make me relax," he said.

"Good. I need something to help me relax too," she said with a sexy smile on her face as she began to walk into the bedroom while taking her blouse off.

By this time in their relationship, they no longer indulged in heavy petting. It was just a little deep kissing, hands all over each other's body and then regular intercourse. Normally, they could make this simple system last for around twenty minutes before one of them couldn't last any longer and had an orgasm.

Right at the beginning of the intercourse phase, Jim's phone wrang, and he reached over and looked to see if it was from anyone important. He rolled over, off of Liz and said," This is an important call from Charlie, the man who is the general contractor on my new house.

It will only take a few minutes."

Jim answered Charlie's call and they talked about things for forty-five minutes. Liz busied herself making sure Jim didn't lose his erection while he talked with Charlie. When he hung up the phone, he looked at Liz and said, "That was almost impossible to talk to him and not make any mistakes on what I wanted him to do. It seems you want to get right back to making love!" Jim said.

Liz gave him a big smile and pulled him back on top of her. This time Jim made sure she would enjoy every moment of what she wanted. When they were both satisfied, they snuggled up to each other and slept for almost two hours.

The hotel provided their evening meal in their dining room. "That wasn't too bad," Jim said.

"That wasn't too good either. We have to get out sometime tomorrow, and get some groceries in this place," Liz said.

The next morning, they went down to the free breakfast and talked about how to fill their day. Jim asked Liz, "My workout at the gym starts at ten am each day. I'll take the car and do my workout while you go shopping?"

"That I can do. But I want you to find a store that you think will be safe for me to shop in," Liz said. "Seeing those three Columbians yesterday makes me think there are more of them spread around the city."

"As soon as we finish here, we'll find a grocery store that's safe for you and I'll drop you off while I go do my workout," Jim said. "I'll shorten my routine and come get you. Does that work for you?"

"That's a good plan. Is there anything in particular you'd like me to pick up?" Liz asked.

"I always like anything you get," Jim said, smiling.

As soon as they'd put the groceries away in their small hotel kitchen, Jim suggested, "Liz, I would like to expand our driving around Salt

Lake City to include the outskirts. I need to get a feel for how far from the center of Salt Lake we might find Columbians. Are you game?"

"Sure. Might as well see the whole place since I may never come here again. Already I don't like the traffic or rude people. Shopping today was a pain in the rear," she said.

"Sorry about that. I just want to see how much territory I might need to become familiar with," he said. "Maybe we'll find a nice place to eat that's free of Columbians." Jim headed north up the east side of greater Salt Lake City, close to the Wasatch mountains. He knew exactly where he wanted to look, but he made it appear as if he'd never been in this part of Salt Lake before.

Liz asked, "I'm getting hungry. Are we looking for some place to have lunch?"

"We are," Jim said as he pulled over to the curb and checked his map again. "I see a lot of restaurants in this area, and one does look inviting. Would you be up for eating at an Olive Garden?"

"Nice job, you old restaurant hunter. How far away is it?" Liz asked.

"We'll be there in ten minutes."

After being seated and checking the 'Classic Entrees' portion of the menu, Liz picked the seafood alfredo and Jim went for spaghetti with meatballs. They selected the Spinach-Artichoke Dip for their appetizer, and they each asked for a beer.

They literally wattled outside and had a good laugh trying to get into the car. "At this rate I'll be over two hundred fifty pounds before we get back to Dallas!" Jim said.

"Somehow, I think you're right," Liz said, laughing.

Once Jim returned to reality and the business at hand, he headed north along highway eighty-nine and eventually onto highway fifteen, where he slowed down until he found the street that went a short way up into the Wasatch Mountains.

Liz asked, "This is quite a ways north of Salt Lake. Are you looking for something special?"

"Not really. I was looking for a place to turn back towards Salt Lake City, and these homes interested me," he said. "Look at these places. Can you imagine how much they must cost?"

"Looks like a lot," she said.

Jim, knowing there was no outlet at the top of the street he was on, turned left on the street just below the top, and made another turn onto a street that offered only a left turn. He let the car slowly descend until he saw the street sign for Lester's house. He was going to drive slowly past the house but stopped when he noticed a 'For Sale' sign near the front gate.

What looked like a man from the real estate company, was just coming from the house to the gate. Jim pulled over and got out to go talk with the fellow. "Hello, can you tell me about this house? Price, availability, and any damage inside? My wife and I might be interested if the price is in our range. It sure has a nice view of the lake from here."

"Well partner, you're about three days too late," said a fellow with a mixed accent. The local authorities have me down here today to switch the sign from 'For Sale' to 'Condemned'.

"No! That's too bad. It looks like a fine house. Why is it being condemned?" Jim asked.

"I'm not sure of all the facts, but I'm told that there must have been a pretty big gun fight inside. There are bullet holes in almost every room in the house. Add to that, it looks like someone was stuffed in a 50-gallon steel barrel and cremated," the man said.

"That must have made the whole house smell to the high heavens," Jim said.

"To say the least. Would you like to take a look around inside?" the man asked.

"I don't think so. I have a weak stomach. Thanks for your time," Jim said as he turned and walked back to his SUV.

When he was at the bottom of the hill waiting to turn south on highway fifteen, Jim told Liz everything that the man said to him. "Pretty gruesome. I can't believe how mixed-up people are. If it was the work of the Columbians, I doubt if they'll still operate this far north of Salt Lake City."

"Liz, we still have a few hours to kill before dinner time. Would you like to visit the site where the east and west transcontinental rail line met? It's about an hour north of us," Jim said.

"I'd be up for about anything after seeing that house back there and hearing what went on there," Liz said with a little shudder.

An hour and ten minutes later they arrived at Promontory Point, parked the car in a lot with meters, and paid their entry fee. Jim asked Liz, after they'd seen all there was to see, "What do you think? Have you seen enough?"

"Well, I know that wasn't much to see. I also know that this was an important accomplishment back in the day. But, about the only thing I can say about it now, is that I've seen it," she said.

"Good. Me too. The drive back to the hotel will be fairly quick once we're on highway fifteen. Just sit back and rest your eyes," Jim said.

27
STRONGER

Each day for the next two weeks were almost the same. Get up late, have a lite breakfast, head to the gym. Then drive around Salt Lake City with Liz, looking for Lester. Jim would finish looking in the city and then they would checkout a new outlying area each day. They got pretty good at recognizing Columbians, but Jim never even saw someone that looked like Lester.

Almost every day, Malika would drop things off for Jim that the Director wanted him to have. One of the things was a salmon bat, which made Jim chuckle to himself. He also received rope, leather gloves, a small 'Old Timer' pocketknife, a military grade stun gun, pepper spray, bear spray and nunchucks. He hid all the things Malika gave him and the disguises he already had under the back floor compartment where the spare tire was kept. It was not real convenient if needed in a hurry, but it was out of site for Liz.

The Director was correct when he told Jim that he would feel better after working out with a martial arts master. He made a mental note to himself to keep doing this workout when they were done capturing Lester and living back in Dallas.

Two days after finishing his work outs with the Master, Jim woke up at three-thirty in the morning and decided to drive into Salt Lake

City and look for any sign of Lester. His first stop was at the Hyatt Place hotel, where Lester used to come to screw his brains out. Jim thought, as bad as Lester looks now, it may be hard for him to get a decent looking prostitute.

Twenty-five minutes after Jim parked his SUV in a nearby lot that offered a good view of the hotel's porte-co-cher, Jim saw a Rolls-Royce Ghost drive under the covering. The car's bronze exterior color with Petra Gold contrast was accented with a Petra Gold single coachline and fitted with 19" Alloy Wheels. Jim was so busy looking at the car, that he almost missed the person getting in the car. He raised his small binoculars up and saw a messed-up Lester. Jim waited a few minutes for the Rolls to drive out onto the street before he tried to follow it. Without much traffic at this time in the morning, Jim decided to follow only a few blocks before he turned off. He tried to follow the Rolls from one street over but got lost immediately. Seeing that it was still dark outside, he headed back to his hotel and was back in bed before five-thirty. Liz rolled over next to him and moaned something unintelligible.

Jim thought for a bit about trying to learn how often and what time at night, Lester made these trips to the hotel for some carnal satisfaction. He didn't think for long, in fact he didn't remember what he had on his mind when he woke up at eleven in the morning.

"Hey sleepy head," Liz asked from the kitchen, "Do you want a late breakfast, or an early lunch?"

"I think I need some loving, then a hot shower, and then I'll have an early lunch," he said, trying to get a rise out of Liz.

"No problem. However, I think a hot shower and early lunch will do you just fine. Maybe you'll get some loving later tonight," she responded.

After lunch, Jim said, "Liz, I've been thinking that this whole time we're in Salt Lake City will make you really bored. What would you say to going to see your family for a while?"

"Believe it or not I was thinking about that while you were sleeping this morning. Are you serious?" she asked.

"Yes, I'm serious. That will get you out of harm's way, if it should happen, and you can spend all the time there that either you or your family wants. Let me check this out with the Director," Jim said. "Or maybe I should start with Malika. As soon as I get an answer, you'll know. Maybe don't say anything to your relatives until we get the go-ahead."

"That would be great. There's not much in Salt Lake City for me to look at anymore. If we get out of this place unharmed, I'll never ask you to bring us back here. These chauvinists are the stupidest, most self-centered people I've ever encountered," Liz said. "The men are only interested in their own gratification and the women are just plain, outright stupid."

Jim called Malika and ran his idea past her, knowing she would need to get the approval from the Director. Malika surprised Jim when she said Liz could go whenever and wherever she wanted to go, but she would need to take two FBI agents along for protection. Jim let Liz know Malika's answer and asked Liz if she still wanted to leave.

"You bet I do, if it's alright with you," she said.

"Ok. Why don't you get in touch with your relatives and find out what they think and when they'd like to see you. As soon as you know all that, let me know and we'll make your travel arrangements," Jim said.

Liz and Jim were both impressed with what Malika arranged for Liz's trip back to Nebraska. She sent Liz and two FBI agents to Lincoln, Nebraska in a private jet and put them up in a hotel in Lincoln. She told Jim, "Liz can stay there as long as you're here zeroing in on Lester, or she can come back here anytime she wants."

"Thank you. You're more than generous. I'm really impressed with you and the whole FBI operation here," Jim said.

Now that he was on his own in the pursuit of Lester, Jim thought about how he would move forward with the capture of the little bastard. He planned to wake up each morning by ten am, and then work out in the gym where the martial arts master practices. He would then determine the disguises he would use for that day, take a long afternoon nap, and after eating dinner he would be out looking for the Rolls. He could pick up Lester's car leaving the hotel on most nights, so he planned on following him for short distances until he'd worked out what roads he took to his hotel.

Once he'd memorized the route Lester took, after getting drunk with the whores, Jim stopped going to the hotel Lester used in downtown Salt Lake City. He spent a few days and nights finding out everything about the hotel Lester was living in, his garage, his property, how many Columbians stayed inside the hotel at night, and how many were there during the day. He began to take photos and make a list of anyone who frequented Lester's hotel during the daylight hours and those he could get after dark.

During his breakfast the next day, Director Campbell called Jim and asked him to come into his office sometime today.

"Good morning, Wilson. I can come in anytime today," Jim said.

"Ok. Make it one o'clock. See you then," the Director said and hung up.

Jim dressed casually for the meeting with Wilson and was outside his office right on time. He asked the Director's secretary, "Please let Director Campbell know that I'm here. He's expecting me."

"Please go in," said the secretary.

As usual, Director Campbell got straight to the point. "Give me an update on where you are in your pursuit of Lester."

"Yes Sir," Jim began. "I located Lester a week or so ago when he was leaving the Hyatt Place Hotel at three in the morning. He got into his car, which is a Rolls Royce Ghost, bronze in color, and headed to the hotel he uses to live in. I followed him for only four blocks so I wouldn't scare him off. But I returned every night to follow him for a short distance, until I was able to put the pieces together and then I found where he lives."

"I'm now in the process of photographing everyone who goes into or out of that hotel, both in daylight and after dark. I'm also keeping track of the times when people are coming and going," Jim said. "When I have all the information I need, I'm going to figure out how I can nab him without either of us getting hurt. That's it so far Wilson," Jim explained.

"That's what I wanted to hear. I like the way you've gone about gathering pertinent information. But you're telling me that you have no plan yet on how you'll capture this guy?" the Director asked.

"I've thought about different ways, but so far, I've come up short on how to get him all alone. I'm sure I could take him down if we were absolutely alone but being alone is what Lester doesn't do! Give me another week and I'll figure it all out," Jim explained.

"Don't worry, you take all the time you need. I'm sure you can figure it out. Thanks for the information so far. Goodbye Jim," Director Campbell said.

On the drive back to his hotel, Jim was pleased that the Director liked the information he'd put together. However, getting Lester alone was more than difficult. Jim was sure Lester learned his lesson the first time about being alone when Jim nabbed him and what happened to him on the island in the river.

Jim began to feel that he was at a disadvantage when it came to trying to capture Lester. The fact that Jim was one person trying to nab Lester, a guy who always had at least three thugs, counting his guards. Despite a wide range of weapons Malika provided him and the physical training he'd been doing, he still felt that he didn't have a chance at finding Lester all alone.

His next tactic would be to get inside the hotel Lester used to satisfy himself and check if the elevator button in the lobby counted the floors the elevator was on as it went up and down. Again, Jim parked outside the Hyatt Place hotel and waited for Lester to arrive, which he did just before midnight. He waited until Lester was inside the hotel, then he put on a disguise that made him look about sixty years old, so he could enter the lobby and see if the elevator was the type with the buttons he was looking for. He walked slowly past the elevator and glanced at the buttons. It was just as he'd anticipated. He walked back past the buttons, just to be sure, and continued on to the bar. He ordered a non-alcoholic drink that looked like a whiskey and found a chair that afforded him a view of the elevator and of the people sitting in the lounge. It didn't take long for a gorgeous young woman to approach Lester's table and motion for him to follow her to the elevators.

Jim picked up his drink, used a cloth napkin to wiped off the glass, and finished the drink. Right after Lester and the hooker got in the elevator, Jim walked over to the men's bathroom door, opposite the elevator buttons, stepped inside and left the door cracked just enough so he could see the button counter. The elevator stopped on the fifth floor. He spent most of an hour in the bathroom waiting for Mr. Romeo to get his rocks off. Lester and the young woman walked out of the elevator on the ground floor. He looked terrible and the hooker looked pissed off. Jim thought to himself that she must not have made much money, especially having to take care of the little, fat, smelly, sliced up foreigner.

Jim was satisfied that he was able to see the floor and room that Lester used that night. However, he knew that he would need to make a few more trips to verify that the same thing happened every time Lester got in the elevator. Especially if he was to conceive a plan to nab him. Jim returned every night for a week, hiding in the bathroom opposite the elevators, and Lester used the elevator five times out of seven.

For the next week, Jim booked the room opposite the one Lester used. Again, Lester used his room five times out of seven, and the nights he did not use two of his rooms were the same as the week before. Jim wondered what Lester was doing or where he was those two nights that he didn't use the two rooms at the Hyatt Place hotel. Jim realized that he would need to follow Lester from his house on those two nights to find out where he went.

When he next began to follow Lester, on the nights that he didn't go to the Hyatt Place hotel, Lester went to one of the most rundown neighborhoods in all of Salt Lake City. The place looked too danger-ous for an older man like Jim to be driving around so he hightailed it back to his own hotel.

The next day he called Director Campbell and said, "Good morn-ing, Wilson, this is Jim."

"You're up early today. What do you need?" he asked.

"I need some sort of camera mounted on my car in a well-hidden place so no one can see it," Jim said."

"And what will this camera be used for?" he asked.

"I've found a place that Lester frequents whenever he doesn't go to the Hyatt Place Hotel downtown. It's in one of the filthiest, most dangerous places I've ever seen. It's at the far south end of the city and it's crawling with Columbians," Jim said.

"You're doing a good job of tracking this Lester prick, but this is one place I need you to stay away from. Don't, and I mean don't, get any closer than half a mile from that place. Do you understand?" the Director said.

"That work's for me. I hated the place when I was there and wished I'd never need to return," Jim replied. "I'll work on getting him where he gets laid."

"Anything else?" Wilson asked.

"Nope. Sorry to have bothered you. Thanks for your time," Jim said as he turned his phone off.

Jim decided to drive all the way to Dallas, without stopping to sleep, so he could see how Charlie was doing. A mile or so from his lot, Jim went straight to the Cramer house to pick up the Sledgehammer shotgun and one pistol, just in case he needed them in Salt Lake City.

Before going to see Charlie, he wanted to visit with Director Talbot to see how things were going while he'd been away. Jim asked his secretary, "Can I speak with the Director for a few minutes?"

"Hello Jim, nice to see you again. He's not available today, or for two more weeks. He and his wife are in East Honolulu in an Airbnb. Directors from the whole conference are meeting in downtown Honolulu this week, and then he and Carol will do a little island hopping the second week. Would you like to speak with Paige?" she asked.

"Yea. That will do just fine, thanks," Jim responded. "Can I just knock on his door, or do you need to tell him I'm coming to see him?"

"You can just go on in. He's not too busy now, if you get my drift," she said with a slight smile on her face.

"Robert, how're you doing. Anything going on as we speak?" Jim asked.

"Nothing that would keep me from visiting with you," Robert said as he got up to shake hands. "What does the FBI have you doing in Salt Lake?"

"The FBI Director of the whole territory, north and south of Salt Lake City to the national borders, and from the Rockies to the west side of Salt Lake itself, is under his control. He is a no bull shit kind of guy that doesn't talk too much and expects things done correctly and without any delay. You know, kind of like Talbot," Jim said, letting out a loud laugh.

"Funny! I'll need to remember that so I can tell Henry when he gets back from learning how to stay on a surfboard," Robert said."

"I really don't have all that much to do. I just need to find the guy who sends all the thugs out to do harm to anyone he doesn't like," Jim said. "That's all I can say. It's really more than I should have said. Mum's the word, ok?"

"I'll never say a word to anyone. I promise," Paige said.

"I'm going over to my new house now to see how it's shaping up. It's been nice talking with you again," Jim said as he walked out of Paige's office.

On arriving at his new house, the garage door was open, but there was no one around outside. Jim pulled his car into the garage and picked up the Sledgehammer shotgun just in case it might be needed. He carefully walked into the mud room and heard people talking, which made Jim feel a bit safer. "Charlie, is that you?" Jim shouted.

"I'm here, but you should make a run for it," Charlie shouted back.

28

DEPLETED

Jim understood what Charlie said and hoped he interpreted it correctly. He slipped outside and made sure the sledgehammer was loaded and ready to fire. He called the Portland FBI office and asked to speak to speak with Agent Cox.

"Agent Cox, may I help you," he asked.

"Agent Cox? This is Jim Sams, from Dallas. I've got a problem here on the lot where I'm having a new house built."

"Hey Jim, nice to hear your voice again. What sort of problem are you refereing to?" Cox questioned."

"Your remember all the Columbian thugs we had to deal with not too long ago?" Jim asked.

"I sure do. What's the problem?"

"The man in charge of building my new house seems to be trapped inside the partially finished structure by the same thugs as before. I walked into the mud room and heard men's voices, but I was unable to see them. I shouted to the general contractor and asked if it was him," Jim explained. "His name is Charlie and he shouted back to me that I should make a run for it. I took that to mean that the thugs had control of him inside the place. That's why I'm calling you now."

Cox responded, "You get your ass out of there now. Find a place where you can hide and see everything that happens until I get there with the calvary. It will take me all of forty-five minutes to get to your lot. Understand?"

"I'll wait for you and your troops," Jim said.

Jim backed his car out of the garage and went around the block looking for a tree near the curb where he could wait for Cox. He got out his binoculars and kept them aimed at the house after positioning the Sledgehammer where he could raise it immediately if needed.

Jim thought to himself that time goes by slowly when you're waiting for a specific time to arrive. He tried to keep his eyes on the house, from the garage in back to the side of the house next to the street. Nothing happened for over half an hour when all of a sudden four Columbian thugs came walking around the house from the front yard. They stopped on the dirt in the side yard and made Charlie sit down, Indian style with his legs crossed, facing the house. Jim quickly checked the time and there was still at least twelve minutes left before the calvary could possibly arrive. Jim looked at how the thugs had arranged themselves behind and around Charlie. It looked to Jim like the thugs were going to kill Charlie out in the open.

As Jim was thinking about how he could kill each thug without hurting his contractor, a fifth thug came walking around from the front of the house, with his fingers interlocked behind his head. He looked at the other thugs and told them, in Spanish, to put down their weapons. The fifth thug walked over to where the other four were and sat in the dirt with them. Jim got out of his car and walked up to the circle of thugs, carrying his Sledgehammer. He went directly to Charlie and asked, "Hey man, are you ok?"

"I'm alright, except for the fact that my wife will need to wash my skivvies and my pants tonight!" he said, smiling.

Cox walked up to Jim, along with six other FBI agents, and greeted him and the older fellow. He first asked Charlie, "Are you ok sir?'

"I'm a little stiff, but otherwise I'm ok. Thanks," Charlie said.

"I'm Agent Cox with the FBI posted out of Portland. I visit Dallas on a regular basis to check if these types of thugs continue to come here looking for trouble. Mr. Sams has helped us in the past. Did any of these goons sitting here ask you anything about Mr. Sams or what you were doing here at this new house?"

"Yes, that grimy looking fellow sitting in front of the other ones could talk a little English and asked when Sams would be coming back," Charlie said.

"And your response was?"

"I told him I just worked here, and I didn't know anyone named Sams," Charlie replied.

"You're pretty smart. Did he buy it," Cox asked.

"Yea. He bought it until Jim came into the mudroom and shouted my name, asking if I was ok," Charlie said, smiling at Jim.

"And what did Sams do?" questioned Cox.

"Nothing. He just got in his car and backed out of the garage, as far as I know," responded Charlie.

"Agent Cox, I think I've got just the solution to make these thugs let us know every last detail of

why they're all here at my house," Jim said as he approached Cox and whispered in his ear, "We'll take all five of them up into the coast range where I know of a gravel pit. We'll put up a plywood target, that has a figure of a man on it, and I'll blow it to smithereens with the Sledgehammer as they watch. Then, we'll replace the target with the thug that speaks English and ask him what he's doing in Dallas. What do you think?"

"It's not the conventional way to obtain information, but I think it's time we had some fun," Cox said with a big smile on his face. "Let's get them loaded and head for the gravel pit."

Forty-five minutes later Jim, Cox, and Charlie put up the target in the gravel pit while two other agents unloaded the Columbians from the vehicles. Cox had his agents sit them down on the ground in the same type of circle they were in back at Jim's new house. The english speaking thug sat a few feet ahead of the other thugs and watched Jim carry in the Sledgehammer.

Jim turned so all the people sitting on the ground could hear as he said, "Amigos! Escuchame," which ment 'listen to me'. "Your leader will be next up there where the target is now. If he does not answer our questions, he, and each of you will die just like the target." Jim turned to the english speaking thug and said, "tell them what I just said. Remember, I too speak Spanish. If you don't tell them exactly what I just said, I'll kill every one of you. compende?"

When Jim was satisfied that each of the Columbians on the ground understood what was going to happen, Jim turned towards the target and said, "Have all of you guys got ear plugs in?"

Cox said, "We're ready when you are Jim."

Jim faced the target, raised the Sledgehammer, and cut loose with the first blast. About twenty-five percent of the upper part of the target disappeared immediately. The second and third blasts completely destroyed the plywood target.

Jim turned and motioned to Cox to have his two agents position the thug that speaks english where the target was just a minute ago. "Ok, agent Cox, go ahead and ask your questions. He may be in the mood to cooperate," Jim said, while smiling.

"Ok." Cox said, looking at the thug eye to eye. "What's your name?"

"Armando, senior," the thug said.

"Where do you live in Salt Lake City and where do you stay when you are here in Dallas?" Cox asked.

"We go to hills and sleep on ground when here. In Salt Lake City we stay in apartment in south end of town," Armando said.

"Who is your boss? You know, your 'jefe,'" asked Cox.

"His name is Lester," the thug said softly.

"What is Lester's full name," Cox asked, in a dissatisfied tone.

"Senior, only name we know is Lester," Armando said, looking frightened.

"Where does Lester live in Salt Lake City?" Cox demanded.

"He stays in a lot of hotels," Armando said.

"Which hotel is he in now," Cox asked, looking at Armando hard, implying his displeasure.

"Now he in Marriott by airport," Armando said quickly.

Cox asked, "How long does he stay in a hotel before he moves to another?"

"He move every month," said a progressively scared Armando.

"Where will he move next?" Cox asked.

"Me no know. It always different," Armando said, as he dropped to his knees crying.

Jim said to Cox, "This guy's not much of a leader."

"Don't worry. Once we get him in custody at our headquarters, he'll sing like a bird. He's not letting us know everything he knows about Lester's habits, because of these other thugs sitting on the ground," Cox said.

"Why don't we just shoot Armando or one of the other thugs. That should loosen their tongue's," Jim asked, with a wink.

"Man, you are really pissed off at these Columbians," Cox said.

"Yep. More than you or the Director in Salt Lake will ever know. But I'm not stupid enough to do that," Jim said.

Cox looked at the other agents and said, "Ok men, put all five of these Columbians into vehicles. We're heading back to Portland."

Jim and Charlie made their way back to Dallas and checked out the house to see if the Columbians did any damage. After walking all through the house Jim said, "Charlie, I'm impressed with all the progress you've made. Why don't you take a week or so off and take your wife on a little vacation?"

"That sounds good. I could use the time to settle down after a day like this. Are we likely to see any more of these pricks again?' he asked.

"I think we're clear of any more Columbians showing up in Dallas. I've got to get back to Salt Lake City in three days. That's when the fireworks are going to begin regarding the rest of the Columbians and the person, they were talking about called Lester," Jim said.

Jim needed to ask Charlie an important question. "After you take some time off, how much longer do you think it will take to finish up the house?"

"Two, maybe three weeks. Your house is at the stage where a lot of little things need to be completed. All the things you asked for are either done or ready to complete. Then it's details with door and window fittings, some touch up painting and then getting the city inspector to issue the Certificate of Occupancy,"

Jim said goodbye to Charlie and again wished him a happy vacation.

It was just a short drive to the Cramer House and all Jim could think about was a quick bite to eat and a good night's sleep. As he parked, he could see a light on the edges of the front window shade. He got out of the car, picked up the Sledgehammer and approached the front door. He hesitated going in the front door and decided to check all three of the other sides of the building. When he was about to move from the last side yard to the front of the house, he saw two FBI agents walking from Cramer House towards the athletic department.

After they walked a little more than halfway to the front of the athletic building, Jim followed a short distance and said, "Hey, you two. What's going on here. Why were you in my house?"

"Oh, hello Mr. Sams. We have the night shift and thought that since you were in Salt Lake City we could use your front room to get some sleep," the oldest agent said.

"I see," Jim said. "Please let this be the last time, ok?"

"Done," said the younger agent said.

Jim turned and walked towards the Cramer House and could see the two agents in the reflection of the house's front windows. He could see that one agent was raising his pistol towards Jim. Jim turned and dropped to his knees and raised the Sledgehammer just as the agent fired. The agent's bullet passed just to the side of Jim's shoulder and struck the side of Cramer House. The next thing anyone in the general territory could hear was the bust from Jim's weapon. Two FBI agents laid dead on the parking lot pavement, bleeding from head to toe.

Jim checked to be sure they were both goners and took out his cell phone and called FBI agent Cox. "Agent Cox, this is Jim Sams. How far away are you from Dallas right now?"

"Hey, Jim. I'm about thirty-five minutes south of Portland. Why do you ask?" Cox questioned.

"I've either got some bad news, or some good news, kind of. When you left my new house, I said goodbye to Charlie and drove over to Cramer House. Approaching the house, I saw that there were lights in the front room. I parked off to the side, got out and checked the sides and back of the house. As I made my way to the front of the house, I saw two FBI agents walking from Cramer House towards the athletic building. I walked a bit towards them and asked in a loud voice what they were doing in my place. They each turned around and said they had the night shift and just wanted to get some shut eye. I bought that and began to return to Cramer House when I saw their reflection off of the windows. They were facing towards me, and one had his pistol raised. I had the Sledgehammer, so I dropped to one knee as I turned to my left and heard their bullet pass next to my right shoulder. I raised my weapon and in just a few seconds there were two supposed FBI agents laying on the ground, bleeding rather badly," Jim described.

Cox asked, "Are you ok? Were you hurt?"

"No. I did go to the ground rather quickly now that you ask. My knee hurts a bit. Would you mind coming back to Dallas so you can identify these two as not being FBI agents? It would sure keep the local police and sheriff's from making a big deal about this whole thing," Jim asked.

"I'll have the people in my car continue to Portland in the other car. I can be at Dallas in about half an hour. Try to keep the deceased from being moved. Don't say a thing about us being there today or being up in the gravel pit. Nobody needs to know the business of the FBI," Cox said. "If they give you any shit, call me and give them your phone. I'll make sure they don't move either of the bodies."

"Thanks for coming back to help me. I appreciate it. I'll see you soon," Jim said.

The Dallas police and the County Sheriff both arrived about twenty minutes later and parked about fifteen feet to the side of the dead bodies. Jim walked over to them and said, "Looks like we've got a problem."

The Sheriff was the first to talk, asking "What the hell hit these two?"

Jim responded, "These two looked like the men who protected the campus a short time ago."

Before he could say anything else, agent Cox pulled up next to the two squad cars and said, as he got out of his SUV, "Gentlemen, I'm FBI agent Cox, out of Portland. These are two imposters that we've been trying to get our hands on for months. I'll take it from here. Ok?"

Both officers nodded in agreement and left the parking lot.

29
NITTY GRITTY

Once the remains of the fake FBI agents were bagged and placed in Cox's car, he said goodbye to Jim and headed back up to Portland. Jim went into the Cramer House and checked everything out hoping not to find any booby traps. Even though Jim was hungry, he just fixed some popcorn and quickly fell asleep in front of the television.

Early the next morning Liz woke Jim up from a nice night of rest. "Jim, this is Liz. Are you awake enough to talk?" she asked.

"I'm getting there. I was sure sleeping sound. Ok, now I'm able to think and talk. How's it going with you?" Jim said, just before he yawned.

"Yea! You sure don't sound like you're awake enough to talk," she said. "Do you want me to sing you back to sleep?"

"No. That's not necessary. How's everything with you?" he asked.

"I've had a great time. It's been a lot of fun, but I'm more than ready to come back to you. Would you be able to set up my return with Malika?" she asked.

"I'll get in touch with Malika as soon as I can this morning and call you back right away. How does that sound?" Jim asked.

"While I wait for your call, I'll begin packing. I'll also give the agents a heads-up. Thank you," she said.

"I can't wait to see you. Oh, I'm not in Salt Lake City now. I had some time off, so I came back to Dallas to check on how Charlie was doing on getting the new house built. Do you want to come to Dallas or Salt Lake City?" he asked.

"How much longer do you have in Dallas before you need to return to Salt Lake City?" Liz asked.

"I've got to return to Salt Lake the day after tomorrow. And I'm driving. I thought I'd need a car while I was in Dallas and did not want to fly here and rent a car," Jim said.

"Then I want to come to Dallas. A day or two on the road with you, driving back to Salt Lake City, will be fun," Liz said.

Jim called Malika's phone number and left a message for her to call him. He went over to his new house and looked around while he waited for her call. He took a piece of paper out of his wallet that he'd written down all the things he asked Charlie to add. Some of the things were already installed, but a lot of the other things had to be discovered wherever Charlie stored them.

As Jim was more focused on finding other items, the ring from his phone startled him. "Hello, this is Jim Sams, may I help you?" he said.

"Hey Jim. I'm returning your call. What's up?" Malika asked.

"Hello Malika, thanks for calling back so quick. I received a call from Liz early this morning and she told me she wanted to leave Nebraska as soon as possible. And she wants to come here to Dallas where I'm waiting for Lester to settle down in Salt Lake City. If you can arrange for her to fly into the Dallas airport today, that would be great. We'd head back to Salt Lake City two days from now," Jim asked.

"That's awfully short notice. Give me some time to check the agents that are with Liz, and also find out if a plane's available. I'll get back to you as quick as I can," she said.

"Thank you very much," Jim responded.

He called Liz immediately and said, "Liz. I just got off of the phone with Malika and she is working to make your trip to Dallas happen. It looks to me like the hardest thing to do is secure the plane. First, it needs to be in Nebraska, two pilots also need to be there, then they will need fuel and then get clearance from Nebraska to Dallas, Oregon. I know she can arrange almost anything, but we'll just need to wait for her call to find out if you can get here this afternoon."

"Oh Jim. It sounds like I've opened a can of worms for her to deal with," she said.

"Don't worry. Remember, they asked us to help them. What's the worst they could do, fire us? Let's just relax and think about what we can do when you get here. OK?" he asked.

"Ok. I'll get all my stuff together and wait for your call. I love you Jim," Liz said and hung up.

Jim felt hungry and realized that the last thing he'd eaten was some popcorn. He showered and got dressed, while deciding where to go for a late breakfast. He decided to visit Oscar's Delicatessen so he could chat with Ellora.

Jim pulled into Oscar's parking lot and immediately saw two black SUV's parked at the far end of the lot. He couldn't believe his eyes, but the one thing he did notice was that both cars had Oregon license plates. He wondered if the Columbians had established permanent residences somewhere near Dallas. He was cautious when he entered Oscar's, trying not to cause people to turn their heads. To his surprise no one was seated at the counters and only three booths were occupied, none being foreigners. As soon as he sat down Ellora brought some water to Jim and said, "Well, well. Why has it taken you so long to come see me again. You know I like to shoot the shit with you. Where's your lady friend? Don't tell me you're done with her?

"Hello Ellora. How've you been doing? And no. I'm not done with my lady friend. She's been out east and will get to Dallas later today," Jim said.

"Oh, that's good. I sure liked that lady. I would have been really pissed if you dumped her," Ellora said, smiling. "What can I get you?"

"First, I'd like peach yogurt with fresh blueberries on top and a glass of Honey Crisp apple juice. Then I'd like two big waffles, with hot maple syrup, and a cup of black, decaf coffee. That's all," he said. "Oh, one more thing. I noticed those two black SUV's at the far end of the parking lot. Those look like the same vehicles that the Columbian thugs drove around in when they were raising hell around here. If their cars are out back, where are they?"

"Jim, listen to this. Those cars now belong to Oscar's Delicatessen. The boss picked them up for a song at an auto auction a couple of months ago. We now deliver breakfast, lunch, and dinner.

Can you believe that?" she asked.

"That's great. Dallas is becoming big time, just like all the big cities," Jim said.

While his food was being prepared, Jim relaxed, as if it was like old times. A simple college town, with enough businesses, parks, banks, and police security to live and raise a family. He was truly happy to be in Dallas again.

Ellora brought Jim his order and just when he started to eat, his phone rang. "Hello, this is Jim

Sams. May I help you?" he asked.

"Jim. Director Campbell sure must like you. Liz will be arriving in Dallas, Oregon at six tonight. Can you believe that?" asked Malika.

"That's great. I'm sure he approved everything because you asked him. I'm very grateful to you for arranging all this for Liz, and me. We'll be in Salt Lake City in two days, around seven at night because we're driving. Thanks again Malika," Jim said.

He finished all the food Ellora brought him, paid his bill, and said goodbye. He looked in the direction of the black SUV's and laughed to himself.

He spent the rest of day in his office working on next season's scheduling and trying to visit with Kristy and Mark. About three-fifteen in the afternoon Henry Talbot, Robert Paige, and Everet Sloan walked it to Jim's office and sat down.

"Hey guys, what's up," Jim asked.

"Jim, do you recall Robert and I discussing your incentive program last winter?" Talbot asked.

"I'm pretty sure I remember. I recall that, by getting into the NCAA Division I Volleyball Tournament, my bonus would be $5,000.00. That's all the farther we went this season. However, we did have two players named Academic All-Americans, which you said would bump the bonus up by $1,000.00. How did I do?" Jim asked.

"You have a good memory. Everet will prepare a bonus check for $6,000.00, which he will include with your next check. It's nice to see you and your team make such strong progress. Each of us hope your team continues to get stronger, not because we like giving money away, but because it brings strong publicity to Cascade University. Congratulations, that's a nice start for your first year in this system of compensation," Talbot said. Each of the men in Jim's office got up and shook his hand.

"I thank each of you for your kind words and support. I'm looking forward to a better record next season. I really like this type of meeting!" Jim said with a big smile on his face.

Jim thought for a few minutes and realized that he was not the only volleyball coach at this university. He made himself a note to give a thousand dollars to both Kristy and Mark. With all of the other things he was doing for the FBI in Salt Lake City, he knew that they were a big part of this season's accomplishment.

He called Kristy and said, "Can you come to my office and ask Mark to come with you?"

"Your request is my command boss," she said in a lighthearted way. "Do I have to bring Mark too?"

"Yes. I hope you're just kidding," Jim said.

Thirty-seven minutes later, both assistant coaches arrived at Jim's office. "Come in you two. I've got something important that I need to discuss with you two," Jim said, trying to sound serious. He began talking to them in a stern voice, "You each have picked up the slack when I've been in Salt Lake City. What I'm doing there is top secret and, very important. I know that our performance in the latter part of this season is totally your fault," Jim said. He then changed his demeanor, and said with a big smile, "You each will receive a thousand-dollar bonus in your next pay period. There is absolutely no way our team could have accomplished what they did during the NCAA championship without your coaching. I'm so proud of each of you. You've earned every cent. I'm wondering if you would be willing to use that money to help us buy new uniforms?" he teased.

Kristy asked, "You are kidding, right?"

"Me? Kidding," Jim said as he chuckled. "I'm not kidding. If and when we win the NCAA's there should be more money coming your way. How much, I don't know at this point. Now, I don't want you to let anyone else in the whole University know about this or what I just said. It's strictly between you and me. Understand?"

Mark answered, "I won't say a word to anyone, even Chris."

"That might be a good idea, come to think of it. Thanks Mark," Jim said. "Kristy. Are you ok with keeping it to yourself?" Jim asked.

"You're serious about keeping quiet, right?" she asked.

"Yes mam. I'm as serious as you've ever seen me," Jim answered. "Are you going to be ok with this?"

"You're the boss, boss. You know you can trust me. I won't say a word to another living person, ever," she said in a serious tone.

"Ok, that's it for now. I'll be returning to Salt Lake City in a couple of days. I'm looking forward to completing my business there and getting back here as soon as possible. I don't have an exact time when that will be. But, whenever you need to talk to me about anything on the team or otherwise, just call my phone. Thanks for this meeting," Jim concluded.

Jim walked back to the Cramer House to make sure everything was clean and tidy. Next, he looked through the refrigerator and the cupboards to see what he could make for dinner. His phone rang as he was making a list of what to buy at the grocery store.

"This is Jim Sams. May I help you?" he asked.

"You sure can. Come and pick me up at the Portland airport," Liz said.

"Wow. They took you to Portland. That's a surprise," Jim said.

"I'll tell you all about it when I see you. OK?" she asked.

"I'm headed for the car as we speak. Give me about thirty-five minutes, depending on traffic," he said.

Evening traffic, as usual, was stop and go once you were within two miles of the Portland airport. Jim pulled over next to the curb in the baggage claim area and got out to go find Liz. Before he could reach the exit door, Liz came out, took Jim's arm, and said, "Please put me in the car and get me out of this airport."

"You had problems getting from Nebraska to Dallas I suspect?" he asked.

"Exactly! Some FBI guy radioed the pilot and told him to switch destinations to the Portland Airport. I asked the pilot to explain why, and he handed me his mic and told me to talk to the Agent. Some FBI agent named Cox told me he had a load of Columbians that needed to be in Salt Lake City as soon as possible. I don't know why they couldn't let me off at Dallas and then fly up to Portland. I just don't understand. I'll be so glad when all this stuff they are asking you to do is finished," Liz said in a frustrated manor.

"Liz, I don't think we have too many more weeks to fulfill our obligation to Wilson Campbell. Let's stop talking about their problems and enjoy our time together. We can pick up something from a Panera and take it to Cramer House to eat. What do you say?" he asked.

"That would be fine. How long is the drive to Cramer House," she asked.

"We should be there in around forty minutes. I think you should lean back and snooze a bit. That will help you forget about what you've been through today. Think about how nice it will feel to sleep together in our bed," Jim said.

30
GET SET

Jim got up once during the night to use the bathroom and fell fast asleep when he got back in bed. Light coming through the edge of a shade and hearing Liz speak softly in his ear, was just enough to wake him up. Liz slowly stroking his penis woke him completely up. "What's going on," he asked in a soft voice.

"Are we going to take off for Salt Lake City this morning?" Liz asked.

"Absolutely. But first things first," Jim said as he reached over and caressed Liz's breasts. "What do you want me to start with?"

"I like that thing you did before, where you started at the bottom of the bed with your tongue and worked your way up," she said with a smile.

"That works for me. Turn over and get rid of the top covers and spread your legs," he said.

The process took about twenty minutes and Jim finished with a long, deep ejaculation. However, Liz pushed Jim over on his back and licked up his sperm. She then took him in her mouth until she got him to cum again. Needless to say, each of them went back to sleep for another hour. They both woke up just before nine-thirty and cleaned up in a hurry.

Jim said, "Let's get some breakfast at Tatters and then we'll swing by the new house before we begin the two-day drive to Salt Lake City."

After they were finished checking out the new house, they got on the road to Salt Lake City. Jim thought to himself that this could be his final trip across Oregon, Idaho, and northern Utah. Before they started on the trip, he'd decided on spending the better part of eight hours driving from Dallas, Oregon to Mountain Home, Idaho. As a surprise for Liz, he'd made a reservation at the Trinity Hot Springs Club, which included a geothermal hot spring pool.

Jim was more than familiar with the drive across Oregon, but most all of it was new to Liz. They stopped in Bend for a light lunch at the Café Sintra and ordered the Shrimp and avocado toast special for both of them.

As Jim was paying the bill, Liz noticed some nice-looking muffins on the counter next to the cash register She asked the waitress helping Jim, "Excuse me, how much are those great looking muffins?"

"They're a dollar fifty each. How many would you like," asked young lady.

She looked at Jim and asked, "What do you think, half a dozen?"

"At least. I've had them before, and they're great!" Jim answered.

Jim settled in for a long drive and was curious about how much Liz would ask about as they made their way across two-thirds of Oregon's wide-open spaces. He knew from experience that there was a long history of the people and places that were in eastern Oregon. Most of those who live in Oregon and people in the rest of the country only have the Willamette Valley in mind when they talk about or think of Oregon.

Liz surprised Jim by falling asleep after eating one of the muffins and looking around for about an hour. There is seldom much traffic from Bend to Burns, where Jim usually tops off the gas tank and loosened up his legs. He nudged Liz and asked, "Do you need to use the rest room or stretch your legs? It will be a long time before we get to Idaho."

She offered up a drowsy answer, mumbling that she wanted to sleep some more. Jim was ok with that and got back on the road, which became somewhat more winding until the Idaho border. They crossed into Idaho, and a short distance east put them on highway eighty-four, which is a good interstate highway through Boise and on to Mountain Home.

Liz finished her nap about an hour before they entered Idaho and the first thing she commented on, once they entered Idaho, was all the traffic. "We just left a road in Oregon that had very little traffic and now we get on an interstate going seventy miles an hour. What gives?" she asked Jim.

"Most of Idaho is covered by mountains. The lower end and west side of the State is fairly flat, which makes for better roads. You'll see before long that most of both sides of highway eighty-four are covered with hay and other grain crops."

Liz asked Jim, "I need to stop and use a restroom. How about we get dinner while we're in Boise?"

"That actually sounds pretty good. Besides being hungry, I need to walk around and loosen up my legs," Jim Said.

Shortly after they exited highway eighty-four, Liz said, "Jim, that Cobby's Sandwich Shop looks interesting. Do you want to take a look?"

"Sure. It's close to the freeway and I'd like to gas up while we're stopped. Let's take a look," Jim said.

When they entered Cobby's it was easy to see that it was just beginning to fill with evening customers. Liz suggested, "Is it ok if we sit by the front window?"

"No problem at all," Jim responded with a smile.

"Good evening," said an older waitress. "What drink would you like to start with?"

"Actually, we're ready to order, if that's alright," asked Jim.

"That's just fine," the waitress said.

Liz ordered first saying, "I'd like the French Dip Sandwich and a cup of hot green tea please."

"And you sir?" the waitress asked with a smile.

"I'll take a chance on the Hot Meatball Sandwich and a glass of root beer, please," Jim said as politely as he could.

With dinner finished, they filled the gas tank, got in the car, and were again heading south on highway eighty-four. They both talked about what they'd just had for dinner and began to laugh.

The drive to the small town of Mountain Home was an easy two-hour drive. When they pulled off of eighty-four into Mountain Home, Jim remembered how to get to the health resort he'd booked. A quick stop at the office to check in, and they looked around to find their private cabin.

"Oh Jim. This is perfect," Liz exclaimed.

"Here's the key. Go on in and check it out," Jim said. He gathered up clothes for tomorrow and went inside to take a look. "I like it. What do you think Liz?"

"What a nice place you picked. Let's walk around outside and locate the heated outdoor spa," she urged.

"I'll follow you," Jim responded, wanting to enjoy Liz's delight at his selection.

They found the spa and continued to walk around the entire resort. "I wonder why there aren't more guests here. This place is so nice," Liz said.

"The fewer guests, the more private time we have to spend in the heated spa," he said.

"You are so right. I'm going to put on a bathrobe and spend my time in the spa naked, "Liz said, looking at Jim while raising her eyebrows.

"This is going to be an interesting hour. Let's just keep our eyes open if we should get carried away," suggested Jim.

"Ok. But you keep your eyes open because you know I'll get carried away!" Liz said with a giggle.

About twenty minutes into getting carried away, Liz looked at Jim and said," This isn't working. I don't understand. With all this water, you'd think I'd be slipperier than anything."

"I'm glad you brought it up. I was thinking that we should go back to the cabin. It will be much more enjoyable for both of us," he offered.

After about thirty minutes of intense, slippery love making, each of them had to cover their mouths when they climaxed.

Jim said, "That was beyond great. You are the sexiest, most passionate woman walking the earth," Jim said, smiling softly.

"Have you had a lot of sexy, passionate woman in your life," Liz asked, rather seriously.

"No. You know that. I've always been a one-woman man," Jim said.

"That makes me really happy. Until you, my sex life was more of a hit and miss thing. My husband was away too much, and when he was at home, he seldom had sex on his mind," she offered. "I don't know what I'd do if I lost you. I don't think any other man on earth could satisfy me like you do."

"Thanks for the generous complement. I hope we're together for the rest of our life's!" Jim said.

They both enjoyed a great night's sleep. After a light breakfast at a small mom and pop joint, they were back on the road by nine-thirty. About two-fifteen in the afternoon Jim pulled the car up to their Salt Lake City hotel and carried everything they had in the car up to their room.

While Liz was putting her things in the chest of drawers, Jim said, "I'm going to go check in with Director Campbell and ask for some equipment I'll be needing in the next few days. Do we have enough in the kitchen for tonight's dinner, or would you like to discover another restaurant here?"

"Let's go out," Liz said, smiling. "You asked."

"That's fine with me. I should be back about four-thirty," he said as he kissed her goodbye.

Jim arrived at the office of Director Campbell at three-twenty and asked the receptionist, "My name is Jim Sams. Is the Director available? I'll only take a few minutes of his time."

"Good afternoon Mr. Sams. Please give me a moment to check if the Director has time to see you now," she said. She cupped her hand over the mouthpiece after asking the Director and waited a minute or so for his reply. "Mr. Sams, Director Campbell would like you to wait until four o'clock to speak with him. Can you wait for him that long?"

"That's not a problem. Thanks for checking," Jim said, looking around for a seat that was next to some magazines.

It seemed to Jim that thirty-five minutes was a long time, especially since he couldn't find a magazine that he was interested in. Trying to keep himself occupied, he walked slowly around the reception area and looked at the paintings and pictures on the wall. Just before the receptionist called his name, Jim's final thought about all the stuff on the walls was that this was clearly where an important FBI person worked.

"Mr. Sams, Director Campbell will see you now. Please go on in," she said.

"Thanks for your help," Jim said.

Upon entering the Director's office, Campbell said, "So, how was your short time off? Are you ready to get back to your mission, capturing Lester alive?" he asked.

"Yes sir. My time off was sorely needed. As for taking Lester alive, I considered a number of ways to accomplish getting him, but only one way was humane. I'm going to need to purchase a number of things, if I can't find what I need already in the FBI's possession," Jim said.

"Do you have a list of what you need? If so, please let me see it," asked the Director.

Jim pulled the list of things out of his back pocket and handed it to him, saying, "After you look at it, please let me explain what I've asked for and why I need them."

The Director looked at the list and said, "I see what you mean. Go ahead and explain this stuff."

"Ok. First, I need a large laundry basket with four-inch wheels, to get Lester out of the hotel that he uses when he's out screwing. Next, I need a large role of ZIP flashing tape. It's a really strong, sticky tape that you need a sharp knife to remove it from the roll. Then, a pack of one hundred, twenty-six-inch stainless steel cable ties, that have a tensile strength of 350 pounds. I want to use these in place of handcuffs. Finally, I need a pharmaceutical drug named Rohypnol, that is not available in the states, but is sold in Mexico," Jim concluded.

"This is a very interesting list after all. Off the top of my head, I doubt if we have any of this stuff in our warehouse's. I'm not going to ask you how all these things intersect to capture one man, but I do need to know about the Rohypnol. That's a drug, right?" Campbell asked.

"Yes. But it is critical to my plan. It's a drug that really relaxes people. Depending on the amount a person drinks, the more they drink the more they relax and usually fall asleep for a short time. However, if they drink too much Rohypnol, they sleep forever. My plan has me fixing some Columbian cocktails so I can make sure no one drinks too much," Jim explained to the Director.

"You do remember that we want him alive and uninjured? Capiche?" Asked Campbell.

"Yes sir. Also, I'll need some help once I get Lester in the laundry basket. He's a fat little porker and I don't want to get a hernia putting him in a car trunk. Can one of your agents help with that?" Jim questioned.

"That won't be a problem," the Director said, as he penciled a phone number on a post-it and handed it to Jim. "This is the phone number of agent Gunnar, who will acquire everything you need, including the Rohypnol. Immediately after you speak with him, destroy this piece of paper. I'll have him contact you when he's ready to hand everything over to you," said Campbell. "I also want you to contact agent Cannon. He'll be the one that helps you move the little pig around. His phone number is on his card. Discard the card when you don't need his help anymore."

"I'll let you know when I get everything from agent Gunnar. Hopefully, I'll have Lester under control and in your custody a few days after that," Jim said. "Thanks for everything," Jim said.

Jim returned to his hotel and asked Liz, "How's the hunt going for a different restaurant?" he asked.

"I've found a couple that we may like. First, there's the Squatters Brew Pub and Market Street Grill and the Oyster Bar, downtown. What do you think?" Liz asked.

"The Oyster Bar sounds interesting and it's my first choice. We could check it out, and if we don't care for it, we can zip over to the Squatters Brew Pub," he offered.

"Good plan my love. Are you ready to go," Liz questioned.

"Give me about twenty minutes to clean up and change clothes," said Jim.

Thirty-five minutes later, they were seated at the Oyster Bar and very happy with their choice. The service and food were better than good, and they both asked each other why they were just now discovering this place. They took their time and realized it was just before nine o'clock.

"Time to go Liz. I'm stuffed and we may have overstayed our welcome," Jim said.

For the next couple of days Jim and Liz went for rides out behind the Wasatch Mountains where they enjoyed the ski resort that followed the 2002 Winter Olympics, and the Sundance Film Festival. Further north, out behind Tremonton on highway thirty, they found a large area of farms which Jim considered as an area that would not hold any thugs.

Three days from when he'd met with Director Campbell, agent Gunnar contacted Jim to let him know everything he asked for was in hand. "Is there any particular place you want to put this stuff?" Gunnar asked.

"Yes. Meet me on the second parking level of the Hyatt Place Hotel, at two-thirty tomorrow.

31

AUDIOS LESTER

At two pm the next day, Jim stopped at the check-in desk of the Hyatt Place Hotel and asked, "I would like to book a room for a couple of days on the fifth floor near the elevator. Is that possible?"

"Yes, we have a very nice room available there. It's a two-bedroom suite, next to the elevator," the receptionist said. "Since it is the middle of the week, that room goes for only one hundred ninety per night, plus tax. Would you like to book that room?"

"Yes, that sounds perfect. When can I check in?" Jim asked the nice-looking young woman.

"It's available now. It was cleaned earlier today and I'm sure you will like it," she said. "Here are the keys to the room. When you check out, you can just leave the keys on the dresser and your receipt will be under your door the morning you depart."

"Thanks for your help," Jim said.

He took the elevator down to the second-floor parking area to meet agent Gunnar. "Ok. I've booked a room on the fifth floor, opposite Lester's playpen. Let's get this stuff out of the car and put everything in that room," Jim said.

That evening Jim went to the Hyatt Place Hotel at eleven pm and parked opposite the porte-cochere. He wanted to see if this was one of the nights when Lester wanted to get laid.

Jim put on a disguise, got out of the car, locked the doors, went inside the hotel, and walked to the bathroom opposite the elevators so he could see if Lester used the same room as before.

The little pig showed up at eleven-thirty, accompanied by three thugs, and spent the first twenty minutes with them drinking at a table in the bar area. As soon as a couple of whores approached Lester's table, he took both of them over to the elevator.

Jim waited until Lester and his night's playthings were in the elevator. Jim counted the floors and saw the elevator stop at the fifth floor, which fit Jim's plan to a tee.

That was all Jim needed to know. He walked back to his car and headed to his own hotel. He crawled into bed, laying close to Liz and was asleep in no time. He woke up smelling pancakes.

"Liz, are you fixing breakfast?" he asked.

"That's correct. It's almost time for you to go work out. You've been looking kind of weak lately," she said, laughing a bit.

Liz and Jim enjoyed an easy-going breakfast and talked about what they were going to do once they returned to Dallas. The first thing Jim wanted to do was to try the McKenzie River to see if the trout had survived the big fire. Lis focused on Jim's new house and her house further south of Dallas. She'd dropped so many hints about wanting to live with Jim, in his new house, that she was beginning to worry that he may not want her to live there.

"Liz, you have nothing to worry about. I want you to live with me for the rest of our lives. I think you will really like all of the things

I've had done to the house that will keep us safe from anything you can think of. It may be the strongest, safest house ever built anywhere in the United States," he bragged. "I better get headed to the gym."

After a good workout, Jim called agent Gunnar to be sure he was still up for meeting him at the Hyatt Place Hotel at two-thirty.

Agent Gunnar was anxious to get this chore off his hands and agreed immediately. "My last question for you Mr. Sams is, once you get Lester, do I still need to assist you getting him into

the laundry basket?" he asked.

"Not at all. Director Campbell took care of that detail by telling Cannon he would need to help me move Lester. I'm worried that he may wake up while were moving him around. I don't want to deliver Lester to the Director any more messed up than he already is," Jim said. "You're finished when we get the stuff put in the room. You did a great job finding and delivering all this stuff to me."

Jim and Gunnar made quick work of putting all the things Jim asked for into the rented room. "Agent Gunnar, thanks again for all your help finding all the things I asked for. I wish you all the best," Jim said, as he shook Gunnar's hand.

Jim went back down to the lobby and walked into the bar, where he sat down opposite the daytime bar tender. "Hey man, would you happen to have any Aguardiente? I think it's usually called Guaro," Jim asked.

"We do, but you don't look like a firewater drinker. What do you need it for?" asked the bar tender.

"I'm going to have a small party at my house in a couple of days, and I thought it would be fun to try something different besides whiskey, vodka, gin, and beer. I'm here today at a company meeting and just thought I'd ask," Jim said.

"All I have are magnums. It's sixty-six dollars US for a magnum. Are you still interested?" the barkeep asked.

"I am but let me check if I've got that much on me," Jim said, as he looked in his wallet. "I've got a total of seventy-five dollars. I'll take a magnum and you can keep the rest. What do you say?

As the bartender placed the magnum of Aguardiente on the bar top, he said, "Here you go buddy. I'll take the tip. Enjoy."

Jim smiled, picked up the booze and headed out to his car, knowing he could put it in the room later.

The balance of the afternoon, Jim stayed in their hotel room and helped Liz with dinner. They again talked about what life would be like after their time in Salt Lake City. "Jim, do you think we could travel more when you're done here?" she asked.

"Yes. I like that idea. I've been so happy in Oregon during my life that I've never thought much about checking out other places. Are you thinking of places like Washington, DC, Maine, Florida, Puerto Rico, Europe, Australia, Alaska or what?"

"I was thinking of starting off looking around closer than those places. I'd like to go down to the bottom of the Grand Canyon in Arizona and go on a float trip. Maybe a train trip from Winnipeg, Canada west to Vancouver would be fun. You know, stuff close like that," she said.

"I'd like to visit those places too. If we're able, as we grow older, I'd like to visit Australia and Washington, DC. What would you think about that?" he asked.

"I can see that happening as we grow older. A lot of what and when we might do things like that depend on how long you coach at the Cascade University."

They continued to talk about traveling during dinner and while cleaning up the kitchen. They watched television for a couple of hours before going to bed, and Jim could see that Liz just wanted to snuggle.

Jim laid in bed and thought about how he was going to nab Lester unharmed. According to his list of the days Lester did not visit the Hyatt Place Hotel, tomorrow night would leave his sex room unoccupied and would be prefect for Jim to set up the room.

Jim woke up early the next morning and drove to the Hyatt Place Hotel. He took the elevator up to the fifth floor and looked for a maid and the cart that she puts her supplies in. The cart was in the hallway in front of a room that was being cleaned. As he walked past the cart, he looked in the open door and could see the maid making the bed. He stopped and quickly checked the supply cart for a master key that would open every room on that floor. The key was laying on top of some white hand towels at the front of the cart. Jim gently picked up the key and put it in his front pocket as he walked to a door leading downstairs. He continued walking down the stairway to the parking area and got in his car. He put the master key up in the sun visor and drove back to his hotel.

When he walked into his hotel room, he could smell breakfast being cooked. "Hey, Liz. That smells great. Am I on time?" he asked.

"It's almost ready," Liz said. "Where have you been this morning. I've been worried."

"I needed to check something out that could only be done early in the morning, which I accomplished. I didn't want to wake you up so early, so I left quietly," he said.

"If you need to do something like that again, please wake me and let me know," she asked.

"I will. I promise. I had no intention of alarming you," he said.

The next afternoon, Jim went back to the Hyatt Place Hotel and moved things from his rented room into Lester's playpen. He placed four glasses and the magnum of Aguardiente on a desk at the far end of the room. Next, he opened the Aguardiente and filled each glass about one-third full and then added a couple of ounces from the vial of Rohypnol to each glass. He also put an ice bucket near the glasses.

Jim called agent Cannon and told him to meet him at his rented room in the Hyatt Place Hotel at nine pm. His next call was to Director Campbell. "Hello. This is Jim Sams. May I speak with the Director please," he asked the lady who answered the phone.

"Let me see if he can take the call. Please hold on for a moment," she said. "He'll be right with you."

"Jim, this is Wilson. What do you need?" he asked, in his regular hurried manner.

"I'd like to ask you how I can present Lester to you around one o'clock in the morning tonight?" he said.

"So. You think you can get him tonight?" he asked.

"I've learned when he's out looking for pussy and when he's down in south Salt Lake City, this is one of his nights to get laid. Agent Cannon and I have everything ready to get him, but I need to know where you want me to bring him at such a late hour."

"If I don't hear from you between now and midnight, I'll be in my office. I'll have three agents with me when you and Agent Cannon bring him in. Just be careful," Director Campbell said.

"There is one thing that I need the FBI to take care of when I'm grabbing Lester," Jim asked.

"I think there should be four FBI agents sitting in the bar area of the Hyatt Place Hotel when I'm upstairs grabbing Lester. The agents would be able to see that the three or four Columbians protecting Lester don't leave the bar area," Jim explained.

"I think you're correct. I'll make that happen. What time do you think the agents should be in place?" asked the Director.

"I'd have two in place by ten and another two at ten forty-five. That way the agents will be sitting at two different tables. I think that would look more natural," Jim offered. "The agents can leave the bar around twelve thirty."

Jim and Liz spent most of the day watching local TV and continuing their discussion about where they would like to explore once Jim retires. It seemed to Jim that the day dragged along slowly. Around four pm he decided to ask Liz, "Would you be in the mood for a little bedroom fun?"

"That would be great. But I think I've contracted a urinary infection. Until I find out for sure, we need to hold off anything like that," she said. "I'm sorry to disappoint you."

"No. Not at all. We'll get you in to see a doctor tomorrow. I'm sorry that you're not feeling well," he said.

"Thanks. That's so sweet of you. I do need to see a doctor tomorrow. We'll look around first thing in the morning for a doctor," she said.

Jim arrived at the Hyatt Place Hotel at eleven pm and parked his car two blocks away. He walked into the garage area of the hotel and climbed the stairway up to the fifth floor and entered the room he'd booked. A knock on the door startled him, so he waited for another knock. He peered through the peep hole and saw that it was Cannon.

"Come on in. How's everything with you tonight?" Jim asked.

"I was getting kind of sleepy waiting to come over here, but I'm ready to get on with it now," Cannon said. "What's our plan tonight?"

"We'll keep an eye up to the peep hole to see when Lester, and his playthings enter the room across the hall. Then we wait about twenty minutes, and we'll take the laundry basket, the Zip tape, and the stainless-steel cable ties into their room. If they drink the Guaro that I put on the desk with the Rohypnol in it, they'll be as quiet as sleeping lambs," Jim said. "I'll take the first shift looking through the peep hole. We'll switch about every fifteen minutes."

At eleven forty-eight Lester waddled up to his door with three women in tow. They all went into the room laughing and tugging at Lester's pants. Shortly after their door closed, Jim walked over to Lester's door and put a reverse peep hole magnifier up to look into the room to see what was going on. Lester was at the desk with the Guaro glasses, as the women on the bed were stripping down. He picked up two glasses and carried them over to the bed and gave

them to two girls who were now completely naked. Jim saw Lester go back to the desk and take a long drink of the Guaro before he picked up another glass and gave it to the third girl on the bed. The first two that got drinks chugged theirs down and were busy playing with the third girls boobs and pussy. Lester walked back to the desk and sat down to watch the girls putting on a show. He reached for his glass of booze and downed the remains in a couple of gulps. He reached for the magnum of Aguardiente and filled his glass again as he whooped and hollered at the girls. In a little over fifteen minute the girls on the bed laid over on their backs and settled down, but still reached over each other feeling around.

Lester got up rather slowly and started to walk in the direction of the bed. He collapsed onto the floor and tried to get up, but finally just laid there, moving his head slowly from side to side and mumbling something. Jim turned and motioned to Cannon to bring the laundry basket and they both went into the room. Jim picked up a few cable ties and put one on each of Lester's ankles. He put a third one on each of the first two cables, thereby securing his feet together. Lester was really woozy as Cannon and Jim rolled him over onto his stomach. Jim pulled one of Lester's arms up on his back and put a cable tie on his wrist. He did the same to Lester's other wrist and then put a cable tie thru each of the wrist cable ties. Finally, Jim put four cable ties together and looped them around Lester's waist, pulling them tight to his fat belly. A final cable tie secured Lester's wrists to the cable ties on his back.

Cannon gathered all the glasses, and the magnum of booze and wrapped them in Zip tape. "We'll put them in the basket with everything else we came in with as we roll this idiot out," Jim instructed.

"Geeze. What happened to this guy. He's got scars all over his body. Did he fall into a meat grinder?" asked Cannon.

Jim was over checking the pulses of the women on the bed to see if the were still alive. He covered them up with a bed sheet and said, "These three are doing ok. We'll let them stay here and sleep it off. When they come to, they'll be out of here in a heartbeat," Jim said.

With Lester in the laundry basket, Jim put a sheet over the top, looked around for any evidence that they'd been in the room, and they departed. They took the elevator down to the second floor of the parking garage. Jim jogged down the street to his car and pulled into the second floor of the garage.

"Give me a hand getting this basket into the trunk of this car," he instructed Agent Cannon. "Then follow me to Directors Campbell's office so you can help me get this back out of the car. Then you're done. OK?"

"No problem. I'm right with you," Cannon said.

32
SUCCESS

At the office building occupied by Director Campbell, Jim and Agent Cannon unloaded the laundry basket and pushed it over to the front of the building.

Before knocking on the door, Jim said, "Agent Cannon, thanks for all your help. I couldn't have done it without you. Go on and head on home."

Jim explained to the night watchman that he was here to see the Director. After a few minutes checking with the Director, the watchman opened the door for Jim. He pushed the basket into the elevator and then to the Director's office. Jim knocked on the door and said, in a loud voice, "Director Campbell, I've got what you asked for."

The door opened immediately and out walked a rather casually dressed Wilson. "So this is Lester," he said. "How's he doing? Is he still among the living?"

Jim reached into the basket and checked Lester's pulse and said, "He's just taking a nap. The Rohypnol is slowly wearing off."

"Geeze, he's an ugly looking creature. All those scares don't make him look any better. How can such a small, ugly person be so responsible for all the problems with the Columbians?" Campbell asked.

"Like they say, '... power tends to corrupt and absolute power corrupts absolutely'," Jim said.

"Well, this piece of crap has corrupted for the last time. Nice work Jim," Campbell said, shaking Jim's hand. "You're now relieved and you and Liz can head back to Oregon. Talk tomorrow to Malika and she will make all the arrangements for your trip home."

"Thanks Wilson. I've enjoyed getting to know you. I liked Malika from the moment I met her. You have a great group of people that are more than efficient. I wish you all the best as you clean out the rest of the Columbians who've caused so much devastation to so many people, Jim said.

Jim walked back to his car and headed for the hotel. Liz was fast asleep when he quietly got into bed. She moved towards him without realizing what she was doing, which Jim always enjoyed.

Liz was up before Jim and cooking breakfast for him, hoping that he would wake up and get going.

As he began to smell the aroma of bacon, he turned onto his back and opened his eyes. A few minutes later he was fully awake and re-membered he needed to call Malika. He fumbled around a bit trying to find his phone and then made the call.

"Hello, this is Malika," she said.

"Good morning, Malika, this is Jim. I've been given the green light by Director Campbell to return to Dallas. My task was concluded late last night without any problems. He seemed very pleased at finally getting Lester. He said I should talk with you about Liz and I returning to Oregon," Jim said.

"Congratulations. I know the Director was becoming anxious to get Lester and begin the roundup of all the Columbians we can get our hands on. So, you and Liz need to fly back to Dallas. When do you want to leave, later today, tomorrow, or another day," she asked.

"Liz and I will be packed and ready to go in forty-five minutes," he said. "What's the quickest you can get us on a plane today," he asked.

"I'll have an agent at your hotel at ten this morning ready to take you to the airport. How does that sound?" she asked.

"That's perfect. Thank you. You have been a real help to Liz and me throughout this whole adventure. Oh, we don't want to fly to Portland. Just to Dallas. OK," Jim asked.

"Dallas it is. I doubt that I'll see you and Liz before you leave, so I want to thank you for all your effort and understanding. Please tell Liz I enjoyed her being here. Goodbye," Malika said.

Jim and Liz finished breakfast and packed up their belongings and were out front of the hotel at ten sharp. A quick trip to the Salt Lake City airport put them airborne at ten-forty. They landed at the small airport in Dallas at eleven-thirty local time.

Jim called Kristy and asked, "Hello Kristy, are you in your office?"

"Hey Coach. Nice to hear from you. Yes, I'm in my office. Is there something you need?" she asked.

"Yes. Liz and I are standing in front of the lobby at the Dallas airport. We need a ride back to the University. Can you com pick us up?" he asked.

"Not a problem. I'll be there as soon as I can," she said.

When Jim and Liz arrived at Cramer House, they put their luggage inside and went out to Jim's car. It took a few minutes to get it started after sitting for so long while he was in Salt Lake City. "Driving this thing around for a while will refresh the battery and it will be a lot easier to start next time," he said, smiling at Liz.

"What's the hurry? Where are we headed?" she asked.

"Be patient, my love. You'll see in a few minutes." Jim took his time driving to his new house, even though he was anxious to show Liz.

He pulled up to the outside of the garage and looked at Liz. She said, "No way. Is this your new house? Why didn't you tell me that it was completed? Can we go in now and look around?"

"That's exactly what I want us to do. There's no furniture or appliances inside yet, so think about what you'd like to have in the house. You and I are going to live here for a long, long time," he said before going inside.

They went in thru the garage and looked in every room in the house. Liz started talking about what she wanted in each room as soon as she entered the kitchen. "Do you want something to write on or will you remember everything for every room?" he asked.

"Don't worry. I'm just talking to myself. I'll need to check out a lot of furniture and appliance stores to see what's out there. I'm sure it will take a while to get everything we need," she said.

"Remember, if you sell your house, you have a lot of nice furniture and appliances down there," Jim reminded her. "There is one thing from your house that I'd like to have here."

"And what's that?" she asked.

"I love the bed in the master bedroom. I'm pretty unhappy whenever I'm traveling and need to sleep in a hotel or motel bed," he said. "What would you say to having that bed up here?" he asked.

"I'm ok with that. I love that bed too. My husband never did like that bed. Since I've met you, I've had a wonderful time in that bed. You bet we'll bring that be up here," she said and gave Jim a big hug.

"We'll have enough time after we finish looking around to drive down to your house, dismantle the bed, and bring it up here. I'd like to sleep here tonight in that bed. Would you be ok with that," he asked.

"You know, I can finish looking around here anytime. Let's go get that bed, some linen, and a few other things. Who knows, we may not need to buy a whole lot if you're ok with the stuff in my house," she said.

With that, they both got in Jim's car and headed down to Liz's house. Jim pulled his car around to the back deck and backed up to the deck stairs.

"Jim, I just remembered Queeny is no longer with us. I may start crying again," she said.

"I'm sure Queeny would understand your crying for her. But nothing will bring her back. I've been thinking that we should start looking for another Lab. What would you say to that?" Jim asked as he hugged her.

"That's probably what I need to help me get over Queeny. When can we do that?" she asked.

"Let's get the stuff we need from your house up to our house in Dallas. We'll put everything in place so we can sleep there tonight, and we'll start looking first thing tomorrow morning."

It was all they could do to get the bed frame and mattresses into Jim's car. "Looks like end tables, some kitchen stuff, and food items will need to wait until our next trip," Jim said.

"At this pace, it will take us a zillion trips to get things from this house up to Dallas. I think we should have a moving van come here, in a day or two, and we'll tell them what to bring up to our new house. Are you ok with that?" Liz asked.

"That works for me. First thing tomorrow morning, you find a moving company and I'll start looking for our new lab," Jim said. "Is it alright with you if I call the new dog 'our' dog?"

"Of course, it's alright with me. After all, it will be our dog. I know we'll both love her. Are we ready to get back to 'our' house now?" she asked with a big smile.

It took time to get the few things they brought with them in just the right spot. Before they put sheets and blankets on the bed, Jim laid on the bed to be sure it still felt good.

"Now I know I'll always get a good night's rest at home. Too bad we can't take it with us wherever we go," Jim said, laughing. "Ok, the final thing to do tonight is food. Where would you like to eat tonight?" he asked.

"Let's just order in a pizza from Abbey's. I'll call it in if it's ok with you?" she said.

"That's fine. I'll have whatever you select. Go ahead with the call and I'll start making the bed,"

Jim said.

After dinner and a shower to take the grunge off, they dried off and looked at each other. Liz smiled and said, "Well, what are you waiting for? I'll race you onto the bed and whoever gets there first can decide what happens next."